2008/0

ANGELA WINTERS

Always
A
CHANCE

ARABESQUE®

ISBN-13: 978-1-58314-804-4
ISBN-10:   1-58314-804-3

ALWAYS A CHANCE

www.kimanipress.com

Printed in U.S.A.

This book is dedicated to all my readers who kept me in line with their encouraging e-mails, constructive criticism and faithful support. I couldn't do this without you!

Chapter 1

Sitting in the backseat of the Lincoln Town Car that had been waiting for her at Atlanta's Hartsfield airport, Lily Wolfe took in the familiar sites of her old neighborhood, Cascade Heights, in the southern part of Atlanta. The finely manicured lawns, the old houses with style right next to the new McMansions and abundant construction.

Nothing much had changed since she left, but that had been only four years ago. Although being admitted to Oxford University's Saïd Business School in England was the longest shot Lily had ever taken, she had been desperate to get away from everything that reminded her of family. After it was over, she made excuses to stay in Europe in order to avoid the real problem in her life. She wasn't going to be able to do that anymore.

The doctor's voice had been disturbingly calm as he explained it to her. "A TIA is short for transient ischemic attack. It's what we call a ministroke."

As the car approached the driveway of the Wolfe home, the older centerpiece in the row of newer homes, Lily's paranoia was getting to her. On a street where everyone had plenty of room to park their SUVs and luxury foreign sedans in their multicar garages and driveways, a simple Chevy parked along the curb reminded her of the familiar FBI presence that used to be a regular outside her family's home six years ago.

So what was she supposed to think as she squinted her large, green eyes to try and get a face on the two sitting in the front seat? Two white guys in cheap suits sitting in a no-frills beige car across the street from where her father lived. Was he in trouble again?

His trouble wasn't what brought Lily back to Atlanta, but it was the reason she left. Adding to this, the death of her mother only two years later had been more than Lily could take. The one thing she had in common with her father was their tendency to avoid problems and pretend they didn't exist.

That was what Lily had done six years ago, when her father's real estate firm came under investigation for real estate fraud, high-pressure sales tactics and property flipping with false documentation. He told her it was all lies and she had nothing to be worried about. Despite the fear and uncertainty swarming inside her, Lily decided to just grin and bare it.

In the end, her father's case was dismissed because of some clever public relations work, misplaced evidence and a grand jury that wouldn't indict. Ward Wolfe considered himself vindicated and Lily went along, ignoring the questions she had about papers she remembered being taken from her own office that had somehow gone missing. As a twenty-four-year-old business analyst, she wasn't privy to the details of Wolfe Realty's business deals, but had based some of her analysis on what the Atlanta FBI had considered doctored information.

It was when her mother, Jessica, died in a car accident two years later, that all of Lily's anger really surfaced. Her rock and foundation was gone and the only way Lily had known to respond was to bring fury on the only person left—her father. After the smoke cleared, permanent damage had been inflicted on her already thin relationship with him. It was then that she decided to run away to England.

Her communications with her father over the past four years had been polite and hollow. How are you? How's your job? How's the company doing? Updates on the neighbors in Atlanta and interesting must-see sights across Europe filled most of their conversations.

That was until five days ago when Lily received a call from her father, who was lying in a hospital bed. He had suffered a temporary interruption of blood flow to the brain, causing a seizure. Not as severe as a stroke, it was considered the precursor to a stroke and Ward's had been severe.

Having seen his life flash before him, Ward wanted the pretenses done with. There was no denial or protest on her part. The fear of God had been placed in Lily at the thought of her father dying with their relationship so muddled.

After conducting some quick personal business, Lily was on the first flight out of Paris. She didn't expect this to be easy, but it wasn't going to be resolved. She had already set her priorities. First was making sure her father was healthy again and had everything he needed. Second was working on repairing their relationship and letting the past go. But now that she saw that car outside the house, Lily was reminded that the second part was going to be harder.

"Thank you." Lily smiled, nodding politely to the driver who'd helped her out of the car.

"I'll take your bags in." He was a fair-skinned man in his fifties and spoke in a Caribbean accent. In a casual blue polo shirt and black slacks instead of the usual dark suit and hat, he looked more like a man on his way to a round of golf on this beautiful mid-May morning.

Lily nodded back anxiously. She would be spending the first few nights at the house, but eventually she was moving back to her condo in Atlanta's midtown neighborhood.

As she approached the front door of a colonial-style brick and columned home that was built in the 1950s, Lily took a deep breath. Before her finger could press the doorbell, the door opened and she stepped back.

"Lily." Brody Saunders stood in the doorway, all six foot four inches of him. He looked down on Lily, who barely made five-five, with that eternal stern look on his face. He was raisin brown, and despite being almost forty, looked like a young *GQ* model in his expensive suit. "It's been a while."

"Hello, Brody." Lily swallowed, trying to fight that tendency to pretend she was close friends with someone she never really liked.

It wasn't that Brody was a bad guy; that stern look was only the face he was born with. He was just fine, although a little cold at times. The tenseness Lily felt around him was based on his relationship with her father. After coming to work for Ward eighteen years ago, Brody was more of a son to him than she had ever been able to be a daughter and Lily was jealous. She sensed he was jealous of her because she actually was Ward's child, something she was certain he would give his life to be.

"Always Dad's right-hand man," she said as she stepped into the house. There was a sense of warmth that hit her at the sight of the familiar decorations in the foyer, but also a sense of pain. They were all her mother's decorations; her style and taste were everywhere. This was why she couldn't stay at this house.

Her father's desire to keep everything of Jessica so tight to his chest had been his way to deal. While Lily dealt with her mother's untimely death by lashing out, Ward dealt with it by forming a shell around himself. He wouldn't connect to anyone or anything, just going further and further inside.

"There is nowhere else I would rather be." Brody smiled proudly as he gestured for her to follow him. "He wanted to receive you in the living room to act as if he was stronger than he really is."

Lily appreciated the gesture. "Brody, please tell me the truth."

Brody turned to her as they reached the stairs. His face held an emotional strain. "He's going to be all right, Lily."

"Your face doesn't say that."

He shrugged. "I haven't been able to shake the fear I felt when I saw him grab his chest in the middle of that meeting."

The impassioned look on Brody's face made Lily want to reach out to him, but she didn't. "I'm so glad you were there for him. He trusts you more than anyone."

Brody laughed. "He called for you."

"I…" Lily shook her head.

"That was the first word he spoke after he grabbed his chest," Brody said. "He looked at me, reached his free hand out to me, but he said your name. He said it twice before he couldn't speak anymore."

Lily had to grip the railing to stay standing. Her full lips began to tremble, but she kept her composure. "I want to see him, please."

Lily felt her chest tighten at the sight of her father lying in the king-size bed. His usually milk-chocolate skin looked several shades lighter and he appeared frailer than usual despite the thirty pounds of extra weight he'd maintained since his wife's death.

Ward Wolfe slowly turned his head away from the television. As his dark eyes set on his approaching daughter, he smiled as if it was painful to do so.

"Little flower," he said just above a whisper as he held his hand out to her.

"Hello, Dad." She took his hand in hers; his skin felt dry. Leaning over to kiss him on the cheek, she chided herself for the first thought that came to mind.

Everything was the same. He hadn't changed even one tiny decoration in four years.

She sat down on the chair next to the bed, feeling several emotions she couldn't explain right now, but guilt was the most dominant. Her father was sixty-seven years old and she hadn't seriously inquired about his health the entire time she'd been in Europe.

"I'm sorry it took me so long to get back," she said, hoping an apology for anything would make things better.

"I understand," Ward said, trying to speak a little louder. He motioned for Brody to turn off the television. "With all the work you've done getting Courtney clean, you couldn't just leave her behind."

Courtney Harris was Lily's twenty-three-year-old cousin whom she had spent the last year trying to get out of the drug and nightclub life. "I dropped her off at the Dunwoody Center before I came here. She'll be there for the next six weeks."

"I'm inconvenient," Ward said. "Just as you got her to agree to treatment, I go and have an attack."

"Don't even think that." Lily reached over and placed her hand on the covers above his leg. "No kidding around, I want to know what's going on."

Ward turned to Brody, who was standing at the foot of the bed. He eyed him sternly until Brody shook his head. Then he relaxed and nodded.

"Lily," he answered, "I won't let you worry about me. The doctor says—"

"He has a twenty-four-hour nurse," Brody said.

"I want to meet her," Lily said.

"She's downstairs," Ward said. "But don't you bother her. She's good and very expensive."

"How long will she be here?" There was a voice inside of Lily that told her the chance to make this more personal had passed and she regretted it. This had become another information exchange and that was what she'd hoped to avoid.

"Lily." Ward strained as he reached out to take her hand in both of his. He seemed to be squeezing hard, but his weakened state made it feel like a slippery grip. "I'm going to be fine. I didn't ask you to come here to be on a death watch."

Lily shifted nervously in her seat. "I know that, Dad. I just…I don't think you're—"

"I called you here." He turned away, setting his attention on Brody.

Lily watched as Brody sighed and nodded reluctantly before leaving the room.

"I called you here," he repeated, "for something much more important than that."

Lily leaned forward, reveling in the belief that her father wanted the same thing she did. If they both wanted to face the truth and become a real family again, nothing could stop them. Not even their own insecurities and fears.

"I need you to come back to Wolfe Realty," he said.

Lily felt her heart fall into the pit of her stomach. She swallowed hard and leaned back. "You want me to come back and work for you?"

"Not for good." A somber expression took over his tired face. "I know you don't want to be a part of the company. You made that clear when you quit after your mother passed."

"Dad, I'm—"

"Don't," he said. "I don't want to get into that. I just need you to be there while I'm not. To stand in for me."

"Dad, I'm a consultant not an operations person. I don't know how to run a company."

"I don't need you to run it," Ward said. "Brody is practically running the place himself. He'll be fine, but he's staying behind the scenes. I need you to be the public face of Wolfe Realty."

After flying nine hours in coach, Lily wasn't quick enough to conceal her instinctual reaction. "Daddy, I... It's been four years."

"It's just a public face, little flower...foundation events and press conferences. Trust me, Brody will handle everything."

"There's no one else you can—"

"Of course there are others, but the name on that door says Wolfe Realty and as long as I'm alive, a Wolfe will be the face of the company." He sighed, turning away. "I know when I decide to retire, the company will no longer be in the family and I don't blame you for that. That's entirely my fault."

He lowered his head. "That's all my damn fault, Lily. I'm so—"

"Not now, Dad." Faced with her first chance to get to the meat of the issue, Lily realized it wasn't the right time. Right now, it was all about making sure her father got well, and rehashing the most painful years of their lives wasn't going to accomplish that. "I'll do whatever you need me to as long as you focus on getting better."

"Thank you. I knew I could count on you. Brody can help you with everything you need. There are a few public events coming up that you should be at."

"Brody is all right with this?" Lily asked.

"Brody is all right with whatever I say," Ward said. "That's loyalty and Brody has always been loyal. Besides, since the investigation, he prefers to stay behind the scenes."

As his right-hand man, Brody was arrested right along with Ward six years ago. They were going to be tried together. Rumors swirled about how they'd swindled the citizens in Atlanta's poorer black and Hispanic neighborhoods as well as a few similar communities in properties the company owned in neighboring South Carolina. Brody got off just as Ward had.

Lily remembered a visit to her parents' house after the trial was over. She'd overheard her mother pleading with her father to fire Brody, but he'd refused. Brody was his man until the end.

Lily stood up and walked to the window. She didn't have the courage to look her father in the eye as she questioned him. She felt guilty even though she had more than enough reason to want answers.

"There's a car outside," she said, tugging on the window curtain.

"I know." There was a pause before, "Come here, Lily."

Lily returned, this time sitting on the edge of the bed next to him. Her eyes apologized as they met his.

"It's too much to ask you to trust me," he said, "but I'm going to do it anyway."

"Why is the car out there?"

"You know why," he answered. "But there is nothing to it. There have been some changes at the company in the last year and a half and they assume I'm—"

"What changes?"

"I can't tell you yet." He smiled. "But it's good, Lily. It's something your—"

"Why can't you tell me?" Lily dreaded a return to this life of secrets and silence. It had been that way between them as long as she could remember. "You want me to be the face of Wolfe Realty but don't want to tell me what's going on?"

"It's good, Lily. I promise." He winced and lowered his head.

"Dad!" Lily jumped up and reached out to him. "What's wrong? Are you… Brody!"

"It's okay." Ward's voice was strained.

"Brody!"

Brody rushed into the room with alarm on his face. Reaching the bed, he practically pushed Lily out of the way and grabbed a wire hanging off the bedpost and pressed it.

"Stop it." Ward pushed him away. "Don't call her. I'm fine."

"That's enough," Brody told him. He turned to Lily. "What happened?"

Lily was shaking her hands nervously and she could hear her heart pounding. "We were talking and…"

"Did you upset him?" Brody asked angrily.

"No, I…" Lily felt as if she was being scolded, but didn't protest. What had she been thinking? She pushed back a suspicious Brody and took her father's outstretched hand in hers. "I'll do it, Dad. I'll do whatever you want."

"Your name is Garrick Pratt," were the first words out of FBI Atlanta head Jamarr Truitt after he greeted Michael. "It's a name you've used before."

Michael didn't believe in wasting time to adjust. From that moment on, he was Garrick Pratt—again. He recycled the name in his mind as he sat at the cold, dark table in a conference room at the FBI's Atlanta office.

Someone had spent a great deal of time with the graphics on the presentation prepared for him. He had heard that the Wolfe Realty case was very important to Pruitt.

Garrick wasn't a fool. He hadn't made his way up in the FBI's white-collar criminal division based solely on his skill. He knew people and he did his research. Jamarr had been assigned the Wolfe case six years ago and was devastated when he failed. So convinced the corruption had come from the inside, whichever agents he couldn't fire, he reassigned to cities like Boise, Idaho, and Louisville, Kentucky.

"We don't need to go through the motions. You know why you're here, don't you?" Jamarr clicked the remote to the next slide of the presentation.

"We're going over that now," Garrick said, placing his hand flat on the stack of folders full of information he had already read on the flight from Chicago yesterday.

"You aren't here because of this case," Jamarr said. "You're here because of you. Your reputation on white-collar crime is stellar. More important, the way you handled that Frasier case is exactly the way we want you to handle the Wolfe case."

Garrick expected as much. "That was an insider-trading case. Wolfe is flipping, and scamming poor people out of their homes."

Jamarr smiled, holding up the remote. "Yes, but you made your way into Jack Frasier's life through his daughter, Carly. Ward Wolfe has… Well, let me show you."

Garrick couldn't deny he was taken aback. He had read about Lily Wolfe, but hadn't seen any recent pictures. She was beautiful; not like a supermodel but in the way he liked. She was a natural beauty with an elusive sexuality. The picture was a frontal view of her as she made her way from the front door of the Wolfe house to a waiting Town Car. Garrick took in her refreshing beauty, caramel-colored skin and long, natural curls.

"Don't be fooled," Jamarr said. "Lily Wolfe is not as innocent as she looks."

"I'm never fooled," Garrick said. "And she doesn't look innocent at all."

As a matter of fact, Garrick thought her beauty made her particularly dangerous. He had to remember who she was if he was going to keep his head about him. "You think her coming back is a sign of something?"

"Yes," Jamarr answered. He gestured to Carolyn Kremins, a tall, California blonde in her mid thirties. She had ocean-blue eyes that stared so intently, they made you blink.

Sitting across the conference table from Garrick, Carolyn stood up and faced him with a serious expression on her face. "Our suspicions that Wolfe might be getting dirty again are encouraged by her return. She was the analyst on many of the bad deals from six years ago."

"He had his own daughter in on it?" Garrick simply shook his head.

Carolyn nodded. "We've explained the secretive nature of Wolfe's business deals that have occurred in the last year. We believe he is confident he's free and clear and has gotten back into—"

"Why do you think you can get him when you didn't get him before?" Garrick asked.

"We don't believe he's committing the same crimes," Carolyn answered. "What we do know is that he's up to something."

Carolyn gestured to Jamarr, who clicked the remote. Garrick was disappointed to see Lily's picture go away. Brody Saunders was not nearly as attractive.

"Wolfe and his sidekick have been selling assets and pulling out of investments over the past year. After the grand jury rejected the case, Wolfe continued the major public relations campaign. You couldn't get the guy away from a camera or mic. He was donating to every charity on the planet and making every business deal as public as possible."

"Then his wife died," Garrick said. "And Lily left."

"She went partying in the drug dens across Europe," Jamarr offered. "While he retreated from the rest of the world. Nothing out of the ordinary for two years, but there is something going on now."

"We need you to get in and find out what that is." Carolyn

pointed to the files underneath Garrick's hand. "When we heard Lily was on her way home, we saw her as the key. She's vulnerable because she's been out of touch, her father is weakened by his recent health problems and she's probably a druggie."

Garrick had read reports furnished by some connection Pruitt used in Paris. There was a rumor that Jamarr had spent his vacation last year following Lily around Europe. She was a regular at nightclubs known for heavy drug use and hard partying. She didn't seem the type, but Garrick had learned his lesson with Carly Frasier. She too seemed incapable of playing a part in her father's investment-banking scheme, but proved him wrong.

It didn't bother him when the FBI asked him to work Frasier's daughter. He had built a reputation for doing whatever it took to get inside, and romancing a woman wasn't a problem. He never took it too far; never had to. Garrick was an attractive, athletically fit man, tall at six foot three, cocoa dark, smooth skin and a finely trimmed goatee. He had dark, piercing eyes, a square jaw his mother referred to as a superhero profile, a Roman nose and full lips.

"I need to be free to do what I have to do," Garrick said.

Jamarr sighed. "I want to give you room, but we can't protect you if you go too far off."

"Violence hasn't played a part in this."

"That isn't necessarily true," Carolyn said. "There were records, now lost, of some physical intimidation of residents who wanted to contest the contracts they signed after realizing the homes were overvalued."

"I know you agents in Chicago like to act like Elliott Ness," Jamarr said.

Garrick laughed. "You're a couple of decades behind."

"That's fine," Jamarr said. "Just as long as you aren't."

"You know the rules, Garrick," Carolyn said.

"You're supposed to be my partner," Garrick said, "not my boss."

"I'm your boss," Jamarr said. "And you know the rules. I can't risk anything with this case."

"I'm not going to do anything that would compromise the case."

"You sure?" Carolyn asked with a wry smile. "It will be hard to resist sleeping with her. She's pretty hot."

"You know what's hot?" Garrick asked. "You saying she's pretty hot."

Carolyn smiled, rolling her eyes. "Just keep it clean."

"Don't worry about me," Garrick said coolly. "Just put everything in place."

"You're good to go." Jamarr clicked the remote and the screen went blank.

Garrick's timing was perfect. He heard the bell to the elevator only a few feet away from his apartment. He tossed the backpack over his shoulder and cupped the doorknob with his hand.

Lily stepped out of the elevator onto the sixteenth floor of her midtown condo, the penthouse floor. It had been four years since she turned over the management of her two-bedroom condo to a private company to rent while she attended business school. For two years it was a great source of income for her, but earlier this year, the tenant lost his job and stopped paying his rent. He moved out and the place had been vacant for six months.

After three nights at the house, Lily had to leave. She was finding it impossible to sleep and felt anxious the entire time. Part of the problem was the surroundings, which made her think at times her mother was still there. It was an eerie feeling she couldn't take. Not to mention, she only seemed to be in the nurse's way when trying to spend awkward moments with her father.

Turning right, she lugged her garment bag over her shoulder and dragged the rolling suitcase behind her. When the door to apartment 1610 opened just before she passed it, Lily expected to see Janice Aiken, who had lived there for all eight years the building had existed, but was halted by the surprise she was met with.

First thought: he was seriously hot. No, the brother was fine and Lily's attention was completely stolen. She stopped, unable to catch the smile that spread across her lips as he stood before her.

"Hi." Garrick had to check himself. Those eyes. He hadn't been expecting those stormy, tempting green eyes.

"Hi." Lily was thinking either Janice, who was about fifty, was the cradle robber of the century, or someone else lived here. "Visiting Janice?"

Garrick frowned, before suddenly remembering. "Oh yeah, Ms. Aiken. She used to live here, right?"

"Not anymore."

"Can I help you with those?" he asked, pointing to the suitcases.

"Um." Inside she was screaming, *hell yeah you can help me,* but she had to appear at least somewhat hesitant. "They aren't that bad."

"I'm sorry," Garrick said. "I don't want to offend your sensibilities. They just look heavy."

"They are. Thanks." She waited for him to drop his backpack before handing him the ultravalet garment bag. "I'm at the end of the hall."

Awkwardly, they both set off at the same time and their arms brushed against each other. They stopped, exchanging childlike nervous glances before smiling and turning away.

"You lead the way," Garrick said, letting her pass.

His mind was trying to get past those eyes, when he got a full view of her from behind. In a pair of low-waist flared-bottomed blue jeans and a tank that stopped just below her belly, he was able to take in a good measure of her curves and felt a rise.

Concentrate, man.

"You bought from Janice?" Despite confidence in her body's figure, Lily felt very uncomfortable with him walking behind her. She moved to the wall, hoping he would come alongside her, but he didn't. *Oh well. I guess this is what all those hours on the treadmill are for.*

"Not directly." Garrick felt the need to be cautious even though this began exactly as he'd wanted. "I'm renting from the management company she was working with."

"ICS," Lily said. "They're my management company too. Janice referred me to them."

Garrick decided to end the conversation there. Don't stress connections that might not connect. The FBI was thorough, but they always missed something. Something such as assuming that a thirty-year-old black woman wouldn't be close enough to a fifty-five-year-old Jewish immigrant to trip them up.

"You planning on selling?" Garrick asked.

"Oh no." Lily tossed her head back and smiled at him. She almost broke her stride by the handsome grin on his face. "I love my place."

Garrick reminded himself who this woman was. He had always been able to prioritize and separate. He wasn't fooled by that textbook toss of her hair and look back with an innocent yet seductive smile. Not at all.

"Oh, I see," he said as they stopped in front of her apartment. "You have an east view."

"Yes, I do." Standing her suitcase up, Lily reached for her

keys. "A perfect view of the arts center, the symphony hall and the best Peachtree Street has to offer."

"Sounds like a…" Garrick pretended to be surprised when she opened the door and all the furniture was covered in white sheets. "You've been gone long?"

The hardwood floors and richly colored walls were dotted with various shades of bedsheets covering all the furniture and bookcases. She hadn't expected to be home within six months.

"Four years." Lily was halfway into the apartment when she turned to see him still standing at the door. "You wanna see it?"

Garrick's eyes widened in surprised. "I'm sorry, I…"

Lily let out a loud laugh, realizing how forward she had to seem. Europeans were much more open and trusting about this sort of thing. She had to remember she was back in Hotlanta. "The view."

"Oh." Garrick laughed nervously, grateful he was mistaken. "Most definitely."

"Here." Lily grabbed the sheet over the sofa and pulled it back. "Toss it there."

He laid her garment bag on the sofa, noticing the careless way in which she did things. He was kind of envious, always having been more toward the anxious side, himself.

"Garrick Pratt," he said, offering her his hand as she stood in front of him. "If I'm going to come into your apartment, you should know my name."

Lily realized she had the careful type here and adjusted herself. All relationships followed the same rule whether business or personal. Assess and adjust. Garrick liked to follow the rules, but once she had escaped her parents' house, Lily felt free, unencumbered, and she liked it that way.

"Lily Wolfe," she answered, taking his hand. His grip was tight and firm and she felt flirty titillation tickle her hand.

Garrick retrieved his hand, not certain what to make of her

unexpected warmness. He hoped she was trying to figure him out. That way, he could keep her interested. He knew he should leave now but didn't want to. The key to every make-them-want-more rule was to cut it short and be the first to move on. He simply didn't want to.

"Come on, Garrick Pratt," Lily said, this time letting him walk before her. It was her turn to get a view and she liked what she saw. He was muscular but trim. He worked out for necessity and health not looks. "Go ahead and open the door."

Garrick unlocked the sliding glass doors and opened them. Walking out onto the balcony, his face was hit with a cool breeze. Lily joined him as they took in the full view. It was an incredibly romantic sunset just behind the centerpiece of midtown Atlanta, Piedmont Park, otherwise called the Central Park of Atlanta.

"Amazing, isn't it?" Lily took a deep breath, closing her eyes. When she opened them, she turned to him and he was looking right at her. She felt that same spark she had when he'd touched her and wondered if there was something there or if her body just responding to not having sex in almost a year.

Garrick knew he had to get out of there as soon as possible. Between the view and this alluring woman sending him a flirtatious smile, things were moving too fast for him. If he let her take control, or even think she was in control, he was in trouble.

"Lily," he said cautiously, "what do you do that affords you the penthouse apartment with this incredible view?"

Lily cleared her throat and turned back to the view. That was faster than usual. In a joking tone, she asked, "Are you a cop?"

Garrick's brows centered for a second, then relaxed as he laughed. Her reaction to his question was textbook suspicious. She liked him and didn't want him to know she was a criminal. All she had to say was real estate, but even mentioning the words made her feel guilty.

"Just because a brother wants some information makes him a cop?"

Lily shrugged. "Don't you enjoy the mystery?"

"I'm not much for mystery," he said sternly. "I like putting my cards on the table."

Lily studied him for a moment. "Because you don't trust anyone."

She was more perceptive than he expected. "I got no problem with trust, Lily Wolfe. I just need some information."

"I can show you my driver's license if you'd like."

"Honestly, you should be doing the same."

Lily rolled her eyes. "You're an honest man. I can tell from your face. Your expressions, your gestures and especially your not wanting to come in without my permission. Psychology 101."

"That's a bunch of B.S."

"Also, I have a gun in my purse."

"Why do you have a gun?" Garrick cringed inside as he caught himself. It was too late. He'd asked it. He should have just laughed.

Lily was puzzled by his expression. This guy was way too serious for his own good. "I don't have a gun, Garrick. I was just—"

"Why would she need a gun?" a voice said.

Garrick wasn't sure how long Brody Saunders had been standing there and that bothered him. He was trained to know when someone was coming up behind him; to feel if he was being watched, but Lily had provided too much of a distraction to his senses.

"We were just kidding." Lily was annoyed that Brody was even here. Her father had ordered him to drive her to her condo and help her move, but she really wanted to be alone. "Did you get my mail?"

Brody leaned against the doorway, keeping his eyes on Garrick. "He couldn't find it. You sure you have some?"

"Yes, I'm sure." Lily had forwarded her mail to her condo on the day she heard about her father's attack. "There should be some."

"Who's your friend?" Brody asked.

"He's my neighbor," Lily said. "Garrick Pratt, this is Brody Saunders."

As the men shook hands, they studied each other intently. Garrick took in his other target. He would have to find a way to get Brody to like him, but that wasn't going to happen anytime soon. Garrick could tell that Brody was more like him: suspicious.

"I can help you move if you have more—"

"We're good," Brody interrupted. "I brought up two bags. There are only two more. I'll get them."

Garrick had already overstayed his welcome according to his own plan. "I have an appointment to get to anyway."

He held his hand out to her, confident that he had done his job despite the unique distractions she caused. "It was nice meeting you."

There was that charge again, but this time Lily felt it even before their hands connected. It was more an anticipation that she savored. His hand was possessive and demanding. It made her imagine him as a lover; the way he would hold her; the way he would take her.

She was entirely too horny for her own good and pulled her hand away. She watched with intrigue as he turned his charming, yet nonplussed, smile to Brody, ignoring Brody's cold response. She could tell there was something about this man in the way he walked; as if he knew everything he was and what he stood for.

"Who is that guy?" Brody followed her back into the living room.

"I don't know." Lily felt a little twinkle in her toes. "But I'm sure as hell going to find out."

As he drove his rented SUV out of the condo's parking garage, Garrick was feeling good about himself. Yes, he was being cocky, but this was his job and he was good. It didn't make any difference how he got the bad guy; he was just going to get him. Or, in this case, he was going to get her.

He had made the right choice to leave when he did, although he was certain if he wanted to stay, Lily would have made that possible regardless of Brody's reaction. It felt as if he had stayed too long, but the truth was, things had moved so fast, it only seemed as though he had been there for a short while.

Lily was going to be one to take notice of; unlike Carly, who was easy to handle. Carly was beautiful, but she had a cold heart. She wasn't any good inside and that was how he was able to keep from sleeping with her, although she'd given him ample opportunity and encouragement. No, Lily had true warmth inside her and it attracted him very much. He just had to remember it was probably the only honest thing about her.

She was hiding something. She was guilty.

He glanced down at his ringing phone, expecting to see Jamarr's number. It was clear that Jamarr had taken Ward Wolfe home with him and was hoping this case could put an end to that. He would want to check in every day, but Garrick had a surprise for him. That wasn't going to happen.

Garrick used his resources at FBI headquarters in Quantico, Virginia, and found out that the brass didn't want anything to do with Ward Wolfe; not anymore. They were giving Jamarr some room as a reward for closing a major insurance fraud case earlier that year.

However, it wasn't Jamarr on the phone. It was his brother,

Dan, the only person who knew where he was and what he was doing.

"Is everything okay?" Garrick asked.

"I'm fine," Dan answered in his usual jovial half-speaking, half-laughing voice. "Thanks for asking. How are you?"

"I told you not to call unless it was important."

"Let's face it, bro, you're not chasing after the mob. All your targets are old, stuffy white guys or bougie black millionaires. You're not in any danger."

"Well, we can't all teach junior-high soccer."

Dan laughed out loud that time. "You got me."

They were the cop and the teacher; two unlikely survivors of the harshest streets on Chicago's west side. Separated by only two years with two different fathers neither had ever seen, and brought together by a hardworking, loving and take-no-crap mother who died too young. They were more than brothers. They were best friends.

"She was over here." Dan's voice suddenly took a serious tone.

Garrick pulled his car over for this. "Melinda came to your apartment?"

"No, she broke into yours. I'm at your place now."

Garrick gritted his teeth. "What did she take?"

"I can't tell," he answered. "She just tore the place apart, but I'm sure she was looking for a trace on you."

"Is she still messing with you?"

"She calls me at least twice a day begging to know where you are. Are you sure you made it clear to her it was over?"

Garrick had done all he could to make it clear to his ex, Melinda Harrow, that it was over. Her jealousy made his job impossible, and giving him a deadline for a wedding ring didn't help the situation. Garrick didn't do deadlines and nothing mattered more to him than his job. He was afraid nothing ever would. It had been almost a month since he'd ended things, but Melinda, a criminal prosecutor, didn't take no for an answer.

"You know I would handle her if I didn't think she'd use it to track me down," Garrick said. "There isn't anything in my place that would lead to me. I've had everything forwarded to your apartment."

"Just wanted you to know," Dan offered. "She's not giving up."

"Duly noted," Garrick said. "These women."

"Tell me about it. Look, Mike, I got to go, but—"

"Garrick."

"Oh, it's Garrick again, huh?"

"Worked the first time," Garrick said. "Besides, I guess the bureau is too lazy to put together a new set of papers."

"Cutting back." Dan laughed again. "You know I'm playing with you man when I joke about what you do. I know it is dangerous and I'm praying for you."

"I know," Garrick said. "And keep it up."

"Make Mom proud," Dan said.

That's what it was all about, and as Garrick started into traffic again, he promised to keep that in mind the next time the beautiful Ms. Wolfe tilted her head his way.

While he was a kid, his mother, Louise, kept him and his brother in line. She did everything she had to do to keep them out of gangs and off drugs. Garrick had certainly gotten into his share of trouble as a kid, but his mother was the one to keep him from joining the dark side, as they used to describe it in the Monroe household. She was all they had in the world and she was the strongest person Garrick had ever known. She stood up to the gangs on her block, but it was a white-collar criminal that did her in.

A pyramid-banking scheme, one of the best the FBI said

it had ever seen even fifteen years after it was taken down, took her entire life's savings. Garrick remembered her anguish when she realized she had been made a fool. With all the courage she had, there was nothing that could be done. She didn't have the resources or the will to fight them, no matter how hard she tried. The law just didn't want to hear from her. She used the resources from the library of the university where she worked as a cafeteria manager to track down the address of the company, and resorted to picketing outside their building every day.

She would rush to the company in between jobs and shout out to the world what they had done to her. After one evening of exhausting protest, she rushed across the street to catch the last bus going home and was hit by a speeding truck.

So while other boys were dreaming of being hoop stars, rappers or hustlers, Garrick was dreaming of the day he could get revenge for his mother and all the other unsuspecting, working-class poor people out there taken advantage of by big companies. It was the only real, true thing that kept Garrick going. It was the only thing that mattered.

It was the reason he would take down Lily Wolfe, and everyone else involved, no matter how beautiful she was.

Chapter 2

"I'm going to hang up on you," Lily warned. She was sitting in the back seat of the chauffeured car on her way to Wolfe Realty's offices for the first time in almost five years. Too busy unpacking over the weekend, she hadn't had time to lease a car yet.

"I'm just giving you tips," Ward said. "It's no strain for me to remind you of things I do every day."

"I'm telling you right now," Lily said, "if you plan on calling me, Brody or the office, I won't go through with this. I'm doing this so you'll rest and won't worry."

"I'm not worried," he insisted. "I'm trying to help you. Now, make sure you hold a press conference within the next two days to—"

"I don't want to do that." Lily understood that her presence at Wolfe would be for PR, but she wasn't going to muck it up.

She was ashamed to feel so suspicious of her father, but

she was. Despite his continuing promises that his secret plan would be good for the company, until she knew about it she would remain suspicious. She didn't want to be used and she couldn't even let herself consider being caught up in another scandal. She had been searching for Chevy sedans everywhere since the first moment she saw the one outside her father's home.

"Lily, it can't hurt you."

"I'll think about it, but only if you stop calling."

Lily could hear him sigh and at first she thought something was wrong. Her chest tightened and she called his name.

"I really appreciate this, Lily." His tone was thick and unsteady. "I know I don't deserve it. I've been no father to you and…"

Lily felt a knot form in her stomach. Were they going to do this now?

"Dad," she said, "not now. I'll come over and we'll…"

"What?" he asked after her pause lasted a second too long.

"Oh my…" The phone almost slipped out of Lily's hand as the car pulled up to the front steps of the building at the intersection of Peachtree Street and Andrew Young International Boulevard in downtown Atlanta where Wolfe Realty occupied three floors.

"How did this… Dad, I have to go. I'll call you later."

As she stepped out of the car, Lily couldn't hold her shock at the sight of Brody standing in front of a camera crew. When he turned to her and smiled, the crew turned as well and one petite Asian reporter with a pink business suit approached ahead of the others.

She shoved her microphone in Lily's face. "Ms. Wolfe, Jenny Tamura with Channel Five. Can you tell us why you've decided to come back to Wolfe Realty?"

"I…" Lily looked to Brody for an explanation, but he

only smiled and stayed frozen in place. "I'm... If you'll excuse me, please."

Lily walked around the members of the press calling for her to respond to their various questions and trying to block her way in order to keep her in front of their cameras. When she reached Brody, before she could say something, someone yelled out.

"Are you confident your father has cleaned up Wolfe Realty?"

Lily didn't turn around so they wouldn't see how the words startled her. She just stared intently at Brody, whose expression became suddenly dark and ominous. He stared the young reporter down for a few more seconds before looking at Lily.

"Was this your idea?" she asked.

"No," he said. "It was my mistake."

She nodded and walked past him inside the building. He was walking alongside her in no time.

"You'll need this," he said.

She took the security card he offered just as they reached the turnstile where only employees could pass. "What were you thinking?"

"It's protection."

"What do we need protection from?"

"Now that Ward's health condition has made the rounds," Brody said as they entered the elevator, "the company could be vulnerable again."

Lily knew what he meant. After her father was arrested six years ago, the company was under attack from its competitors. They wanted to buy Wolfe Realty up and tear it apart so it couldn't come back and be a threat again. The company held on by a thread.

"Seeing you would let people know things are still...tight."

"You should have warned me," Lily said. "I could have prepared a comment instead of looking like an idiot."

"You would have refused."

"Don't assume that about me." Lily followed him as the elevators opened up. Looking around, she immediately noticed the place had been completely redecorated. Gone was the eclectic, modernist style, replaced by cherry wood, granite and marble. It looked more like a law firm.

Lily only wished her father could do the same in his private life. "I made a promise. I want to help, but I need to know what's going on."

"I'll tell you everything you need to know."

Lily stopped, waiting for Brody to realize she wasn't following him anymore. He turned around and walked back to her.

"What?" he asked.

"This isn't the military," she said. "Don't talk to me like that. I need to know what's going on and that it's all kosher."

Brody shook his head. "I'm disappointed, Lily. Do you think your father would bring you back to this if he thought you could get hurt legally?"

"He let me sign off research reports he knew were false," she said. Looking around, she was curious as to why the halls were so empty at 9:00 a.m. "Where is everyone?"

"I'm sorry you want to go backward," Brody said. "Your father is moving forward and has gone through painstaking efforts to make Wolfe Realty beyond reproach."

Lilly wanted so badly to believe that. It would make things so much easier. "I just hope…"

"Lily." He placed his hand on the doorknob to Ward's office door. "You don't have to worry. Trust me. When things are revealed to you, you will be happy."

"What does that…?"

"Welcome back!"

Lily jumped sky high in the face of an office full of people circling her father's large mahogany desk.

"We'll talk about it later," Brody whispered to her as he veered to the left.

Sabrina Dunkle was the first to rush to an astonished Lily with open arms. She looked all business in her plantain-yellow Tahari suit and perfectly styled glamour-girl hair.

"Hey, girl!"

"Sabrina!" Before Sabrina's arms closed around her, Lily remembered that the woman worked out daily and her hugs were usually more like a body choke. She was pleased when she realized that Sabrina was taking it very easy on her. She was barely squeezing.

Among other things, Sabrina was into perfection and that was the one sticking point between her and Lily. Sabrina came to Wolfe Realty at the same time Lily formally started her role after college. Although Lily had been interning there for three previous years, she and Sabrina were on the same level. They made fast friends despite Lily's head stuck in research papers all day and Sabrina always knee deep in finance.

Lily teased Sabrina for her style, claiming it was a sickness not to be able to leave the house to pick up the newspaper sitting right on the front step, without some makeup on. Sabrina teased Lily for believing in true love instead of going after a brother with the dollars.

"We all thought you would never come back," Sabrina said, almost as much as an accusation as anything else.

"Come on in, girl!" Angela Wachtel, her father's longtime executive assistant, waved her over. She had lost weight since the last time Lily had seen her. She remembered her father mentioning that Angela's low-carb craze was getting on his nerves. "Tell us what you've been up to."

Most of the faces were foreign to Lily. Then there were familiars such as Becky Weldi in accounting, Wendell Osteen in Actuaries and Sherry Laggen in Human Resources, people who had been there since she was just a kid.

Lily felt a mixture of warmth at their kindness and anxiety at her own feelings of expectation. She felt as if she had deserted them; as if she was under some genetic obligation to stick around no matter what happened. She had wondered if they all thought she was cold and callous for leaving her father behind after the death of his wife. Mostly, she feared they might believe she was back to stay.

After well-wishes, brief stories of European travels and doughnuts, the employees made their way back to their cubicles until only Sabrina was left.

"I'm surprised to see you're still here," Lily said as they both sat on the leather sofa against the wall. "When I left, you said you were leaving, too. You've always wanted to do the big time."

"I did," Sabrina said. "After you left, I got a job at a Fortune 500 in Midtown. It was glamorous, great money and all that."

"But?"

"I was nobody." Sabrina shrugged, her smile showing perfectly white teeth that sparkled against her dark brown skin. "I was just one of many and I felt invisible. So, when Brody asked me back, I came back."

"He's always taken a liking to you."

Sabrina shrugged again. "It came in handy that time I guess. So, there I was a manager among many. Here, I'm vice president of finance for human resources."

"So you came back for a bigger title on your business card."

"Titles mean everything, Lily. You're not in loose Paris anymore. It's uptight Atlanta. Title, college, neighborhood and car, that's all people want to know."

"I know where I am," Lily said. "I was just hoping I would miss it more."

"Well, I'll get you back in step." Sabrina scooted closer

with a mischievous smile on her face. "First things first. I'm going to find you a man 'cause I know those French boys don't know how to throw down like a southern brother."

"Nobody throws down like a southern brother," Lily said, laughing. "But I think I've already got someone in mind."

She hadn't been able to stop thinking of Garrick Pratt all weekend. She had knocked on his door twice over the weekend, but he wasn't home. Feeling that was brazen enough, Lily decided against leaving a note.

"What does he do?" was Sabrina's first question, always keeping it real when it came to what mattered.

"I don't know," Lily said, realizing how clueless she was about him. "But he's fine and he's just the right kind of uptight that makes him a challenge. I'm going to loosen him up."

Sanctuary was only a few seconds away, Lily said to herself as the elevator doors to her building closed and the elevator started up.

It had been one hell of a day. After a few peaceful moments with Sabrina, Lily went in search of Brody, who loaded her desk with business reports, articles and other documents to keep her busy. She had been unable to make much progress as one person after another stuck their head in the door to ask about her father, make introductions or engage in small talk.

Starting at ten, Lily was called into a series of meetings from departments such as Project Management, Marketing and Human Resources, only broken by a lunch served in her office as she and Brody watched a congressional session on C-SPAN 2 of the Senate's Banking, Housing and Urban Affairs Committee. Returning to her father's office, the pile on her desk had somehow grown in her absence.

All the while, she continued to feel apprehensive about being there. At some point in the day, the new decorations ceased to quell her memories of some of the worst days in her life. She remembered walking down the hallway to her father's office with the eyes of the company's employees on her, all of them wondering what her family was hiding from them.

All she'd wanted today was to get inside her home and take a long, steaming hot bath with a glass...no, a bottle of wine and thoughts of...

Lily blinked as the elevator door opened on the fourth floor to reveal a barely clothed and not too profusely sweating Garrick.

"Lily." Garrick said her name as a hello, glad that he had timed this right. From the gym, he could see the front of the building perfectly when Lily stepped out of her chauffeured car. He carefully made sure he would be there waiting when her elevator made its way up.

"Hi." Lily swallowed nervously as if he could read her mind; her dirty mind. She couldn't help but react to the sight of his trim, dark body in a gray tank and black shorts. "You were, uh...um."

"Working out. Yeah, I like the gym here. It's big enough not to be crowded after work hours. You use it?"

Lily looked away, wondering how much of a toll the wear of the day had taken on her looks. "I um...have in the past for weights. I have a...a treadmill in my apartment."

"I remember," he said, taking the opportunity to get a good look at her. She looked incredibly sharp in a lavender pantsuit. The fabric was soft, but the lines were sharp, indicating she was all woman but meant business. Although her hair was still loose and wild, wearing makeup made her look more sophisticated and serious.

Garrick would be careful not to underestimate this woman. She possessed more than the necessary tools to force his hand and allow him to make a mistake. And when she turned back to him, he saw that the intimacy of his response had affected her.

Who did he think he was? Lily wondered. His deep voice

and classic smile made him prime player material, but she sensed he wasn't trying to be that. Still, he was trying to be something. Or maybe she was reading him wrong.

"I owe you an apology," she said, finally confident that she could complete a sentence without embarrassing herself again. The way he carried himself, Lily felt he was used to classy women and she seemed to be anything but in his presence.

Garrick's brow centered.

"For Brody," she explained. "The way he acted Saturday. He was really rude."

Garrick shrugged. "I wouldn't want any man near you either."

It was Lily's turn to frown. "You… No, he's not my man."

Garrick pretended to be pleasantly surprised. "You sure he knows that?"

"We work together," she answered, happy to have that cleared up. "He's just the suspicious type."

"Is there a reason?" Garrick wasn't so sure that came out as natural as he needed it to. He had to gauge his windows and he might have been hasty with that one.

Lily lowered her head, looking at the floor. She laughed as if at an inside joke and secretly thanked God as the bell sounded and the elevator opened up. "Here we are."

She wasn't too crafty, Garrick thought, but she was good enough. "After you."

"So what do you do, Garrick? It's Garrick, right?" As if she had forgotten.

He nodded as he walked alongside her toward his apartment. "I'm a development director. Or well, I used to be."

"What do you mean?" They stopped at his door.

"It's a long story." Garrick knew that it was too soon to connect that part of the plan. "How about you?"

Lily swallowed again and pasted on her worthiest smile. "I'm a business analyst."

At least that wasn't a complete lie. That was what she did for a living. She was just taking a short sabbatical at Wolfe Realty.

"Sounds interesting." Garrick blamed himself for her reluctance. He wasn't doing a good enough job of making her act on her interest. He had to get some room on her mental list of preoccupations. "I'd love to hear about it sometime."

He noticed her eyes widen a bit. She was hesitant, but he wouldn't give her a chance to ponder. "It's nice seeing you again. I'm sorry I look like such a scrub."

Lily thought it was a shame how just a hint of interest from a man she didn't even know could wipe away a bad day. "You don't look like a scrub."

"Next to you," he said, looking her over, "I look…"

"Good." A smooth smile formed across her lips. "You look real good."

Garrick was speechless and this time it wasn't an act. The twinkle in her eyes and the easy flow of her lips made him pause. He recovered quickly, pleased and more confident that he was on her mental preoccupations list. Knowing he had to end this interaction before it seemed all too convenient, he was struck by that same desire he'd had before not to. He had to work past it.

"You have a good day, Lily."

"Sure," was all she got out before he was inside and the door closed behind him.

Standing at his door, Lily didn't know why she felt as if she'd just been rejected. It was him who gave the I-want-to-see-you-again cues. Shaking her head, she turned down the hallway and started for her place. Had she been away too long to remember how confusing American brothers were?

Later, lying back against the neck cushion at the head of her tub, Lily closed her eyes and savored the vision of

Garrick's sweating, muscular arms and thighs. She imagined his chiseled stomach and that indention between his stomach and the tops of his hips. It added heat to the already scalding water. She cooled herself with a sip from the chilled glass of wine in her hand.

Basking in the freedom, she thought of throwing caution to the wind and asking him out. Selfishly, she felt she deserved some release, but only for a second. The truth was, she had come home to focus on her father's health and their relationship and hadn't done much for either so far. As fine as he was, Garrick would have to move to the back burner.

"Gin on the rocks."

Lily ignored the look on the waiter's face as she gave him her drink order. She knew what he was thinking. That was a man's drink. Little did he know she'd had another encounter with the press asking uncomfortable questions; mainly if she was going to take over Wolfe Realty and clean it up now that it seemed as if her father was going to die.

"That's what I'm talking about," Sabrina said as she leaned back in the plush camel leather chair. "You learned how to drink in Paris."

They were sitting at a corner table in one of the hottest jazz clubs in Midtown. In the brief time she had been at Wolfe Realty, Lily had found herself able to slip back in much easier than she'd thought. Not much had changed and she wasn't so sure that was a good thing.

The one thing she found relaxing and reassuring was Sabrina. They had never been the best of friends, but Sabrina was helpful when it came to social events going on over the next few weeks; the events her father needed her to attend. It was Sabrina who'd decided to go out for drinks after work. Lily had agreed, hopeful she could let loose after the pressure of being the "face" of Wolfe Realty really got to her.

"They don't drink like this in Paris," Lily said, avoiding eye contact with a smarmy brother who was passing by and looking her way. "But wine just wouldn't cut it after this day."

"The press has to go for the jugular," Sabrina explained. "Don't let it get to you. You've done good this week. You're sliding right back in."

Lily tried to smile, but couldn't quite make it happen. "Thanks."

"I know what you're thinking," Sabrina said. "Things are different."

"I'm not thinking…" Lily sighed, unable to pull off a lie. "It's just that I was planning on being here just for Dad and…"

"That's what you're doing."

Lily nodded. "Yes, just not… You're right. I mean, every time I go over to my dad's house, all we do is talk about everything that doesn't mean anything. At least at Wolfe Realty, I can do something for him."

Sabrina leaned forward with a long face. "It was real hard here after you left."

"I didn't have a choice."

"I know you were dealing with your stuff, Lil." Sabrina lowered her head, staring at her open palms. "It was just…I mean, after the arrests and the trial, I thought it couldn't get worse. I felt like I was trapped, you know."

"You should have quit earlier," Lily said.

"I couldn't desert your father like that. I respected him too much."

"But did you believe him?" Lily asked.

Looking up, Sabrina blinked before turning away as the waiter returned with their drinks. After he left, she began to nod without saying a word.

"You stayed out of loyalty," Lily said. "You think I was disloyal?"

"I'm not judging you, Lil. Your mother just died. You had to do what you thought you—"

"I thought he was guilty." Lily took a hard swig of her drink after she heard herself say the words.

Sabrina leaned back, her lips parted but not speaking a word.

"All that time I was speaking up for him and telling you how he was being targeted because he was a successful black businessman…" Lily felt too ashamed to finish.

"Well…what…what do you think now?"

"I don't think much of anything," Lily said. "I know that I love him and I want to make peace with him. I want to help him."

"You're helping him by what you're doing and you're sure as hell helping me."

"I know you're overloaded," Lily said. "You should hire someone."

"Your dad has nixed that. Salary, benefits, paperwork. With the changes coming, he doesn't want to add—"

"What changes?" Lily leaned forward.

Sabrina's eyes widened as she shrugged her shoulders. "Talk to Brody."

Lily had already had two arguments that week with Brody over missing files he had removed from her father's office. "I'm asking you."

"I don't have anything to tell you," Sabrina said. "I just know things are changing. Your father has frozen all hiring, cut spending, contributions and has limited what financial information even I have access to. It's like the Ward and Brody Show and the rest of us are just along for the ride."

Lily didn't like the sound of that. It was something a smaller company could do, but not one that had been so recently under legal suspicion. "What do you think it's for?"

"Something worth keeping from everyone," Sabrina said.

"Just like last time," Lily said, noting Sabrina's cautious expression. "I don't want to talk about this anymore either."

"Damn." Sabrina finished her drink. "I don't know how it got that heavy anyway."

"We came to unwind." Lily wasn't surprised that her first thought was of Garrick. "Look at some of these men like they're pieces of meat. Maybe make a few lewd comments."

"These brothers tire me," Sabrina said with a disaffected tone.

Lily remembered Sabrina as being sort of man crazy. Her disinterest had to mean she already had someone; or had them in mind. "What's his name?"

Sabrina blushed, shaking her head. "Nuh-uh. You first. Tell me about this new neighbor."

"There's nothing to tell," Lily said. "Like I said, I'm here for Dad."

Sabrina laughed. "Word of advice, Lil."

"What's so funny?"

"Don't play the sacrificing, self-denying sistah. It doesn't work for you."

"Between Dad and work, I just don't have the time."

"If he's the right man, you'll find the time. Fit him in."

"Fit him into what?"

"Either your dad or work or both. If you want him, you'll find a way."

"I guess I don't really want him," Lily said.

The girls caught eyes and they both threw their heads back in laughter.

"You were never a good liar, Lily."

"You need to tell me that you understand," Garrick said in a stern, resolute tone.

He only heard a sigh on the other end of the line and his patience was wearing thin.

He had never been in love with Melinda Harrow because he was never given the chance to. The way he met her was ideal—at a picnic in Chicago's famous Grant Park. She was introduced to him by his cousin, Louis. Garrick had just finished an insurance-scam case and was looking to blow off some steam. An intelligent sister, she was beautiful, tall, glamorous and recently divorced.

He should have paid more attention to that last point.

Melinda was cool to be with at first, but once the Frasier case came and Garrick threw himself into it, things changed. She became suspicious and extremely high maintenance, making his life incredibly difficult for two months. He thought of ending it, but her beauty made him hesitate and he enjoyed the sex. Just as the Frasier case wound down and he thought he might be able to make a real relationship out it, he came upon her, a criminal prosecutor, rummaging through his bedroom drawers after breaking into his home.

He ended it, and found out that Melinda wasn't interested in being dumped so soon after being left by her husband. Garrick was grateful to get out of Chicago, which was part of the reason he agreed to work on the Wolfe case with just two days' notice. He thought he could get away from Melinda.

Now, if she would just leave his brother alone. She was trying to track him down and knew that Dan was the only person who knew where he was. For the second time since leaving, Garrick had gotten a call from his brother that she was harassing him for information.

"You're not listening to me, Michael." Melinda's voice made it seem as if she was trying to cry for effect, but she wasn't quite cutting it.

"Just tell me you understand," he ordered. "You're going to stay away from Dan."

"Give me a reason to." Her voice was suddenly cold and completely void of emotion.

Garrick took a deep breath. The threats would come soon. "Don't push me, Melinda. You're not going to win…"

"We'll see about that."

There was a click and Garrick knew she'd hung up. Melinda always had to get the last word.

"Must be a woman."

He turned to see Carolyn standing in the doorway of the private room he had excused himself to at the FBI office. She held a very pleased smirk on her face in response to his frustration.

Garrick stuffed the phone in his back pocket. "You ready?"

Carolyn tossed her file on the table and stood across from him, both hands on her hips. "You'll have to do better than that to evade me."

Garrick smiled, appreciating Carolyn's attempts to form a friendship. He hadn't been that responsive. "Okay, yes… It's a woman. An ex."

"Ohhh, the best kind."

"Don't tease," he said. "You remember being single."

"It's been ten years, but yes, I do." She sat down. "I remember how it was impossible to do this job and date. Dating was the worst."

"Not worse than breaking up." He envied her marriage. In his twenties, Garrick had thought he would push getting married back to forty, but at thirty-five, he would give anything to have something stable, something real like marriage. Only, he knew he wasn't living a life that made it possible. Still, it didn't stop him from wanting someone he could trust with his secrets; somewhere he could rest his head.

She frowned suspiciously. "You okay with this?"

"Don't question where my head is," Garrick said. "I'm a professional."

"Even the most professional of us can get caught up."

"The ex is history."

"I'm not talking about her."

They stared at each other for a second before Garrick rolled his eyes and reached forward, grabbing the folder. "What you got for me?"

"Just a trace of everywhere Lily Wolfe and Brody Saunders have been and what they've been doing for the past three days. Basically there's nothing."

"They're white-collar criminals. You won't find anything following them on the street. All their crimes are done in the safety of their offices and over their cell phones and BlackBerries."

Garrick opened the folder and cursed Carolyn under his breath because he was having a hard time concentrating. He looked up and saw the satisfied look on her face and slammed the folder shut.

"What?" he asked.

"Carly Frasier," she said. "Now Lily Wolfe. How do you do it?"

Garrick smiled and nodded. "It's my job."

"Yes, but you're not a Casanova," she said.

"You want to know how I get these women to let me into their lives?"

"Oh no." She leaned back, waving her hands with palms out. "I know how you do it. You're handsome as hell and have a great ass. I want to know how you keep from falling. How you keep from hitting the sheets."

Garrick laughed, slapping his hand on the table. "You're funny, Carolyn."

"Tell me," she urged.

Garrick became very serious. "I just remember who they really are. I remember why I'm doing this."

"Is that working with Lily Wolfe?"

Garrick nodded, not sure what words he could find.

"And you don't feel guilty?" she asked. "I mean, we all feel guilty for some of the lies we tell, but you get these women to fall in love with you."

Garrick looked down at the folder again. He didn't want to talk about it anymore. "I just do what I have to do to get justice."

"I know," she said. "I just also know it gets hard, so I hope you won't shut me out. I'm here to help you."

He looked up at her and grinned. "That's good to hear, 'cause I have a feeling I'll be calling you on that."

Here she was, after fifteen minutes of reminding herself it was the twenty-first century, standing at Garrick's door. A commitment Lily had made to Sabrina after several drinks seemed so simple at the time. She was able to convince herself that asking Garrick to dinner was what he wanted. He was the one to say he wanted to hear more about what she did sometime. That was still code for *I'd like to go out,* wasn't it?

Sober and two days later, things weren't quite as clear. Lily's own relationship mistakes made her more cautious, and even though she was very attracted to Garrick, she didn't trust herself. Was she genuinely interested in him or just horny? Would that show? He seemed to be a cautious person; introspective and perceptive. Would she seem too forward, too loose?

Why did she care so much? It wasn't as if she was in love with him. She was just interested. The worst that could happen, he would say no. Of course, followed by running into him absolutely every day, with the best days being the ones she ran into him with his girlfriend, who would of course be younger and prettier with a squeaky-clean family past.

"Stop it," she whispered to herself.

Yes, there were reasons for her to be cautious, but she couldn't be this person anymore. Ignoring her feelings; passing on opportunities. What happened to gaining sexual confidence with age? Something about this man made her nervous just thinking of him, and maybe that was why she was so interested.

As she raised her fist to the door, her action was halted by the sounds she heard. Laughing, but not just laughing. Two people were laughing and one was a woman. Lily felt her stomach tighten as she heard the laughter getting louder, closer. Her brain was telling her to run, but she was frozen in place.

Garrick looked surprised when he opened the door, but he was really relieved. Watching through the peephole, he had been afraid she would change her mind and go back to her apartment.

"Lily." He smiled, taking a moment to appreciate how shapely her figure looked in a red satin tank top and low-rise jean shorts.

"Hi." Lily's fingers dug into her palms as she smiled as wide as she could. Her eyes darted to his right, noticing the attractive white woman with a blond ponytail smiling while sipping a glass of wine.

"Did you... Are you stopping by for a visit?" Garrick was working hard to read her expression at the sight of Carolyn.

"No, I..." She stammered for words. "Just thought I'd say hi. I'm on my way out, running errands. I..."

"I'm sorry." Garrick stepped aside, opening the door wide. "Come on in."

"No, it's okay." She got a better look at the woman, who was dressed in a very casual top and shorts. The easy way with which she stood there made Lily uncomfortable. "I have to get going. I just wanted to make sure you were getting along well."

"I'm doing great," Garrick said. "Annette, this is my neighbor down the hall, Lily Wolfe. Lily, this is my friend Annette."

Annette approached her with such a confident smile, it made Lily feel as if the woman was welcoming Lily into her home. It was stupid for her to think that Garrick didn't have a woman.

"It's nice to meet you," Annette said, holding out her hand.

Lily shook her hand, trying to meet her aggressive grip. "Same here. I really should…"

"That name." Annette leaned back, frowning. "Wolfe. It sounds…familiar."

Lily felt her nerves stand on end as her eyes shifted to Garrick.

"Annie's a journalist," Garrick said, not sure he liked what Carolyn was trying. He told her to follow his lead. He should have known something was wrong when she agreed too quickly. "She's naturally inquisitive."

"Were you in the news recently?" Annette asked.

"I don't think so." Lily hated lying, but she felt on the spot and wanted nothing more than to get as far away from this woman as possible.

"She just got back in the country," Garrick said. "She hasn't had time to make the news."

Garrick realized his mistake the second he spoke. Lily never told him where she'd been, just that she'd been gone four years. Everything around him slowed to a standstill as he studied her, waiting to see if she'd noticed his gaffe.

"Sorry," Lily said as she began backing out. "I really have to go. Someone is waiting. We have…um it's lunch."

Garrick was grateful that she seemed too uncomfortable to notice his slipup. "Well, okay, but I…"

She didn't wait to hear more, as she was halfway to the elevator. She didn't look back until she heard the door close. She let out a breath and her shoulders fell.

"Damn," she whispered to herself, feeling completely defeated. So much for taking a chance.

"What in the hell did you do that for?" Garrick asked.

Carolyn shrugged. "It was natural."

"That's not what I asked you to do."

"You're the one letting things slip," Carolyn said. "Why didn't you just give her address in Paris while you were at it? I think she makes you nervous."

He pointed to her. "*You* made me nervous. This is why I like working alone."

"You asked me here. Remember that."

"I told you exactly what I wanted you to do." Garrick sat down on the sofa, wondering if maybe Carolyn was right. There was more to his apprehension about Lily than was on the surface.

"Why would you want to make her jealous anyway? I mean, if she thinks you're dating, she won't be interested."

"She's not jealous," Garrick said. "She's just more curious now. When she finds out I'm not dating anyone, she'll be relieved and I'll make my move."

Carolyn stood at the edge of the sofa, her arms folded across her chest. "I underestimated you. You are smooth at this."

"That's what I've been telling you."

"A real jerk," she added, "but good."

Garrick knew that was the truth. So why was he still worried?

Chapter 3

Never had Lily been so grateful for a Monday. Actually, she had never been grateful for a Monday ever, until today.

After dropping in on Garrick and his lovefest with long-legged Barbie early Saturday, Lily went out of her way to avoid running into him again. She even considered staying at her father's house over the weekend because the fear of running into him, or even worse—him with her, in the elevator made her almost nauseous.

Even this morning, as she tiptoed down the hall, after peeking out and making sure he wasn't there, the noise of a door unlocking, ready to open, made her jump. She was ready to turn and run back to her apartment until she realized it wasn't his door.

After staying hostage in her apartment over the previous day, Lily was eager to get back to work for the distraction and escape. Having crossed Garrick off her list, she felt confident that she could return to focusing on work and dealing with her father. She was going to be hopeful. As she entered her office, however, what she saw dampened her spirits and made her angry.

They didn't seem too excited to see her either.

"What are you doing here?" she asked, storming to the desk.

Brody was hastily gathering up papers as her father sat in his chair, looking annoyed.

"I could ask you the same thing," Ward said. "It's seven-thirty. Since when did you become a morning person?"

"Not important." Lily didn't want to admit that she was here early because she hoped leaving early would help her avoid Garrick. "Answer me."

Ward smiled. "I raised a feisty one, Brody."

Brody grumbled, offering a quick, fake smile while he continued collecting the papers.

Looking down, Lily could only catch glimpses of the property management reports on properties for sale. She did spot an invoice from a name she didn't recognize: AFC Corporation.

Reaching for the document, Lily was surprised by Brody's quick reaction. He dropped everything in his hand just in time to grab it out from under her. The move was too obvious to even pretend not to notice.

"That's not for you," Brody said.

Lily's eyes shot to her father, whose uncomfortable look told her everything she needed to know. They were up to something and her heart wanted to break.

"I want to know what that invoice is," she said. "Who is AFC?"

"It's for Brody to handle." Ward pushed against the desk to back up.

A pained looked on his face made her rush around to him, but Brody held his hand out to stop her.

"I got him," he said, reaching out to Ward.

"This is ridiculous," Lily said. "You're not supposed to be

working at all. You're still in recovery. If you show bad signs at your next checkup, you'll have to have surgery."

"I'm fine," Ward said. "Besides, I'm not working. I just came to sign some documents and I'm on my way back."

"What documents?" she asked.

Brody and her father looked at each other before her father responded. "We've talked about this, Lily. Brody and I are handling it."

"That wasn't my question," she said. Her father's stern stare tempered her challenge. "Why couldn't he come to you?"

"It was his idea," Brody said. All the papers gathered, he stuffed them in his briefcase and slammed it shut. "I have to go now. Late for a meeting in Dunwoody."

"Wait a second!" Lily was shaking her head in disbelief. "You can't expect me to just ignore this very suspicious scene."

"I expect you to do as you agreed to," Ward said with a hardline expression. "I'm disappointed that you think I'm doing something wrong. I made it clear to you that isn't the case this time."

"Even though you can't tell me anything?" she asked sarcastically. "Yes, no reason to question that at all. After all, blind belief has worked so well for me here."

Looking at the expression on her father's face, Lily knew she had pushed him too far. As he stood up, she could see his hand grab tightly to Brody's arm. She was stressing him and even though she had a right to an answer, it wasn't worth making things worse.

"You can't come here," she said, turning away to avoid eye contact. She reached into her in-box, pretending to care about what was on the cover of the morning's *Atlanta Journal Constitution*. "What you need, Brody can bring to you."

"That's what I said." Brody turned to Ward. "You ready? The car is outside."

Ward nodded. "You know the annual Atlanta Cancer Foundation ball is in two weeks. We are a major sponsor, Lily."

Lily nodded. "I'll be there. Don't worry."

"I'm not worried." As he passed her, Ward stopped, sighed and then continued. "I know I can count on you."

Lily wondered if he had considered hugging her or touching her at all when he'd stopped and thought against it. She blamed herself, but blamed him even more.

Who was this man? She called him Dad, but there were times, like just now, when she didn't even know him and wasn't sure she wanted to. Yes, she loved him, but no matter how hard she tried, she couldn't trust him. He was keeping something from her, and after everything that they had been through, Lily couldn't understand how he could say he loved her and take this route.

Then she realized she couldn't remember the last time her father actually told her he loved her. What a mess.

"I think you're being paranoid," Sabrina said as she and Lily sat down in the corner they made for themselves at Dream, a trendy nightclub in Midtown.

"Don't you think I have a right to be?" Lily asked. She wasn't ready to let go of the disturbing information she had received earlier that day.

After trying to calm down from the earlier scene she had walked in on, Lily was unable to let her suspicions go. She wanted to find out what papers Brody had taken from the office; papers he didn't want her to see. When she went to his office to ask who he was meeting with in Dunwoody, Trisha, his executive assistant, looked at her with a blank stare.

"Trish is a goofball," Sabrina said. "Who knows what she got right."

"She specifically said Brody was in the West End," Lily

said. "That's on the complete opposite side of Atlanta than Dunwoody."

"So maybe he was going to Dunwoody first or after." Sabrina shrugged before tilting her head in the direction of two men walking by.

Lily ignored them, men being the last thing on her mind right now. "I made her show me his calendar. He had nothing in Dunwoody today. He was lying to me."

"Maybe he was lying to Trish."

"Either way," Lily said. "he's lying and he did not want me to see those papers."

Sabrina studied her, nodding slowly. "I'll give you he's acting suspiciously, but I think it's because he's nervous about you being back."

"Oh please. I'm not a threat to him and he knows it. He's closer to my father than I am. Hell, Dad doesn't even talk to me." Lily leaned back with a defeated sigh. "This was all a mistake."

"Don't say that," Sabrina said. "You came back to salvage some semblance of family. That can't be a mistake."

"You want to know what's pitiful?" Lily asked, lowering her head to focus on her hands placed on her lap. "Since I've been here, I've been alone with my father countless times and we haven't even touched on our shell of a relationship."

"Merry Christmas."

Lily looked up to find why Sabrina wasn't paying her any attention. A wide, mischievous smile was framing her face and Lily knew that was the universal look for *I've spotted the hottest guy in the room.* Never one to be too depressed to enjoy some eye candy, Lily tracked down Sabrina's discovery and found him right away.

"What?" Sabrina asked in response to Lily's loud gasp.

"The one in the purple polo and blue jeans?" Lily asked. "That's who you're eyeing?"

"That's who every woman in this club is eyeing."

Garrick did look good. He had the preppy look down pat and wore it nice and clean. As he sat down at the bar, he seemed oblivious to the approving stares of all the women, and a few men, around him.

"That's him," Lily said, feeling as if she wanted to hide.

It seemed to take Sabrina a few moments, but she quickly caught on. "That's the neighbor? The brother you... *ooohhhhh,* where's the white girl?"

"Don't go there, Sabrina."

"Go on and talk to him, girl. Bring the brother back home where he belongs."

Lily smiled, but shook her head. "I don't think so. I think walking in on him with that woman was a sign for me not to be distracted."

"Which you are anyway," Sabrina said. "Just say hello. Get us a free drink."

Lily was shaking her head although she already knew she was going to go over. She just had to work up the nerve. There was no real justification for her to feel awkward. There was nothing between them besides her attraction and mistaken belief that he had asked her out. No harm could be done in just saying hello.

Or so she thought. The second Lily approached, saying his name, the look on his face as he turned to her told her she was going to smack Sabrina for talking her into this.

"Lily." Garrick's lips formed a half smile as he gripped his drink tight. "How are you?"

"Not great," she said, "but it looks like better than you."

He nodded, a wider smile this time. The softness of her features was very soothing to him. "Is it that obvious?"

"Just thought I would come by and say hello," Lily offered. "My friend and I are just having a few drinks. It's pretty private where we're at, so if you'd..."

"Actually, I…" He shrugged apologetically. "I just want to be alone right now, but thanks."

"Oh." Lily swallowed, hoping she was smiling, even though that kick to her gut hurt something awful. "Okay, that's fine. I understand. Have a nice evening."

She heard him say something as she quickly turned and walked away, but the pounding in her ears drowned it out. What a fool!

"What happened?" Sabrina asked as soon as Lily returned.

Certain he wasn't looking, but just in case he was, Lily kept that smile on her face as she sat delicately back in her chair. "He blew me off."

"He what?"

"He basically asked me to get the hell away from him." Fool me twice, Lily thought. That was that. No more with the hot Mr. Pratt.

"He did not." Sabrina scooted her chair closer to Lily's, looking in Garrick's direction. "What did he say?"

"He asked to be left alone." Lily simply wasn't used to rejection, but this one in particular stung like a bee.

Sabrina's eyes widened. "No, he did not just kick you to the curb. He must play for the other team."

That would be some solace to Lily, but she knew that wasn't true. Romance hadn't been high on her list of priorities while in Paris. She was too busy chasing after her young cousin, with the death wish of working her butt off for an ultracompetitive consulting firm. Had she lost her touch? Was thirty over the hill? Had she forgotten how to read American men?

"He must be playing some game," Sabrina said, rolling her eyes. She made a smacking sound with her lips. "You know what I'm talking about?"

Lily knew all too well. Men who played as if they weren't

interested in order to get a woman more interested. Women, like men, enjoyed a challenge and men would have these women so tied up, they would do anything to get him to ac-knowledge them. Once they did, the woman was putty in his hands. If that was his game, Lily was not that girl.

"I don't think that's what he's doing," Lily said. She wasn't sure what he was up to, but there was something up with him. "I don't care."

Sabrina's dubious expression wouldn't let up. "You sure about that, 'cause…"

"'Cause what?" Lily asked. "'Cause some brother didn't want to be bothered? I don't care about him. I don't even know him. I was just trying to be nice because he looked a mess. All I was going to do was say hello. It was your fault, anyway. I—"

She stopped as Sabrina's head lowered to the ground as she cleared her throat. Lily felt her stomach tightening and wondered if bad luck was the only kind of luck she had.

"Lily?" Garrick waited patiently for her to look up. He believed he might have overplayed his hand. Sometimes he hated this crap.

Lily just stared at him, not saying a word. She didn't look angry or hurt. She just looked…nothing. She wanted it to seem as if she didn't care. She wouldn't give him the pleasure of knowing she did; she really did.

"I'm sorry," Garrick said, standing there awkwardly. He shared an uncomfortable glance with her friend, who clearly did not approve. "Hi."

Sabrina stood up. "I have to go to the ladies' room, but I'll be back."

Those last words were clearly a warning for him, and Garrick nodded his understanding. As the woman left, he took her seat.

"I'm sorry," Garrick repeated.

"You said that already," Lily answered. "Although I'm not sure what you're apologizing for."

"I was rude to you earlier."

"You were honest." Lily shrugged. "You wanted to be left alone. No big deal."

"I've had a bad day," Garrick said. "I shouldn't have taken that out on you."

"You didn't take it out on me," Lily protested. "No need for apologies. If you want to be alone, then…"

"I'm done pouting," he said. "I moved all the way out here from Raleigh for a job that turns out not to exist."

"Sorry to hear that."

"Do you know anything about corporate takeovers?"

"I know they can come without warning. If a company doesn't expect to be taken over, they'll go on with business as usual."

"Well, I'm business as usual. Only one month into the job I'm told my position has been eliminated."

"You might have some legal recourse."

"I just got off the phone with my lawyer. It's not looking good." He shook his head and smiled. "When I saw you walk over, I was like…shit."

"Well that's not the response I'm used to getting."

He laughed. "No, I mean, I was thinking here comes a beautiful, has-herself-together sister I'm attracted to and… damn, a brother ain't got a job."

Lily was more flattered than she expected she should be by his confession. "Why would I care about that?"

"You know how you sisters can be when a man steps to you. A black man without a job? Loser, no good for nothing are the common terms I think used. I wouldn't have a chance with you."

"Are you looking for a chance with me?"

Their eyes locked and Garrick felt his attraction to her was all too real. He didn't need to actually care about someone to be convincing, but this feeling was completely different from anything before. She had a sparkle in her eyes, a tenderness to her lips that made him believe he could know her soul.

"You could say that."

Lily wasn't buying it. "So you were pulling a preemptive strike. Turn me down before I turn you down."

"Very childish, I know, but I wasn't really in the mood for more rejection."

She leaned back in her chair with an austere expression on her face. "So now that you're done feeling sorry for yourself, you thought you'd give me another chance?"

"It's not like that," he answered, getting her point. She wasn't as eager as he may have thought she was. "I'm just here to apologize. If I can stay and talk, I'd be grateful, but I'd understand if…"

"Don't you have a girlfriend to talk to?"

Garrick paused, grateful that she was at least interested enough to ask. "Annette isn't my girlfriend."

"Annette?" Lily asked, knowing that she was playing games despite saying she wouldn't bother.

"Yes, the woman you saw at my apartment Saturday. She's not my…We only have a professional relationship; she works at the company I was just let go from."

Lily accepted the feelings of relief his words placed on her and quickly recovered. "She seemed so familiar with you at your home."

"That's just her style." Garrick wished he could be closer to her. "No, I'm flying solo right now. How about you?"

Lily just smiled and tilted her head.

"Aw, come on," Garrick said. "You've got to offer up more than that."

"I don't have to offer up anything," she corrected.

"You are upset with me."

"I'm not." She waved a dismissing hand. "Get over it."

"Then talk to me."

"What do you want me to talk to you about?" she asked. "My personal life? I don't have one. I've spent the last year working live a slave in Paris."

"See, now *that* sounds interesting." He leaned forward. "Tell me more about that."

"My life in a cubicle? Give me a break."

"You had to have been doing something else," Garrick said.

"No, I didn't." She wasn't going to tell him about spending her nights in shady bars and clubs chasing after her drug-addicted cousin.

Garrick didn't expect much of the truth from her, but he couldn't accuse her of lying if she didn't tell him anything. "You mean to say you were in Paris for a year and didn't find a way to get into any trouble? I don't believe it."

She blinked and looked away, which told him she was guilty as hell, and it made him angry. Garrick stood up. "Let's dance."

Lily's eyes widened as she looked up. "What? I…"

"Don't waste time, woman. They haven't played an R&B tune since I walked in here. If we don't hurry now, they'll get back to hip-hop and I don't think you want me on the dance floor when that happens."

He held out his hand to her and Lily didn't hesitate to take it. Maybe she should have been more tentative, but she didn't want to be. When his hand touched hers, he gripped it tightly, but not too tightly. She felt his strength as he pulled her up effortlessly, and it made her fell small and feminine.

A tingle rushed over the skin on her arm as she came face-to-face with him. She was turned on by the fierce look in his eyes even though they told her he was hiding something. It was something she needed to know.

"One dance," she offered.

He led her to the dance floor, trying to figure out why holding her hand was having this effect on him. He purposefully hadn't had anything to drink because he already sensed this woman could get past him if he wasn't completely clear. Yes, she was pretty, sexy and all that, but she was also a liar and probably worse.

Remember that, he told himself as they began to dance. *Please remember that,* he reminded himself, because the way she was moving right now, so dangerously, made him want to forget.

Maybe it was the club atmosphere or maybe it had just been too long, but Lily was feeling something. It was a dangerous kind of something that told her she was probably better off without it but would never want to be. She felt a charge igniting between them as they danced to the fast beat without words. Their eyes stayed connected and the rest of the dance floor disappeared. She hadn't even noticed that the music had switched to a slow tune until he reached out and took her by the arms.

When he pulled her to him, Lily was taken over by a sensuous urgency. She wanted him to pull her all the way so their bodies would touch, but she came to only inches from him. His head tilted slightly down as hers tilted slightly up. When he started to move, she followed suit and felt a clear tingling sensation in the pit of her stomach.

"Damn," Garrick said, not sure of what else to say. He wasn't playing a part right now. This woman had him with no push and his fifteen years in law enforcement hadn't prepared him for that.

"Am I supposed to reply?" Lily felt it was unfair to ask, considering he was only saying what she was thinking.

"Did I say that out loud?" Garrick laughed. "Sorry 'bout

that. Holding things in has never been my strong point. Not so for you, I guess."

Lily got the message. "I had family stuff going on. That's why I didn't get into any...trouble, as you call it, in Paris. I was dealing with some family drama. Didn't need any more trouble."

"What kind?"

"Nothing that would interest you."

"How do you know what would interest me?"

"You're right," she said. "So, why don't you just tell me?"

"Honesty." Garrick could see she was taken off guard because she stopped dancing.

"What is that supposed to mean?" Lily asked.

"Honesty goes both ways, Lily. I have to be honest with you and tell you that I know about your father."

Lily sighed, suddenly not in the mood to dance anymore. "I doubt you really know about him. You're referring to what you've read in the papers, right? Did you Google me?"

"After I read about your return in the paper, I was curious."

"Is that what you want to know about?" Lily asked. "My father?"

Garrick leaned in, his lips forming the most convincing smile. "No, I just wanted you to know that I know. I sensed apprehension on your part and thought that might be why."

"I'm not apprehensive." Lily felt unexpectedly calmed by his tone and the reassuring look in his eyes. "I'm just private."

"Fine." Garrick accepted that this would take time. Usually impatient to get to the guts of a case, he was willing now to wait. He'd admit it to himself; he was incredibly attracted to Lily Wolfe and he wanted to get to know her better. A lot better.

"Fine," he repeated. "Then we'll save the private for another time. Tell me whatever you want to."

She said nothing but kept her eyes steady on his. Slowly, her hips began to sway again and as he followed her lead, Lily felt powerful, the ultimate aphrodisiac. She had a good feeling about this one and she hadn't had a good feeling about anything in a long time.

More than a few drinks and several dances later, Lily's head was swimming as the elevator to her floor opened up and she and Garrick stepped out. There was a sense of dread that this evening was coming to an end. It had been so fantastic.

After a few more dances, Lily and Garrick returned to their corner, where Sabrina was already engrossed in conversation with two other women she recognized from her health club. Although Sabrina seemed a little suspicious at first, she quickly warmed to Garrick, and Lily was able to sit back and watch him work his considerable charm on her as well.

The only uncomfortable moment came when Lily mentioned Garrick's background and Sabrina suggested he send his résumé to Wolfe Realty. Lily knew she should have been enthusiastic, but she was the last person to encourage anyone to come work for her father's company. It was a shame that she would think that, but she covered it up, giving Garrick one of her business cards, which had just been delivered to her that morning. He seemed interested, but not too eager, and she had to wonder if it was because of what he'd mentioned before about her father.

Despite his talking the overwhelming majority of the time, Lily still sensed there was a mysterious part of Garrick he was holding back from her, but it didn't matter. He made her forget her troubles with his jokes and attention. She enjoyed the way his flirtations were lighthearted with kind smiles, while interspersed with glances that lasted just a second or two too long, long enough to make her uncomfortable in a sexual way. She appreciated the subtle way these looks told her that although he was a good guy and wanted to get to know her, there was no mistaking what else was on his mind.

As each hour passed, Lily felt as if she was connecting more and more with him.

It was midnight when they decided to call it quits and share a cab home. Sabrina took a separate cab, since she was going in a separate direction. Finally alone with him, Lily wanted desperately to kiss him, but he purposefully kept his distance, maintaining that undeniable smile as he told her the story of how he broke his leg playing baseball in college, thus ending his Major League hopes.

Not once had he asked her about her father or any of the mess that she hated talking about. Lily wanted to believe he was being considerate and she was grateful for that. It was embarrassing not being able to talk about one's family, but that was a reality that Lily had gotten used to over the past six years.

She liked Garrick, but there was something about him and the way he had spoken that night that told her this man was black and white when it came to right and wrong. Whether it was his views on the law, politics or culture, everything he'd said that night screamed that he was a man of principle.

On the other hand, he had mentioned that he knew about her father and still seemed interested in her. So, she was hopeful the explanation was that he was honest but fair. If he proved to be that, Lily hoped she could soon tell him the truth about everything. He could be the one man she could trust not to judge her by it.

"This is where we part?" she asked as they stopped at his door first.

Garrick turned to her, all pretenses aside. He was desperately fighting the biting chemistry that had grown between them throughout the evening. It took everything he had to keep his distance in the cab, and now, he just didn't think he had what it took to deny himself what he wanted.

"I can walk you to your door," he said, stepping closer. Her tired eyes only made her look sexier and more seductive. His body was telling him he wanted to sleep with this woman now, and his mind, which he had hoped to rely on, wasn't doing much to combat the desire. "It will give us a few more minutes."

Despite her body wanting him to keep coming closer, Lily lifted her hand to halt his advance. The look in his eyes was hungry and it made her think she might do something she would regret.

"We've had a little too much to drink." She heard her voice crack a little.

Garrick could feel his breathing pick up as his body reacted to her. It was as if he was watching himself, just standing by as he made a huge mistake. This was too soon, but he didn't care at all.

"I want to kiss you," he said with passion in his voice. He took another step forward to where they were only inches apart. Her hand came flat against his chest and the touch set him on fire.

"Careful," was all Lily could whisper, but it was more to herself than Garrick. Her pulse was pounding and she felt a dizzying current rush through her.

"Say yes or no," he whispered to her. "I won't be angry, but I want…"

He was taken aback at first when her lips came to his, but immediately exploded in heat at their soft touch. As if instinct hit him, he reached out for her, pulling her to him. The feel of her body against his sent a shock through his system.

When his fingers pressed against her arms, Lily's flesh pricked at the touch. The pit of her stomach churned as his kiss grew in demand with every passing second. Currents of passion shot through her so quickly, Lily was just as frightened as she was aroused.

Feeling himself getting drunk on her lips, Garrick pressed

harder and let out a slight moan as they separated. His body, urging and pleading for more, was sent a jolt as he felt Lily push away. How quickly he had forgotten himself.

"I'm sorry." Garrick was breathing loudly and quickly as he stepped back. "I just wanted to kiss you, but…"

"It's okay." Lily's hand went to the wall to steady herself. She felt off balance. Was it because of the wine or that kiss? All she knew was that every inch of her was tingling.

"I'm a good guy," Garrick said, reeling from how quickly he had lost himself just now. This was not a good thing.

"I know you're a good guy." She smiled tenderly, getting her wits about her again. "I just need you to know that I'm a good girl."

"There is no misunderstanding." He bent down to retrieve her purse, which she'd apparently let go of during the embrace.

"Good." Lily accepted the purse, making certain to avoid any skin contact. "I think I should say goodnight."

"Sounds like a good idea, but only on one condition."

"What?"

With a look of undeniable determination on his face, he said, "That I can see you again, like dinner later this week."

Lily sighed, hopefully not appearing too eager. "Call me. We'll talk."

"I'll do that."

"Good night, Garrick." Taking a few steps, Lily turned back to him. He was still standing in the same spot, watching her leave, and it made her regret having to walk away. "You'll remember what I said?"

"What?" Garrick couldn't remember much of anything right now.

"Your résumé," she answered. "I might have something for you."

It all came back to him and Garrick suddenly felt like the

biggest jerk in the world. Why should he? After all, she was the criminal. Wasn't she? He wasn't sure of anything right now, except that he wanted to see this woman again as soon as possible.

"Oh yeah," he answered. "I'll get it to you right away."

As he watched her turn and leave again, the sway of her hips giving him a preview of what he would be dreaming about tonight, Garrick tried to refocus. Jamarr would be pleased. He was on his way in.

"I cannot believe you didn't hit that," Sabrina said as she hopped onto the edge of Ward's desk in his office.

Lily was sitting in the chair facing the desk, not yet comfortable with sitting in her father's chair behind the desk. "You don't know me, girl."

"I know what I saw."

"What did you see?" Lily sipped her morning coffee, still feeling the excitement from last night. Sabrina was waiting for her in the office when she arrived that morning, expecting a much juicier story than what she was getting.

"I saw two people who were going to hit it the second they got a chance." Sabrina set her cup of coffee down on the desk. "I saw those glances and smiles. You were committing gesture fornication. Not to mention the dancing."

"All we did was kiss." Lily closed her eyes for a moment, savoring the memory of his lips pressed against hers. "It was a pretty incredible kiss, but nothing more."

"You're the only person on this planet who can spend a year in France and come back sexually repressed."

Lily rolled her eyes. "I'm am not… Look, girl, you let me worry about my sexuality and you worry about what you're going to do when he sends his résumé in."

"Who?"

Both women turned around to see Brody standing in the doorway. Lily distinctly remembered closing the door but hadn't heard the handle click. Brody was a sneaky one and she hadn't forgotten about his lies.

"Girl talk," Sabrina said. "You're not invited."

"I'm COO of this company," Brody said. "If I'm not invited to a conversation, it shouldn't be going on."

He entered the room, standing at the desk. He looked down at Lily, who didn't bother to smile for him. "Still sharing your time between this seat and the sofa?"

"I work where I want," Lily said. "You're the one who wants that chair so much, why don't you sit there?"

Lily was looking straight ahead, but she could feel Brody's eyes dig into her.

Sabrina nervously cleared her throat. "We…we were talking about this man that Lily hooked up with last night, her neighbor."

"I didn't hook up with him," Lily said. "It wasn't like that."

"I wasn't concerned about that part," Brody said. "You were talking about a résumé. Are you considering bringing someone on?"

"It's the same guy," Lily said. "And yes, I am."

"We aren't hiring. You would have known that if you had spoken with me first."

"Since when do I need your permission?" Lily asked.

"What is your problem?" Brody huffed.

As Lily stood up, Sabrina hopped off the desk and headed for the door.

"I think I hear my phone ringing." And with that, she was gone.

"My problem is that I can't trust you," Lily said, "so I'm not inclined to get your permission for anything."

"Get off it," he said. "Your father told you there were things going on that you don't need to know about yet. Why can't you trust him?"

"I'm not talking about him."

"You are if you're talking about me." Brody made his way to the cabinet against the wall and leaned back against his elbows. "Everything I do is based on what he wants, Lily. So you are accusing him if you're accusing me."

Lily fought the urge to back down, knowing that he was probably right. She was all ready to expose Brody for his lies, but not her father.

"Now, tell me about this man," Brody said.

"There's nothing to know," she said. "He does fund development work and I know Sabrina is a little overloaded with all of the changes going on."

"We don't need anyone there," he answered curtly. "We're cutting back our funding."

"I want to wait until we get a look at his résumé."

"Don't you know what it says? You were talking about him as if you were intimate with—"

"Don't go there, Brody."

"Well, I need to check him out."

"A little inappropriate for you to be playing big brother."

"Not for you," he said. "For Wolfe Realty. I have to make sure he isn't kissing up to you with ulterior motives. Your father is vulnerable right now and—"

"Don't repeat the sermon to me." Lily walked over to the sofa and sat down. She found it ironic that Brody would want to investigate Garrick when she felt as if she was the one with something to hide. "You leave him alone. I know what I'm doing."

Brody's tone held his frustration. "Lily, you are not here to run this company. You are here as a figure—"

"You weren't in Dunwoody!" Lily almost surprised herself with her outburst, and from Brody's reaction, she had done the same to him.

Brody lifted his head a bit and relaxed his shoulders. Leaning forward, he stuffed his hands in his coat pockets. "I know you were asking Trish about where I was yesterday."

"You might want to let her in on the lie next time. She left you ass out, buddy."

Brody's lips formed a wry, lopsided smile. "Well, it appears little Lily Wolfe has grown up. She's gotten quite an edge to her."

Lily appreciated the acknowledgment. Now maybe he wouldn't talk down to her so much. "Who is AFC Corp and what do they do?"

"You've gotten very nosy as well." Pulling his left arm out of his pocket, he looked at his watch. "You want answers, talk to your father. I promised him secrecy and unlike you, I'm completely loyal to the man."

Lily shot up from the sofa. "How dare you!"

"Quiet easily, princess." Brody started for the door, doing a half turn to face her. "While you were out getting laid, I was with him trying to help him through those horrible headaches he's been having lately."

"What…" Lily didn't remember headaches as a side effect of his medication. She rushed for her purse. "Why didn't you tell me? Why didn't you call me?"

"I asked him." Brody's voice held a satisfied tone. "After the way you acted in here yesterday morning, he said you wouldn't care."

"You should have called anyway." Grabbing her purse, she headed out the door feeling more guilty than she could have imagined for all the fun she'd had last night.

"What about this guy?" Brody called after her. "I need his—"

"You stay out of my business," she yelled back, "and I'll stay out of yours."

Chapter 4

"So I helped you out, huh?" Carolyn tried to keep pace with Garrick as he walked down the hallway of FBI Atlanta headquarters. "I made her jealous."

"I didn't want you there to make her jealous," Garrick said. "I wanted you there to make her curious. I needed the subject of significant others to come up so I could clear the air. I needed her to bring it up."

"So your objective is to have this woman panting after you so bad that she'll tell you anything you want, give you access to all her files."

"I just want her to trust me." Garrick wasn't really interested in talking about Lily.

He had gone too far with her too soon. Now he seemed too desperate for her attention and that could come back to haunt him very soon. He could decide to pull back now, but it might seem too awkward. It would either make her suspicious or turn her off completely. He had to do damage control.

"Does she?"

Garrick shrugged. "I'm getting there."

Carolyn frowned. "What are you holding back from me?"

"Nothing you need to know."

"We're working together on this, right?"

Garrick nodded. "I told you what happened."

"She kissed you?

"I kissed back." Boy, had he kissed back. He hadn't been able to stop thinking about it.

"You're attracted to her," Carolyn said. "So what? Like I said, she's hot."

Garrick smiled. "You really get me going with that."

Carolyn socked him in the arm. "All men are perverts."

"I won't argue with you there."

"What I'm saying is—" Carolyn stopped as they reached Jamarr's office "—no one expected you not to be hot for her, so I have to believe that worried look on your face is because there is more to it."

"I would just prefer it if she was a selfish witch like Carly Frasier was. It helped me keep my perspective."

"Whatever you do," Carolyn admonished, "don't let it get so far it jeopardizes the case against her. The case comes first."

"I know that."

Before Garrick could knock, the door swung open and Jamarr was stopped in his tracks. "I've been looking for you."

"I'm right here," Garrick said.

"You've been hit."

Garrick lowered his head, surveying himself. "Funny, I feel fine."

"Your identity, joker. A private investigator in Marietta has done a full, bona fide, FBI background search on Garrick

Pratt. He must have used some connections within the agency to get it as detailed as he did. We can't figure out yet who ordered it, but Wolfe Realty is a client. Your girlfriend wants to know what your story is."

"We expected this," Carolyn said. "She wouldn't be doing it if she didn't have something to be paranoid about."

"The good news," Garrick said, not feeling at all happy about this, although he knew he should be, "is that my background will clear and she'll trust me."

"But will she hire you?" Jamarr asked.

"From the way he's putting the moves on her," Carolyn said, "Lily Wolfe will be giving Garrick a key to her house, the office safe and whatever else she's got very soon."

Garrick smiled as the other two laughed, wishing he didn't hate himself right now. Despite his current state of emotion, he knew this was good news. It was common these days for people to Google, the buzzword for Internet search, the latest girl or guy they met at a bar, but this was some serious stuff.

This was beyond a potential employment checkup. Lily was suspicious of anyone coming into her life and Garrick's experience told him that meant she had something to hide.

This was the last straw. The last thing Lily wanted to do was upset her father more, but there was about to be a showdown between her and Brody and the outcome was not going to go well.

When she arrived in her office that morning, a corporate folder was placed directly in the center of her desk with the words PRATT, G. typed in big bold letters. Opening the folder, Lily found herself reading the life story of Garrick Pratt and she was livid.

"What do you…" Trisha shot up from her chair outside Brody's office as Lily passed her by, ignoring her. "Hey!"

When she entered the office, it was empty. She turned to Trisha, who was standing in the doorway with a nervous look on her face. "Where is he?"

"What are you mad about?" Trisha asked.

"Where is he?"

"The bathroom, I guess. He just left two minutes ago."

"I'll wait here." Lily was immovable as she stared Trisha down.

"He doesn't want anyone in his office while he's out."

"I'll wait here," she repeated.

Rolling her eyes, Trisha turned and left.

"Like I care what he wants," Lily whispered to herself. Turning around, she approached Brody's desk and shamelessly started looking through the documents scattered about.

She was struck curious by the first-draft budget reports Brody had tucked underneath an open folder for administrative forms. Midyear reports were due next month and she was curious about the financial situation after her last conversation with Sabrina. Placing her folder down, Lily picked up one of the reports and scanned it. Everything looked in place, but she had very little to gauge on since this wasn't her area. She thought of asking Sabrina for help.

Lily was ready to place the report down, before the last page on the report caught her eye. It had a sticky note attached. Tony Sund, Wolfe Realty's CFO, had a question:

OVERBUDGET WITH PAYMENTS TO AFC. WE SHOULD DISCUSS.

Lily recognized the name as the same on the invoice Brody had been so quick to grab away from her the morning her father showed up at the office. Maybe it was paranoia, but she didn't think so. Putting the report down, she grabbed a pad and wrote the name down. She looked for any other information on the sheet that indicated who AFC was, but found nothing. Only that tens of thousands of dollars had been given to them over the last six months.

Hearing voices in the hallway, Lily ripped off the sheet of paper, stuffed it in her folder and moved from around the desk.

"What are you doing in here?" Brody's expression was dark and threatening as he eyed Lily on his way to his desk.

Lily watched as he looked over his desk for anything suspicious. Like hell this man didn't have something to hide. "You have a lot of nerve."

"Your statements are laced with irony." Seeming satisfied, Brody sat down at his desk. His anger transferred to his usually annoyed look. "I assume it's on purpose."

Lily waved the folder in her hand. "I told you to leave Garrick alone. What is this?"

"I forgot to ask you," Brody said sarcastically.

"I *am* acting CEO."

Brody laughed. "Please, little girl. You're wasting my time."

"How did you even find out who he is?"

"Your little girlfriend loves to hear the sound of her own voice."

Lily assumed Sabrina was behind it. She couldn't keep her mouth shut for a million dollars. "You had no right to do this. You completely stripped him naked. This is a hundred times more than the usual background check we make for employees."

"Is that what you think I was looking for?" Brody asked. "His potential as a worker bee?"

"No, I'm assuming you're afraid and suspicious because you're up to something."

Brody's lips pressed together as his eyes narrowed. "I've had enough of your accusations. Get out of my office."

"I'll leave when I'm finished."

Brody slammed his fist on the desk. "Then you need to be finished, now!"

Lily gasped at the action, feeling a sense of fear briefly rush through her.

Brody got ahold of himself and sighed. "Lily, I'm busy. If all you have to do is accuse me of something I haven't done, which you don't know what it is anyway, you really need to leave."

"I won't be dismissed by you." Her voice sounded more confident than she felt at the moment.

"I did you a favor with that background check."

"How do you figure?"

"Your lover boy is clean," he answered.

"What does that mean?"

"He's a real person."

"You were checking to see if he was FBI, police or something like that? How can you do that and expect someone to think you're not trying to hide something?"

"I didn't say I wasn't trying to hide anything," Brody answered. "I'm just saying I haven't done anything wrong."

"If it isn't wrong, then why would you care if he was a cop?"

Brody shook his head. "You are so naive, Lily. That FBI agent, Pruitt, that went after your father six years ago still has a personal vendetta against him, against you, for Pete's sake. Don't think he doesn't know you're back in town."

Lily had an uneasy feeling about the direction this conversation was taking. She didn't want to accept there was still a taint on her. She wanted to believe that it had all been erased when she left Atlanta, but that was too much to ask.

"Pruitt would try anything to bring Wolf Realty down," Brody said. "You can't trust anyone."

"You can't," Lily said. "But I'm not you."

This was all a mistake. This was all a mistake. Lily wanted to kick herself as she walked down the long hallway from Brody's office to hers. She had left abruptly because his words jarred her. *You can't trust anybody.* Is that what she had come back to? Is that what she'd agreed to? She wanted to believe that nothing was more important than her father's health, but what had she gotten herself into? What had her father gotten her back into?

When she'd agreed to come back to Wolfe Realty there was no mistaking it was a temporary arrangement. Only now she was beginning to believe temporary would have a permanent stain to it.

Standing outside her father's office, Lily couldn't find it in herself to enter.

"What's wrong?" Angela asked as she casually filed her nails at her desk.

Lily looked at her, feeling her chest tighten. "Nothing."

With that, she turned and headed toward the lobby. She needed to get outside. She needed some fresh air. She took the elevator down to the first floor and rushed outside the revolving doors onto the sidewalk. It was hustling with the leftover morning crowd; too busy for her to see Garrick until he was right up on her.

"Lily."

She stammered for her voice. "Uh…Garrick. I… What are you doing here?"

"I came to see you." The angry look on his face was uncompromising.

"What's wrong?" Lily's happiness to see him for the first time since they'd kissed was quickly replaced by a feeling she was about to get in trouble.

"About that!" Garrick pointed to the folder in her hand, his name prominent on the cover.

Lily looked down at the folder she didn't even realize she was still holding. Feeling completely embarrassed, she looked back at Garrick. "Garrick, I…"

"Why would you do that?" he asked. "You completely invaded my privacy."

She felt so guilty because of the injured tone in his voice. "How did you know?"

"I haven't even given you my résumé yet, so is this a personal thing?"

"Garrick, I…" Unsure of what to do, she offered the folder to him. "Here, take it. I didn't…"

Garrick took the folder, confused by her display. She was either a really bad liar or she wasn't lying. "If you didn't, who did?"

Lily would love to give Brody up, but she knew she couldn't do that to Wolfe Realty. "Someone at work heard me mention your name. The funding department handles thousands of dollars. There is so much opportunity for fraud."

"Now I'm a criminal?" Garrick found it ironic that this was her defense.

"I didn't think that for a second. I told them not to do it."

"Then why do you have the background check?"

"It's hard to explain."

"The truth is very simple."

Lily's mood veered sharply to anger. "Don't call me a liar."

"I'm not calling you a liar." Garrick shook his head, turning away. He sighed convincingly and turned back to her. "Lily, I'm sorry. I was just so damn offended to know you had done a background search on me. I mean, Google is one thing, but…"

"How did you know?"

"I have fraud alert with all the credit agencies," he said. "They call me every time my social security and financial records are accessed. I was an identity-theft victim once."

"I know what you must be thinking," Lily said, "but I didn't initiate this. The report was given to me this morning.

That's why I came out here. I needed to blow off some steam because I was so angry about Brody going—"

"Brody did this?" Garrick's mind was racing. If it was Brody who pulled the report without Lily's knowledge, it was possible she was telling the truth.

"It's not important," Lily said. "In a very wrong way, someone thought they were looking out for me. I would never…I mean, I know you must feel violated."

Garrick took a step closer to her, reaching out. As his hand gently touched the wayward strand of hair falling over her face, moving it out of the way, he was taken by the tenderness and calm that came over him. He was supposed to pretend to comfort her now, but this was all wrong. He genuinely wanted to comfort her more than anything in the world.

"It's okay." His finger brushed slightly against her soft cheek before he removed his hand. "I'm sorry to act up so much. It's just not a good feeling."

"I know." Lily wanted him to touch her again. Just that brief contact warmed her entire face and sent a shiver down the front of her chest. "I really am sorry."

"Stop apologizing," he said. "You make me feel like an asshole. You know, I'll tell you anything you want to know."

She felt her breath catch as he took another step closer. Looking into his eyes, she wanted nothing more than for him to kiss her.

He didn't make her wait any longer, because he simply couldn't wait another second. His lips came to hers tenderly as he kissed her. They separated before kissing softly again. Garrick didn't know what to think, as he was consumed with the need to be solace for her. It scared him enough to make him stop.

When their lips parted, their foreheads leaned against each other. With all the hustle around them, the only sound was both of their hearts pounding in their eardrums.

Garrick was the first to lean away. He took a deep breath and held up the folder. "Here, take it back."

"No." Lily felt as if she was ready to fall to the ground any second, her knees weakened by the tenderness of the kiss. "It's your private information. No one else should have it but you."

"I tend to overreact on trust issues," he said. "I think you've picked up on that."

Lily smiled shyly. "I think I have. It's important to everyone."

"I want you to trust me." He reached out and rubbed her arm in a reassuring gesture. "I want to trust you."

Lily felt apprehension sneak in. She wanted to believe it was because he was getting too intimate, too early in the relationship, but she knew it was more likely her own misgivings about herself.

"I take it you're not interested in giving me your résumé anymore."

"No, I'm not, but not for the reason you're probably thinking."

"Not because you hate Wolfe Realty and everything we stand for?"

Garrick shook his head. "Because I don't think it's a good idea to date someone you work for."

"We're dating?"

"I hope we are." Garrick laughed. "If I haven't completely turned you off with that outburst, I'd like to take you to dinner."

"Shouldn't I be taking you to dinner to make up for all this?"

"You think a brother can't afford dinner 'cause he's out of a job?"

Lily laughed. "Oh no, the male ego. I don't want to go up against that. Yes, you can take me to dinner and I'd prefer someplace expensive."

"I'll be down the hall at seven."

"Sounds fine." She put her hand up to stop him as he leaned

forward. "Save some of that for later. Don't get ahead of yourself."

Garrick watched her walk back into the building, waiting for her to turn around and see if he was still there, still looking. When she did, he smiled and she smiled back. Yes, he was still there, looking at her, just like she wanted. It was all about trust, he knew. It was all part of the game. Soon, she would be telling him everything.

That is, if she knew everything.

Maybe it was the feelings he was developing for her that were all too real, but Garrick was beginning to sense he might have gotten Lily wrong. There was no real proof she was in on her father's schemes. Yes, she'd been the lead analyst on the false reports and forged documents, but that didn't mean she knew about it.

He looked down at the folder in his hand, thinking about what she'd said. If it was Brody who'd ordered the background check against her urging, then the belief that she had something to hide was even weaker.

As he opened the folder to see just how perfectly the FBI had created the life of Garrick Pratt, a small slip of paper fell out. Bending down to pick it up, he read the message. The letters AFC were underlined with four question marks, followed by WHERE IS THE MONEY GOING?

An expert on his character, Garrick knew this had nothing to do with his background check and it made him curious. No, it made him suspicious.

Garrick could tell from the blank stare on Jamarr's face that he was about to blow up. It was the calm before the storm and in the short time he'd gotten to know the man, he could read him well. Sitting across from him at this desk, he had just told him about his encounter with Lily that morning.

Jamarr took a deep breath, looked away and sighed. Then, turning back to Garrick, he spoke in a calm, cool voice. "You said what?"

"Don't explode on me, man."

"You're too late!"

Garrick held his hand up. "Hold on, brother. I'm trying to tell you—"

Jamarr stood up, kicking his chair back. Leaning over his desk with both hands in fists against the table, he said, "This has all been about you getting into that company and you said what?"

"You heard me right. I said no."

Jamarr laughed, shaking his head. "Okay, I get it. I get it. It's the girl. You have a problem with going after—"

"Don't question my integrity," Garrick warned. "My only objective is to get to the truth."

"You say that as if you aren't sure what it is anymore."

"Well…"

"Well, nothing! I'm sure, and I thought you were too before you started messing around with this girl."

"Messing around with this girl is what I'm supposed to be doing." Garrick didn't like the sound of that, but it was the truth. "I'm not losing sight of my priorities here. I'll admit, this is harder than before, but I know what I'm doing."

Jamarr leaned back against the wall, his shoulder touching the picture of the president of the United States. "So how am I going to get you into this company if you turned her down?"

"She'll offer again."

"How do you know that?"

"I just do." Despite the misgivings he was having about Lily, Garrick knew he had to trust his instincts. "I'm certain that Brody Saunders initiated the background check."

Jamarr threw his hands in the air. "Oh, here we go with her being innocent again."

"I never said she was innocent," Garrick said. "I just said I believed her when she said she didn't run the check. If it was Brody who called for the check, then I need her to go back to him and tell him that I turned her down."

"And you know she will."

"She seemed angry enough when I first saw her outside that building."

"When will she ask you again?"

"I'm not sure," Garrick said. "Maybe tonight. Maybe later this weekend."

"You're certain she likes you that much?"

Garrick nodded. "There's great chemistry between us."

"Is it real or fabricated?"

Garrick just looked at Jamarr, unable to answer. It was all too real and both of them knew that wasn't the objective.

"I need you in there," Jamarr stressed. "Don't let your feelings for her mess up this case for me."

There wasn't yet any case at all, but Garrick had a feeling mentioning that wouldn't go over well right now. "The case comes first."

"Where are you going?" Jamarr asked as Garrick stood up.

Garrick waved the slip of paper that had fallen out of the background report Lily gave him. "I have to check on this. I have a hunch it means something."

Part of him was hoping it would mean something because he needed anything he could get to keep his mind straight. His emotions were trying to convince his mind that he was wrong about Lily Wolfe, but he knew he probably wasn't. He had a job and this was about justice. He couldn't let a physical attraction compromise the reputation he had worked so hard to get.

* * *

When Lily arrived in Sabrina's office, she was on the phone talking with her back to the door. Thinking she might be interrupting something, she turned to walk away but was struck by what she heard.

"Do you want me to die?" Sabrina asked.

Lily turned back, hoping she'd heard her wrong.

"I'm telling you, I can't find it." Sabrina sighed. "I know I've lost it before, but I could very likely die if I don't have the medication, so what do you want me to do?"

Lily was frozen in place as Sabrina swung around in her chair and saw her. There was a sudden look of surprise on her face, but then it calmed as she returned her attention to the phone.

"But I could die, right? That's what you said." She waved Lily farther in. "Well, I'm telling you I'll be running out in two weeks, so call my pharmacy now."

Lily sat down in the chair, feeling guilty for the fact that she had come here to get on Sabrina for giving Garrick's information to Brody.

"Thank you." Sabrina rolled her eyes. "Goodbye."

Hanging up the phone, Sabrina seemed to sense Lily's discomfort. "I guess I forgot to tell you. I have a fatal disease."

"Are you joking with me?" Lily asked. "Because that's not funny."

Sabrina smiled. "I'm not joking and I've decided it is funny. Don't worry, it isn't inoperable cancer or HIV. It's hepatitis C."

"What…? How?"

"I started getting symptoms after I left Wolfe Realty. I thought I was just tired, but then I started getting stomachaches and…well, I guess my ex gave it to me."

"That's the most severe kind." Lily tried not to freak out. She didn't know much about the disease but knew it was a serious disease of the liver.

"Just out of the damn blue," Sabrina said. "My doctor diagnosed me and I didn't want to believe it. I have the long-term chronic kind."

"Are you…" Lily was searching for the right words. "Are you going to be okay?"

"I will be," she answered nonchalantly. "As long as I stay relaxed, eat well and take my medication."

"Your medication… Is there a lot? Is it difficult?"

"Interferon and ribavirin. Interferons and Ribavirin." Sabrina repeated the words over and over again with a singing tone. "I have to take them if I want to stay alive. They're supposed to keep my liver healthy or something like that."

Their eyes met and Sabrina's head fell back, laughing.

"You're so textbook, Lily. You don't know what to say, right? You're searching for the words? Whatever you decide, please don't say I'm sorry. I couldn't bare it if you said that."

"I should say something," Lily suggested.

Sabrina tossed her hair to the side and lifted her chin. "Honey, I am way too fabulous to let a little disease get me down. My life is changing for the better and my future is great. My man is going to take me away from all of this. We're going to go to Belize and…"

Lily waited as Sabrina suddenly became anxious and distracted.

"What is it?" Lily asked.

"Nothing."

"You were on a roll there," Lily said. "Tell me about him."

"I've really said too much, but I'm just moved by how much he loves me even though he knows I'm a burden."

"That's wonderful." Lily wondered why she was so secretive about this man of hers. "He isn't married, is he?"

Sabrina swallowed with an innocent tilt of her head. "He's in transition."

"Sabrina."

"He was already in transition when I met him, so don't blame me." She waved her hand. "I'm done talking about him, the disease, all that. What did you want?"

"Uh." Lily looked down at her hands on her lap. "I just wanted to see what you were up to."

"No you didn't. What's going on?"

"Well." Lily got up the nerve. "I was just, kind of, well…you know, I was sort of…"

"Don't treat me like a wounded bird, Lily. I'm tougher than you."

Lily's left eyebrow lifted a fraction. "You think so?"

Sabrina nodded, pressing her lips together.

"Well, in that case…I'm pissed at you for telling Brody about Garrick. He had him checked out."

Sabrina sat back in her chair, her shoulders lowered. "I know. I feel bad about that….Brody can be a real bully sometimes."

"Garrick was very upset."

"How did he find out?" Sabrina asked. "You tell him?"

Lily explained her morning encounter with Garrick on the steps of the building, including the kiss and dinner invitation.

"I'm really interested in the kiss," Sabrina said, frowning, "but I'm curious as to how he found out about the background check so quickly."

"He said he has a fraud alert or something like that."

Sabrina seemed unsatisfied. "Fraud alerts aren't supposed to flag on this kind of check. And how would they be able to update him that soon?"

"It doesn't matter," Lily said. "He doesn't want to work here."

Sabrina pouted mockingly. "Did we hurt his wittle feelings?"

Lily laughed. "No, he said he doesn't want to date his boss."

"Cheesy, but charming enough. So, what are you going to wear?"

"I'm going for the best. I'm on my way to Lenox Square in Buckhead now." Lily stood up. "But I wanted to ask you a favor first."

"You came to rip into me and ask me a favor?" she asked. "You got some nerve."

Lily handed her a sheet of paper where she had written down the name AFC Corp. Once she'd remembered she left it in the folder she gave Garrick, she quickly jotted the name down before she could forget.

"Do you know who that is?"

Sabrina studied the paper. "It looks familiar. Why?"

"I looked it up on the Net and couldn't find anything. There were a lot of AFCs, but nothing related to real estate in Georgia. There wasn't anything in any of the files in my dad's office. At least not the ones Brody hasn't locked."

"Brody is big on locking files," Sabrina said. "What about Ward's computer?"

"I can't access his personal files. You have access to our financial records. I need to know who AFC is and why we're paying them so much money."

"No problem," Sabrina said. "Why are you so curious?"

"I just am." Lily noticed Sabrina's doubtful expression. "I know you think I'm paranoid, but I just need this."

"Tony's a pretty meticulous CFO," Sabrina says. "He dots his i's and crosses his…"

"He was curious too." Lily relayed the note Tony Sund left for Brody.

Sabrina seemed more interested. "Did you talk to him?"

"He's not in today, but I will as soon as I can." Lily grinned. "Unless you can do it for me."

"But when I do," Sabrina said, "I get an explanation."

"Sounds fair."

Carolyn's advice paid off. Desperate to impress, Garrick solicited a restaurant referral, one with class, a romantic and, most important, a private, atmosphere. She suggested Bluepointe, a contemporary restaurant with an Asian influence in Buckhead. It was hard to get a table, but Carolyn used her connections and got him a prime reservation that evening in the most private space in the restaurant where they were mostly concealed by thin white curtains.

Fortunately, it was a place that Lily had never been to but had heard great things about. Garrick was glad he was able to spark her interest with the restaurant selection because she completely blew him out of the water when it came to dressing to impress. He heard the carnal growl inside of him at first sight of her upon opening her apartment door.

Her naturally curly hair was up in a loose-fitting bun with tendrils that fell down the sides of her face, and her makeup was soft and understated. But it was the dress…that dress. The formfitting olive-green charmeuse trim wrap dress with a deep, around-the-shoulders, sleeveless V-neck front and low to-the-waist scoop back looked perfect on her. The sash around her waist was a darker green shimmering silk.

Garrick felt like a punk for being so affected by her. Beautiful women were like bullies in that sense, and he felt like a teenage boy intimidated by her looks. For only a second, though. When he wrapped his arm around her waist to lead her through the restaurant, he felt a heat in his groin that reminded him he wasn't at all a boy. And when she turned her head to him with a promising smile, Garrick felt like a man on top of the world.

"Does that bother you?" Garrick asked after the hostess left them alone.

Lily slid into the half-circle table, admiring the presentation. She appreciated the effort, but hoped Garrick didn't think she was high maintenance. To meet a man who was handsome, sexy, smart and had principles, she would have been happy to eat at McDonald's.

When she opened her door and came face-to-face with Garrick, all cleaned up, Lily literally felt her breath taken away. Brother was looking fine in a blue oxford shirt and casual pants, but it was the fashionable Italian jacket that really made him stand out. It was a smooth gray, hand-stitched and perfectly tailored notched-collar wool/silk combination, perfect for his trim, muscular physique. He looked clean cut and confident and made Lily glad she'd decided to go with the more expensive dress among the two she'd picked out earlier that day.

"Does what bother me?" she asked, his vitality drawing her like a magnet. She wanted to be as close to him as possible. His masculinity wasn't overwhelming, but he wore it so well it made her feel more feminine.

"All of these men staring at you," he said. "Don't tell me you don't notice. Some of their dates had to tell them to close their mouths."

Lily laughed. "Men are all pigs. I ignore them."

"All right, now, wait a second. Are you including me in that group?"

"You're a man, aren't you?" She laid her napkin across her lap.

"Last I checked."

"I'm just playing with you, of course."

"I certainly hope so. Granted, the overwhelming majority of us are pigs, but a few of us know how to hold it down right."

"Hold it down?"

"It's a phrase," he said. "Haven't you heard it?"

"I've been in Europe for the past four years," she said. "I'm not up on the latest jargon."

"You have to tell me about that," he said as the waiter returned to their table. "About what you've been doing out there."

While the waiter was taking their drink orders, Lily contemplated what to tell him. She wanted so badly to trust him with the truth. She had no reason to be ashamed, but there was just this pang inside her, wishing she had a better story to tell.

Well, here goes.

"I went to school at Oxford for three years before getting the job in Paris I told you about. When I wasn't working, I was trying to detox my cousin, Courtney, who's addicted to meth."

For some reason, entirely unknown to her, Lily smiled at Garrick, whose wide eyes just stared. He seemed speechless and she assumed that was probably one of the better responses she could have expected.

Garrick blinked, shaking his head. "Wanna run that by me again?"

She repeated what her life had consisted of the last four years. "Didn't I tell you about this at the club that night?"

"I would have remembered." Garrick had taken for granted that Jamarr was telling the truth when he'd said Lily was involved in the drug scene. "You just talked about your job and the sights you saw in Paris. Is your cousin okay?"

She nodded. "She's on her way. I had her in rehab before I had to come home, so I brought her with me and put her up at the Dunwoody Center."

"That's commitment." Garrick was impressed even though he couldn't tell if she was telling the truth. "You must be close."

"We used to be as kids." Lily was feeling a little bit more comfortable now that she had gotten started. Maybe the worst was over. "Then she started running with a bad crowd and...well, we got separated. Then my aunt Jonelle called me, frantic, telling me Courtney was in Paris, club hopping with a drug crowd. So, it kind of became a mission for me."

Even though he intended to check for himself, everything inside him told Garrick she was telling the absolute truth. "You had to dredge through all those clubs looking for her? It's amazing you didn't get pulled in yourself. That's how it happens to a lot of people. You know, getting caught up while trying to get someone out."

"It was never a temptation to me," Lily said. "That scene was sickening and it made me so angry, I wanted to give up on her."

"But you didn't."

Her eyes softened with emotion, thinking of the tears and prayers, remembering how much her mother had loved Courtney. "With the exception of my aunt Jonelle, Courtney is the only relative on my mother's side I have left."

"Your mother?"

"She died four years ago," Lily said, feeling a slight choke in her throat. It would never be an easy thing to say. "Car accident."

Garrick remembered reading about her mother's death in the report, but it wasn't until he heard Lily say it with the emotion of a daughter that he really felt the connection. "My mother was hit by a truck when I was fourteen."

Lily could tell from the raw pain glittering in his dark eyes that he was telling the truth. The sense of loss shared between them reflected in their gaze touched her so deeply that Lily didn't know how to respond.

"I'm sorry." Garrick looked away, his compassion frightening him. He needed to pull away, but he couldn't. He needed the information. "I never knew my father, so you should be grateful you still have yours at least."

Lily's brows drew together in an agonized expression.

"What's that for?" he asked.

She turned to him. "What?"

"That." He mimicked her expression as best he could.

"Nothing."

"You can't lie to me," he said. "I'm familiar with that look. I get the same one when someone mentions my brother. I love him, but…we aren't as close as we should be. Is that what I was getting?"

"Perceptive, you are."

"Why aren't you close?"

She gave him a look that asked, *Why do you think?*

Garrick bent his head slightly forward. "I got the distinct feeling you didn't want to talk about your father when I mentioned the article. I don't blame you. The piece wasn't exactly flattering, but it did seem like a bunch of circumstantial rumors."

"Most of it was." Lily swallowed hard. "And my relationship with my father isn't all about the…"

"Scandal?"

Lily nodded. She had overestimated her comfort level in telling the truth. It wasn't just about fearing Garrick's impression. She just wasn't ready to talk about it.

"I would think if it was all lies, it would have brought you closer." Garrick looked away, feeling as if Lily might be able to tell how much he hated himself right now.

He knew it was normal to feel bad at times doing this job, but this was more than that. This sympathetic character he found in himself for her was almost overwhelming. The pained look in her eyes and the way her voice was quivering was staking its claim inside him.

"You would think." Lily's voice was distinctly fragile. "Don't get me wrong. He's my father and I love him. He's the reason I'm home, because he's sick and I'll do anything to make sure he gets better. It's just that there has been this thing between us since I was a kid. What happened just…" Her voice trailed off.

Slowly, he covered her hand with his as it lay flat on the table. When she looked deeply into his eyes, he took her hand to his mouth and kissed the inside of her palm. The fluttering in her belly made her eyes close as she savored the moment. She opened them just in time to receive his lips with her own.

Escaping in the caressing movement of his lips, Lily felt a fire gently growing inside her. She felt wrapped inside an invisible cloak of warmth as his mouth possessed hers. She reached out, her hands taking hold of his face, as she pressed her mouth against his to feed the hunger she was feeling.

The sound of the waiter clearing his throat forced them to separate immediately, but their eyes lingered for a few moments longer.

"I'm sorry…" The waiter's eyes moved from the ground to Garrick. "I can come back if you'd like, but…"

"It's okay," Garrick said. "I think we need the supervision."

He shook his head and made a whistling sound with his lips. When he turned to her, she smiled and he laughed. He laughed despite this aching feeling inside that told him he was about to ruin the entire case against Wolfe Realty and seriously screw up his career.

For the rest of the evening, Garrick worked hard to steer the conversation to superficial topics, even though he should have been fishing for more information on Ward. Halfway through the bottle of wine and sushi appetizers, he forgave himself for getting off track. Part of it was because he just wanted to taste her lips again, but there was a part of him that wanted to stop her. He wanted to stop her from talking about anything that caused her pain, no matter how much he needed to know.

He felt slightly redeemed when she asked him again if he wanted to give her his résumé and he reluctantly agreed. At least he would have something to submit to Jamarr.

Lily was in heaven and she didn't want to trust it. Maybe

because of all the years of being disappointed by every man in her life or this nagging feeling that she didn't deserve to be this happy right now.

She'd always dreamed of a kiss that would take her breath away, by a man she could respect as much as she could desire. She was both confused and intrigued by him. He made it clear he wanted her, but he also tried to keep her distance, even though she didn't want him too. It had been a while since she'd had this good kind of drama in her life—impromptu kisses and mysterious behavior.

A girl could get used to this.

Chapter 5

Garrick was in ground zero and all he could think of was how sexy Lily looked in her peach-colored, miniskirt business suit. That should have been the last thing on his mind when he stepped inside Ward's office, but what was he to do, with this gorgeous woman walking toward him with a smile that softened his soul.

"I'm glad you could come." Lily reached out to touch his arm and the butterflies that had began to flutter at the sight of her went into overdrive. "Come over here."

As she led him to the sofa, Lily felt the sweet anticipation tickle through her body as she thought of last night. After dinner, they took a walk along Lenox Road, holding hands and stealing innocent kisses that quickly became not so innocent. He was quiet while she talked about her father's illness and it amazed Lily how much better she felt after sharing her concerns with someone.

Her heart made a decision about Garrick last night, but she would keep it to herself for a while. A girl couldn't lay all her cards on the table so soon.

The romantic evening ended with him at her front door, saying good-night. She was grateful he hadn't asked to come inside, because Lily knew she would have let him. She would have let him do anything he wanted. She couldn't imagine regretting it, but she knew it was possible she would, because she wanted things to go the right way with Garrick too much to screw it up by moving too fast.

Garrick sat down on the sofa, thinking that he should be getting the lay of the land to see if there were any documents out that could be useful to the investigation, but he was too preoccupied with the soothing smell of Lily's perfume as she slid closer to him.

"Are you planning on acting inappropriately for the workplace?" he joked.

Lily laughed gently. "One of the perks of being a useless figurehead."

"What does that mean?"

"I'm just here so someone with the last name Wolfe is employed while my father recovers."

"I thought you were in charge." Garrick found this incredibly curious and was unexpectedly hopeful. "What are you doing here?"

Lily sighed, looking down. "There is a lot I haven't told you."

Garrick waited patiently with an understanding expression on his face as she looked back up at him.

"I want to tell you the truth," she said. "You should know what's going on."

"Are we talking about that article again?"

Lily shook her head. She would tell him the truth about that, but not here; not now. "My title is acting CEO, but all I do is show up at meetings, repeat a script and make sure the media and competitors know Wolfe Realty is still in the family. My biggest job is showing up at events."

"So your father is running things from home." There were no words for how much Garrick wanted to believe that.

"Brody Saunders is running things," she answered with a roll of her eyes. "That very polite brother who walked in on us after we first met."

"Yeah. He likes me in particular. He's the one who vetted me."

"Vetted?" she asked, confused.

He'd just slipped again. "Checked out. You know, the background check. Should I be worried about him?"

"No need to worry," Lily said. "I'll protect you."

Garrick's gaze dropped from her eyes to her figure. "A strong, sexy woman watching over me? I feel…I feel so delicate."

Lily leaned in closer, grabbing at his tie. "Now, I will need payment for my protection. I hope we can work something out."

"I'm sure we can." Garrick looked around before leaning in and giving Lily a quick kiss on the cheek.

"What was that?" Lily didn't bother to hide her disappointment.

"A down payment," he answered. "I'll give you the rest when we're in a more private setting."

"My office is safe."

"Your door is wide open."

She gives him a teasing grin. "Aw, is the baby scared?"

"Don't." He waved a warning finger.

"Don't what?" she asked. "Don't dare you?"

"I always won truth or dare as a kid." Garrick relished his body's fiery reaction to her playful mood. "You gonna mess around and find yourself in a sticky situation."

"Interesting choice of words." Lily pulled him closer. "Kiss me."

Garrick was fighting himself, but he knew which side would win. He only had his pride and wanted to hold out as long as possible. "Lily, it's…"

"And oh yeah," she said, feeling the excitement of what was soon to come as his hand came to her thigh. With a sultry tone, she puckered her lips and said, "Call me Ms. Wolfe."

That was it for Garrick. He grabbed her and his lips came down hard on hers. His kiss was greedy, taking possession of her, fueled by a fire that had never left him since the night before. As her lips opened to receive him, his tongue didn't hesitate to explore her mouth. As she met his kiss with her own fervor, his body was hit with sharp currents of desire and he quickly lost himself inside her.

When she began to lean away, he resisted, pulling her back to him. He didn't want to think about anything. He just wanted to feel her. This woman made him do things he didn't want to, shouldn't want to.

"Garrick." His name came between heavy breaths as Lily pushed away harder this time.

Despite the furnace raging inside her, she knew they weren't alone any longer. The risk of getting caught had seemed exciting at the time, but as Sabrina stood in the doorway with one hand on her hip and a get-a-room look on her face, Lily wished she had locked the door.

"What?" Garrick leaned back, not yet ready to give up.

Lily gestured her head toward the door. When Garrick saw Sabrina standing there, he let Lily go and came back to the world.

"Hello." He stayed seated, unable to stand up at the moment.

"It's nice to see you again, Mr. Pratt." Sabrina slowly walked toward them. Instead of joining them on the sofa, she grabbed a chair from the small table in the center of the office and dragged it over to them. "Lily, I thought we had a meeting."

"We did," Lily said, reluctantly recovering. "Garrick is that meeting. Fortunately, he's changed his mind about Wolfe Realty."

"Oh really?" Sabrina was unsuccessful in concealing her surprise. "I thought the personal thing was…"

"I'm only interested in a consulting opportunity," Garrick said. "That is if there is a need for my skills."

Sabrina nodded. "Well, I'm sure we do need them. I heard Tony mention we have some subsidy-funding issues that we need to deal with. It's government stuff."

Garrick was grateful she'd touched on something he knew. At least he wouldn't have to completely B-S his way through this meeting. "Most of what I do is seeking out funding, but I have dealt with a few public-policy issues."

"Well, it's not my area," Sabrina said, "but I can give you the right contact info."

Garrick pulled a résumé out of the portfolio case he had with him and offered it to her. "Can you get this to the right person?"

He had full confidence that everything would check out. The FBI was reliable in that sense. Sabrina studied the document without responding.

He stood up. "Why don't I excuse myself to the men's room as you two talk about me. I can tell you want to."

Lily appreciated the gesture and was curious about Sabrina's seeming hesitation. "A left out of the office and two doors down."

She waited until he was gone to ask Sabrina what the problem was.

"Well, first," she answered, finally looking up from the résumé. "He's going to be expensive. Look at the stuff he's done."

"He's looking for a job, so he won't have too much time to commit to us anyway." Lily sat up straight, smoothing out her breast jacket. "I know I sound like some desperate hoochie trying to hook her man up to get some dollars, but I'm not. He is clearly brilliant."

"You're thinking with your you-know-what on that," Sabrina said. "You don't even know him well enough to say he's brilliant."

"I thought you were impressed."

"I'm thinking with my you-know-what too." Sabrina smiled. "You sure he isn't taking advantage of you?"

"Garrick is not that person," Lily insisted. "Besides, Brody's check came back clean. You know, if Brody said he's okay, then…"

"Brody said he was okay to date you, not work here."

"I didn't see it that way," Lily said. "Does the work need to get done or not?"

Sabrina's expression still held some hesitation. "He doesn't really help me out, but…"

Gratefully, Lily's assistant was nowhere to be found and the hallway was clear. He knew his opportunity to listen in wouldn't last long, so he hoped they would say something good soon. Their voices were soft, but he could hear every word.

"What is it?" Lily asked. "If you have a good reason to say no, then I'll respect that, but I think it was asking a lot of his ego to come in here. You know how men are."

"Girl, do I." Sabrina rolled her eyes. "It's just Brody has turned into the cheapest man alive."

"That reminds me," Lily said. "Did you find out more about AFC?"

"I tried, but I got the runaround. All Tony could tell me is that they broker for us and the person he deals with is a woman named Ann Raines or something like that."

"Why doesn't he know more?" Lily asked. "He's the CFO."

"He says it's an account that Brody handles. I'm telling you, Lily, he and Ward have become a two-person company.

The rest of us are just administrative support. If even the CFO has questions about where the money is going, you might as well give up."

Lily knew Tony wasn't going to be much help. "Tony is spineless, and if Brody has him up to something, he won't tell. I'll try to ruffle some feathers on my own, starting with Brody's office."

"Hey, I haven't given up yet." Sabrina's voice gave away her determination.

"I'm not doubting you." Lily sensed that Sabrina's insistence was in part because she felt Lily pitied her.

"I'll search the files myself," Sabrina said. "I wanted to follow proper protocol, but that turned into a dead end. Besides, I know how to handle Brody better than you. You two only know how to argue."

Lily couldn't argue that. "Well, when you speak to him make sure you find out why he's cutting money everywhere while he's spending a boatload with AFC."

"Maybe it's connected," Sabrina suggested. "Don't look so worried. Brody told me whatever it is they're working on is a good thing."

"Yeah, that's what Dad said, but good for who?"

"Your father isn't stupid enough to make the same mistake twice."

"Why not?" Lily asked. "He got away with it, didn't he? We all did."

Garrick wished he hadn't heard Lily's last words. It went to his gut like a brick.

We all did.

He heard noises in the distance and sensed someone coming down the hall. He would have to make himself known and he knew that would be the end of the very useful conversation. That was fine. He didn't want to hear any more anyway.

* * *

"This has got to be the most fashionable office I've ever seen." Garrick followed Sabrina's instructions to sit across from her desk.

The office looked more like a den with maroon curtains on the windows, abstract paintings on the walls and modern sculptures for art. Sabrina's desk was covered with items more suitable for a bedroom vanity than an office table.

"I like to give it my touch." Sabrina sat down and swiveled around in her chair. "It's real estate. It needs a little color, you know?"

"It clashes with the rest of the firm's decors."

"That was all part of the PR plan. After the…"

Garrick sensed her hesitation. He'd pegged Sabrina right. She didn't trust people. She had a lot of secrets of her own and assumed everyone else did as well. "I know about the scandal."

"Of course you do." Sabrina shrugged. "No need to keep that secret. You should know what you're getting into if you want to consult here."

"You were saying?"

Sabrina gestured toward the walls. "This wouldn't look so unusual six years ago. Only, after the scandal hit, Ward wanted to go superconservative. He wanted a law-firm look 'cause he thought it would add polish and prestige. When I came back, he let me be the exception."

"You came back?"

"Yes, I left the company for a while."

"After the scandal."

"It was rough."

"Ignore me if I'm being too forward," Garrick said, "but you weren't part of that scandal, were you?"

"No. I was just a little nobody, managing finance in Community Relations. Ward didn't even bother to learn my name back then. He certainly wouldn't have included me in anything like…like that."

"But the scandal had to reflect on anyone who worked here," he said. "You couldn't stick around."

Sabrina appeared to be searching for the right words. "Like I said, it was rough."

Garrick leaned back in the chair. "Why are you back, Sabrina?"

"What do you mean?"

"I'm not an expert, but I'm reading your body language, your tone, and I get the feeling you don't trust or like Ward Wolfe very much."

"Ward is…" Sabrina sighed. "Ward is just fine with me. He's a lucky son of a bitch, I know that much. But I didn't come back for him. I came back because I have an ego and I prefer to be a big fish in a little pond."

"Even though you could risk your reputation if something bad went down again?"

"Things are different here now," she said with an optimistic grin. "Wolfe Realty has recovered its reputation and the future is going to be bright."

"How do you know that?"

She tilted her head to the side. "For me at least, I just do."

Garrick wondered if her optimism was faked for his benefit or just stupidity on her part. It wasn't important. What mattered was that he was in, and although this was the messiest *in* he had ever made, it was where he needed to be.

"Let's get down to business," he said, pulling his chair to the desk.

The sound of her cell phone ringing in her purse on the chair next to her interrupted the uncomfortable silence between Lily and her father as they sat down for dinner in his dining room. Since she had been back, the only other dinner they'd shared had been with the benefit of cable-network news in the background so they could be distracted from discussing anything meaningful about themselves.

Sitting across from him over the antique table her mother bought from a luxury-estate sale in Druid Hills ten years ago, Lily wasn't sure what to say. She focused on the stuffed chicken and rice she'd prepared for them.

"You want to get that?" Ward asked.

Lily shook her head. "Voice mail will pick it up."

"It might be your new boyfriend." He smiled at her surprise. "Brody told me."

"He isn't my boyfriend," she said. "And Brody doesn't know enough to tell anyone anything."

"I hear Brody knows more about him than you do."

"Did you have something to do with that?" she asked, even though she wasn't sure she wanted to know the answer.

"I was told after the fact," he answered, "but I would have approved either way. With me…out of commission, Wolfe Realty is vulnerable."

"It seems…" She paused at the sound of her voice mail beeping. "It seems like we have something to hide."

"It's more like something to protect." Ward took a sip of water. "Can't I have just one glass of wine?"

"Not at all," she answered quickly. "Garrick doesn't want to hurt Wolfe Realty. He just wants to keep busy while he looks for a permanent position."

"You're interested in a brother without a job?"

"It's not what you think."

The voice mail beeped again and Ward said, "You can answer that if—"

"What did Brody tell you anyway?"

"Just that you've taken a shine to this young man who has had a lot of jobs in a lot of different places."

Lily smiled at the old-fashioned term. "I have taken a—what did you call it?—shine to Garrick. He's a great guy and I enjoy his company. We aren't serious or anything. I just got here."

"And you don't plan on staying long, do you?"

Their eyes caught and Lily thought she saw pain. She wondered if it was the result of his physical discomfort or because of what she was saying.

"Atlanta isn't my home anymore."

"Lily." He placed his knife and fork down and looked at her squarely. "Atlanta is where you were born and raised. It is where I was born and raised. It is where your mother was born, raised and where she died. Atlanta will always be your home."

The emotion welled in her throat. "You know what I mean."

"I hope you know what *I* mean."

"I don't want to argue with you, Dad. I came here to have dinner, to talk to you."

"But you'd rather be with Garrick."

Lily could sense him pushing her away. It was always one of them that did it before things got too serious. "If I would rather be with Garrick, I'd be with him."

"Don't get smart with me, young lady."

Lily lowered her head, playing around with her food. "Sorry."

"It may not seem like it," Ward advised, "but I do appreciate all you're doing for me, for the company, the family."

"I believe you, Dad."

"You don't have to lie to me."

"Are you sure?" Lily hadn't expected to say those words but was grateful she had. The look on his face told her there was no going back from them and that was what she needed. "Because if I tell the truth, then I'll expect you to tell the truth, and where will we be?"

The way he was staring at her made Lily feel like a little girl about to be scolded, but she knew that she wasn't, so she stood her ground. "Something is going on that doesn't feel right."

"What would feel right to you?" he asked. "Would anything?"

"Transparency," she offered in a definitive tone.

"Not everything is your business."

"It appears as if nothing is."

"That's enough."

"Enough of what?"

"Enough of you questioning me." Ward returned to his meal. "I've made mistakes, but...Jesse's death changed things for me."

"Don't bring Mom into this," Lily insisted. "This is about the company and how you and Brody—"

"Her death and you hating me." Ward spoke as if Lily hadn't said anything. "That's what did it."

Lily was stopped in her tracks as her fork fell out of her hand. "I don't...I never said I hated you."

"You didn't have to say it, Lily. Your hateful rampage against me before you fled to England said it for you."

"I was angry because you lied to me." She gripped the edges of the table, leaning forward. "You used me."

"I never used you," he said. "Not deliberately."

"You knew those reports you had me analyze were fake." Lily's psychological desire not to broach the subject made her stomach tighten and her head begin to hurt.

"I'm atoning for my mistakes. The company is completely legitimate and what I'm planning now is going to make up for everything that has happened in the past."

"I want to know what that is," Lily demanded.

"It's going to change Wolfe Realty forever." He placed his hands flat on the table and smiled proudly. "Lily, you'll be proud. Most important, Jesse will be proud."

Lily felt a single tear trail down her cheek. She could hear what he was saying but not feel past her resentment. "Stop mentioning her, please."

"I can't," he said. "There's still some ridiculous part of me that feels that if I keep mentioning her, her spirit will stay here. She is still with me, you know."

"We could really use her now," Lily said, letting the emotion soften her. "She was our mediator. That's why things were so hard after she died. She was always the one that got us through hard times."

"Hard times." Ward laughed bitterly. "Hell, she got us through dinner."

"This gaping hole between us…" Lily sighed regrettably. "It was always there. Why?"

His head fell shamefully. "I'm the father. It was my responsibility. Jesse would get on me about it all the time."

"Really?"

"You know, your mother was a good woman. She would never get on me in front of anyone, not even you. But when we were alone, she let me have it. She was a spicy one."

As the room fell silent, they both indulged in their fondest memories of the one thing they had in common—their love for Jessica Wolfe. That was until the sound of Lily's cell phone started ringing again.

Lily apologized and reached into her purse to get it. She checked the display, hoping it was Garrick. Instead, it was Sabrina. Assuming she just wanted to talk, Lily answered to tell her she would call later.

"Sabrina?"

Sabrina's voice was hurried and agitated. "Lily, what have you gotten me into with this? Tony is useless and Brody couldn't help me, so I did some searching myself."

"What's wrong?"

"I found…"

There was noise in the background and Lily felt the hair on the back of her neck stand up. "Sabrina, where are you?"

"Home, I…I think we should have left alone. I… What the… I have to go, I'll call you later."

The line went dead after that. Lily tried to call back, but she went directly to voice mail.

"What's wrong?" Ward asked in response to Lily's expression.

Lily placed the phone back in her purse, feeling a shiver run down her spine.

"I don't know," she said, "but I have to go."

She was touched by the regretful expression on his face. "I…I'm sorry if I made things ugly, Dad. I just…"

"You don't have to say it, Lily."

"But I do, Dad. We both have to share our part of what needs to be said if we're ever going to do anything about this gigantic hole between us."

With a resigned sigh, he nodded his head once. "Drop by this weekend, will you?"

"I will."

Lily didn't have time to find joy in the token of progress they had just made. There was something about the tension in Sabrina's voice that hit her radar, and she needed to get to her.

"What are you still doing here?" Jamarr looked at his watch. "It's after eight."

Garrick looked up from the computer. "I'm trying to dig deeper for AFC and Ann Raines."

"What are you finding?"

"I've pulled a few companies with the AFC moniker that are related to real estate and construction in the Southeast, but not in a very generous Atlanta metro area. None are public, so I'll have to do some more research. None of them have an Ann Raines connected to them."

"So Wolfe Realty is sending checks to a local company that doesn't seem to exist run by a woman who we can't find."

"Sounds like enough to pull bank records. Someone is cashing those checks."

"Hey, guys." Carolyn, purse in hand, ready to go, stopped in the doorway to the computer room. "Why are you still here?"

They both looked at her.

"Stupid question." She entered the office, tossing her purse on the table. She grabbed a chair. "Do we have enough to get a warrant and search those records?"

"We need proof that Wolfe Realty is even paying a suspicious company before we can get a warrant," Garrick said. "I can try to get it when I'm in next week."

"No," Jamarr said.

"You don't want the records?" Carolyn asked.

"I do," he answered, "but that's just the beginning. This girl is going to get us closer."

Garrick leaned back, his expression still and serious. "I don't think she can help us."

"When did this happen?" Carolyn asked, skeptically surprised.

"Think with your other head, buddy." Jamarr straightened his shoulders and cleared his throat. "She isn't innocent. You overheard her conversation with the other woman."

"You're only listening to the back end," Garrick said. "If you pay attention to the entire conversation, she seems too curious to be guilty."

After overhearing Lily's conversation with Sabrina, Garrick had to deal with internal conflict that took him off his focus all day. He kept repeating her last words over and over again. *He got away with it, didn't he? We all did.* It took him a while to get past all the implications of that statement, but once he had, the entire conversation began to bring him some perspective.

Like he was then, Jamarr was still too focused on the end to take in the whole.

"You mean guilty this time?" Carolyn asked.

"Are you against me, too?" Garrick asked.

Carolyn shrugged, leaning back.

Jamarr stepped farther into the room. "I think I need to be asking that question, considering I'm in charge of this investigation."

"I'm not against you," Garrick said. "I just feel like Lily can help us."

"She can help us now?" Jamarr laughed as he spoke. "This is rich."

Garrick stood up. "Jamarr, who do we want?"

"I want everyone!"

Garrick stared him down until Jamarr's shoulders lowered and he took a deep breath. "You have to keep perspective."

"You're telling *me* to keep perspective? You're the one letting a piece of—"

"Okay." Carolyn stood up, holding her hand out. "Let's not go there."

"No," Jamarr said. "Let's go there. If it demeans you, Carolyn, you can leave."

"Actually, it demeans you," she said. "You're both losing perspective here. You, for your obsession with all things Wolfe, and Garrick for his affection for Lily."

"I have never let my personal feelings make me lose sight of the objective of a case," Garrick said at the same time he knew he had never let it get this far before. "If I thought Lily was in the middle of this, I would still go after her as a target."

"You go after her until I tell you that you don't," Jamarr ordered.

"What if he's right?" Carolyn asked. "What if she is the key, not the mark?"

"She's never been the mark," Garrick said. "It's always been Ward and Brody."

Jamarr threw his hands in the air. "This is unbelievable. Okay, even if I concede that she might be innocent this time— and I stress the words *this time*—even then, she's not going to turn on her father. Or do you think you have it so good you can get her to do that?"

"Give me time to collect enough evidence and I'll convince her to do the right thing," Garrick said, more hopeful than confident. "You know my record, Jamarr. I've done it before."

"That was when you had time," Jamarr said. "I don't have time. The feds don't want to hear another update on how we're romancing Ward Wolfe's daughter."

"I know what I'm doing."

"You'd better," Jamarr demanded. "I want Wolfe and Saunders and I want them now."

Carolyn waited until Jamarr was gone to grab her purse and head for the door. "You should call it a night."

"Just another half hour." He looked up at her, taking in her skepticism. "Don't tell me you think I'm losing it too."

Carolyn sighed, brushing away strands of wayward flaxen-blond hair. "I believe that you'll do whatever it takes to get to the truth and make this case happen. Only, you argue for her like she's your woman or something."

"I don't agree with that."

"Oh well, then I guess that makes it untrue."

"Good night, Carolyn."

"You'll lose her," she said.

Garrick paused, staring blankly at the computer screen.

Thinking of the inevitability of Carolyn's words made him feel angry and frustrated. "I know."

"Either way," she said.

"I know," he repeated with urgency. "Which is why you can count on me to do this right. There is no future for me and Lily Wolfe, so I'm not going to let the idea of one poison my efforts and alter my intentions."

"Good night."

When she was gone, Garrick leaned back in his chair, running his hand over his head. Lily wasn't even his, would never be, but the thought of losing her still bothered him. It made no sense. They had barely spent any time together, but he felt a clear connection to her and that was beyond the physical. The physical, well, that was as inexorable as the inevitability of losing her. Lily would hate him once he told her the truth, no matter how it turned out for her. Like Carolyn said, either way.

All Garrick could hope to do was make sure that Lily didn't have to suffer for her father's sins.

This wasn't a good sign.

The second Lily reached the top of the steps to Sabrina's town house in the Virginia Highlands neighborhood, she noticed that the door was slightly open. She was worried that Sabrina wasn't answering her phone as she tried to call her several times from the road, and fought the urge to call the police. She was worried that Sabrina might be sick, but it was the thought of something else that had her speeding over to her place.

There was no reason for her to believe that she had placed Sabrina in danger by asking her to investigate AFC further, but Lily couldn't fight the gut reaction that told her Sabrina's quick hang-up was somehow related.

It wasn't so unusual that her door was unlocked. The previous two times Lily had been to Sabrina's place, the door was unlocked and Lily got after her for it. Sabrina considered herself forgetful. She forgot things, lost things, but Lily warned her not to let it happen again.

When she glanced to her left and saw the parking space for Sabrina's BMW empty, Lily wasn't further encouraged.

"Sabrina!" Only a few steps into the apartment, Lily stopped in her tracks. The place had been ransacked. Something had gone terribly wrong here. "Sabrina!"

Then she heard footsteps from around the corner. Hitting the hardwood floors hard, Lily knew it wasn't Sabrina. She knew it wasn't a woman and she was suddenly scared to death.

Not waiting to test her theory, Lily turned to hightail it out of there. When she reached the door, a voice calling out her name made her stop. Turning around, she was shocked to come face-to-face with Brody standing in the foyer. His expression made it seem as if he was just as surprised to see her.

"What are you doing here?" he asked.

"What…" Lily's voice caught in her throat. She couldn't hide that she was afraid. "Where is Sabrina?"

"She's gone."

"Gone where? What happened here?"

"I asked you a question." He took a step toward her, but stopped as she backed up. "What's wrong with you?"

"What have you done?" she asked.

After taking a second, Brody sighed and rolled his eyes. With an annoyed tone, he said, "You can't be serious."

Lily stepped forward and in a forceful tone demanded, "Where is she?"

"I don't know," he answered, "but something went wrong. She left me a message. She was frantic."

"She called me about forty-five minutes ago. She was very

upset. There was something…" Lily's apprehension warned her against saying anything more.

"What?" Brody asked.

"What are you doing here?"

"I told you. She left me a message asking for help. She was crying. Saying Tony Sund bit into her about going through files she didn't have password access to. She mentioned you."

"No," Lily said. "Tony Sund barks but he doesn't bite."

"Well, apparently, he bit this time. I saw blood."

Lily gasped, her hand coming to her chest. "Blood? Where? How much?"

"In the bedroom." Boyd grabbed Lily as she tried to pass him.

"Get your hands off me." She pushed him away. "Don't touch me."

"I got here just a few minutes before you." He reached into his pocket.

"What are you doing?" Lily backed up, Boyd's disturbing description filling her with distress. "Stop."

"I'm getting my phone." He reached out, offering his cell phone. "You can listen to the message she left me."

Lily didn't accept the offer. "How much blood?"

"Enough to know she didn't cut herself shaving her legs."

"She could still be here."

"She's not," he said. "I've looked all over. Her purse and car are gone. Something went down, but I didn't have anything to do with it."

"You won't let me look around," Lily said. "How can I believe you?"

"I'm trying to protect you, Lily. Now get out."

"Get out?" she asked. "Protect me from what?"

"Just get out. Who knows who else she called? She could have called the cops. You can't be here, neither of us can."

"I'm calling the police now." Lily reached into her purse for her phone.

"You can't."

"You can't stop me."

"I won't try, but you should know what it's going to do to Wolfe Realty. What it will do to your father."

Lily's finger stopped just as she pushed the nine.

"What are you going to tell them?" he asked. "You know whatever it is, which I'm sure is wrong, it will lead to your father."

"No." Lily was trying to ignore the images of her father from earlier that night. "This is not about Dad. It's about…"

"You don't know what it's about," Brody argued. "How long have you been back? You don't know the stuff she's been into."

"Please." She pressed the nine.

She was thinking of Sabrina's boyfriend. The mysterious man she seemed to get uncomfortable about whenever Lily wanted to know more. The one whose initials she wrote inside a heart on sticky pads.

"You're going to kill him."

When she looked up, Lily could see a hint of desperation on his face. "We can't just walk away."

"We have to," he said. "Even if we call the police and say nothing, you know it's going to come back to your father. They'll trace her calls and—"

"Stop." Lily felt her chest compressing. She couldn't be thinking about this. "Dad assured me the company isn't doing anything wrong."

"So what are you going to say to the police?"

Lily put the phone back in her purse, fighting not to give in to the anxiety and confusion that was circling her.

"Get out of here, Lily. I'm going to call the cops from a public phone somewhere far from where either of us live."

"But she could be hurt," Lily urged. "She needs someone to call now."

"The sooner you're out of here, the sooner I'll call."

Lily wanted to listen but she didn't. "This is wrong, Brody."

"Dragging Wolfe Realty and your father into this is only going to make it worse. Lily, he can't take it right now. Not from you."

"But I'm not…" Just a glimpse of the guilt she felt at considering Brody's suggestion made Lily sick to her stomach. "I don't trust you."

"I don't need you to trust me," he said. "I need you to believe that I would never hurt your father. He's…he's like my own."

Lily did believe that, but it did nothing to ease the ache she was feeling inside. "Brody…"

"Go, Lily." Grabbing her by the arms, he forced her out of the house.

She pushed away, turning to him as he stood in the doorway. "I don't understand. If Dad is telling the truth, then…"

"Then this probably isn't about you. Be glad for that and leave."

"Glad?" Lily couldn't believe the coldness, even for Brody.

As she drove away in her car, her hands shaking and tears streaming down her cheeks, Brody's words just wouldn't sink in. Despite her thoughts of the mysterious boyfriend, something told Lily that Sabrina had met with trouble and she was to blame. If what she thought turned out to be true, not only would she never forgive herself, she would have no choice but to believe that it all led back to Wolfe Realty and to her father.

Chapter 6

From what Garrick heard, drinking was what had done his father in. It was hard to know who was telling the truth when he'd listened in on stories discussing this imposingly absent man in his life. The Satan Sauce, as his grandmother had called it, was the consensus when it came to the man's wrongdoings, disappearances and crimes. It was for this reason that Garrick made the choice to keep liquor at a good distance for most of his life. He would nurse a glass of wine on social occasions at times, but generally passed when offered.

So, it didn't make sense that he was so tempted to have a drink. As he leaned into the empty refrigerator in his kitchen, he felt the thirst call at his throat and really wondered if it was a hereditary thing.

This situation with Lily was not as big a deal as he was making it out to be. Neither was it complicated. He simply could not be with her. That was it. She was the case and that was that.

No matter. He couldn't get her off his mind and there was no explaining it. Yes, she was beautiful and held a tenderness about her that softened him to his core. Yes, she was sexy and her kisses made him want to give in to his most carnal desires.

But she was the case and that was that.

Garrick was beginning to second-guess himself, something that a man in his position simply did not have the luxury of doing. When she told him she was having dinner with her father that night, his professional instinct told him to find a way to tag along. What stopped him, he wasn't sure. He wanted to go, but for professional reasons. He was going to confuse himself to death.

"Stop thinking!" he yelled to himself as he reached for his cell phone on top of the kitchen counter.

"Hello?"

"Don't panic," Dan said.

"So my panic begins. What happened?"

"I've been robbed, brother. Someone broke into my place."

"Did you call the cops?"

"I wanted to call you first," he said. "It's kind of weird."

"Weird how?"

"Nothing was taken. Well, almost nothing."

Garrick had an uneasy feeling this was going to become about him. "What is almost nothing?"

"I think they were messing with my desk. My bills…your bills…your mail."

Garrick didn't bother to ask if the forwarding post-office box to Atlanta was among the bills. "Why in the hell do you have that lying around? You aren't supposed to."

"I was going to put it away, but you know how stuff piles on and you forget the little things. Or what you thought were little things."

Garrick took a second to calm down. "What else is missing?"

"Absolutely nothing," he answered. "I've racked my brains and it's nothing. Look, man…I, uh… Whatever this case is you're working on… Maybe they traced you back here."

"I don't think so."

"Are they the mob or something like that?" Dan asked. "'Cause, if you're in danger and I'm…"

"I'm white-collar crime, Dan. You know that."

"Well, yeah, but they can be worse than the mob sometimes, you know."

"You watch too many movies," Garrick said. "They aren't violent and they have no reason to go to your place. I think it was Melinda. So do you."

"So, what do you think she's going to do?"

"She's going to try and track me down." Garrick knew he hadn't ended things well with Melinda, but this psycho game she was pulling had moved beyond inconvenient. I'll have some Chicago FBI stop by and talk to her."

"Strong-arm her?" Dan sounded almost excited.

"Talk to her."

"About what?" Dan asked. "We don't know for sure she was the one who broke in. Besides, it would just lead her to a P.O. box, not you."

"Trust me, we know how to handle this type of thing." Garrick suddenly felt like a thug. The call-waiting beep sounded and he looked at the display. "I have to go, man. It's the boss."

He pressed the Send button. "Hey, Jamarr, a little late for a phone—"

"Sabrina Dunkle is missing," he interrupted in a cold tone.

"Who?" It took a second to register. "What happened?"

"Emergency got an anonymous call from someone worried about her."

"Lily?" Garrick rushed to the living room to grab a pen and paper for notes.

"No, a man. We think it was Brody Saunders."

"Go on."

"When the cops went to her place, it was ransacked and there was blood in the bedroom. A good amount."

"But no Sabrina." Garrick wasn't sure what to think. Murder was never expected to be a factor in this case. He was worried about Lily. "What is the detective saying?"

"Nothing yet," Jamarr said. "He's with Carolyn now."

"How did you find out?" Garrick had an ominous feeling in response to Jamarr's silence. "Is Lily all right?"

"Lily's fine, as far as I know, but maybe she can tell you why she was at Sabrina's last night with Brody Saunders."

"No," Garrick said. "She had dinner at her father's."

"We saw her there."

"You're leaving something out."

"We've been following her."

"Dammit, Jamarr!" Garrick slammed his fist against the wall. "Since when?"

"Since I wasn't sure I could trust you to be impartial."

Garrick bit his lower lip to contain his words. He took a deep breath before continuing. "If you don't trust me then assign this case to someone else. You had no right to do this without telling me. What if she caught on?"

"If she knew she was being followed, do you think she would have showed up at Sabrina Dunkle's?"

"So now you think she and Brody hurt Sabrina?" There was no way Garrick would believe Lily was violent. Now, Brody was another story, but Lily would never back him up if he'd done something to her friend.

"We don't know. We followed her from her father's house to Sabrina's. She and Brody had some kind of argument outside and then she left. We followed her home, but he must have left right after 'cause the call to 911 came from a pay phone about twenty miles away."

Garrick felt as if a brick had been dropped in his stomach.

Jamarr continued. "We have everyone close to the Wolfe case flagged with the station, so when SVU got the case, they called us right away."

"Something's wrong, Jamarr."

"Something's wrong, all right. The girl is probably dead."

"Why?"

"That's what you need to find out first thing tomorrow. SVU is going to do their thing and they know she is tagged to our case, but I left out what we knew about Lily and Brody. You need to get to the truth."

"It might not be related. Sabrina has nothing to do—"

"Is this the same man who mentioned the disturbing conversation he overhead just earlier this week? You were the one who said we might be able to work Sabrina."

"I know what I said!" Garrick was letting his frustration get to him.

"You're not listening to me," Jamarr said. "Your mark was there and Brody Saunders was with her. Between the time she left, the 911 call and the cops showing up was less than forty minutes. Either she saw the girl before something happened, made it happen or showed up after it happened. We think that third choice is what went down, but either way, she didn't call the cops."

"Maybe she was scared," Garrick said.

"Or maybe you're scared that she wasn't."

Garrick's frustration quickly turned to fury. "Jamarr, don't ever question me again."

"After this," he said, "I don't think I'll need to anymore."

After he hung up, Garrick tried to quell the rage inside him.

Gripping the phone so hard his hand hurt, he paced the living room, not sure what to do or where to go.

What kind of fool had he been? What kind of fool was he being? Still, after everything, there was a voice that was telling him Lily had to have been too scared to call the police. That had to be it.

He would see her tomorrow morning and she would tell him the truth. She had one last chance.

"Lily?"

With the haze around her, Lily stared out the window overlooking Andrew Young International Boulevard. She didn't bother to fight back tears as Sabrina's face appeared all around her.

"Lily?"

Then there was all the blood that, although Lily hadn't seen any, tainted her visions and assailed her with guilt. What had she caused? Who had done this? What had they done?

"Lily?"

When the touch came to her shoulder, Lily jumped into the air and screamed. She turned to see Angela, who had jumped back with a scream as well.

"Angela." Lily held on to the wall to stay up straight. "I'm sorry, I…"

It was then that Garrick came busting through the door, looking ready to take on anyone. "What is it?"

"Garrick!" Lily felt her heart leap at the sight of him. She rushed to him and fell into his arms, alarming herself by how happy she was to see him. "Thank God you're here."

She'd wanted to call him so many times during her sleepless night, but didn't. She'd even made her way to his front door before rushing back to her apartment in shame. She couldn't tell him; she couldn't tell anyone. So she'd lay on the sofa, crying, worrying and cursing Brody under her breath.

"What was that screaming for?" Garrick had to fight that sympathetic urge inside him. He saw the pain on her face and only wanted to comfort her.

"I guess I scared her," Angela said. "I know she sure as hell scared me."

"I'm sorry, Angela." Lily stood up straight but never let go of Garrick. "I'm just upset. We all are."

"I just wanted to know if you were accepting visitors."

"Yes, and Garrick isn't a visitor. He's a contractor with Wolfe Realty now. He…" With a sigh, she looked up at him. His expression was blank and it bothered her. She wasn't sure what she expected, considering she hadn't told him anything. "He is working with Sabrina."

Angela's hand went to her chest and her face fell somber. "Have you heard?"

Garrick nodded. "Sabrina's missing. It's what everyone here is talking about."

"There was foul play," Angela insisted.

Garrick turned to Lily. "How long have you all known?"

Lily turned away, trying to hide her lying eyes. "We were told this morning."

That wasn't what he'd asked, but Garrick shouldn't have expected the truth from her. He felt his anger returning.

"It was such a shock." Angela was shaking her head as she left the office.

"Sit down, Lily." Garrick took her by the arm, ignoring the electricity he felt from touching her, and led her to the sofa. "Tell me what happened."

"We don't know." She wanted to lean into his chest, but he sat down too far from her. "She's missing. Her car is gone. There were signs of struggle in her house and evidence of foul play."

"Is that all you know?" he asked, still giving her a chance at the truth.

Lily shook her head in denial, confused by the cold tone in his voice. "Garrick, what—"

Brody knocked on the door as he walked inside. The expression on his face at the sight of Garrick was not a happy one. "Hello, Garrick."

Garrick nodded a hello to the man he would prefer to blame this all on exclusively, despite having no proof of anything.

"Can I speak to you in private?" Brody asked Lily.

Garrick noticed that Lily wouldn't even look at him. He turned back to Brody, whose uncomfortable grin made things all the more confusing.

"This isn't really a good time," Garrick said.

Brody ignored him. "Lily."

Lily looked up, unable to hide her rage through her tears. "Not now, Brody. Please leave."

"You heard her," Garrick said.

Brody just rolled his eyes. "It's about tonight, Lily. We have to discuss it."

"What's tonight?" Garrick asked as Lily let out an exasperated sigh.

"It's a charity gala." Brody explained. "It's an annual event and Wolfe Realty has been a major sponsor for years. Ward's mother died of breast cancer."

"We can't do that," Lily said. "Sabrina's… She could be dead."

"You don't know that," Garrick said, although he suspected the two people in the room with him were the only ones who did know Sabrina's true state.

"But…" Lily shook her head vigorously.

"Lily, when Ward suffered his attack, he hastily asked Sabrina to handle our PR because she is so well known on the social circuit. She volunteered to give out some awards. Someone has to go in her place. It should be you, since you were going anyway."

"I can't now."

"What about your father?" Brody's tone showed his irritation. "This is what you agreed to. You…"

Garrick noticed Brody's unpleasant stare. "I'm not leaving."

"Fine," he said. "Then you make sure she gets there tonight. A Wolfe has to be there."

Lily stood up, her hands clenched in fists. "Fine, Brody. Just leave."

"You don't have to do this." Garrick stood up. "It's just a ball. There will be others."

"No." Lily's shoulders slumped as she felt as if her head was going to explode from all the pounding. "It will be a big deal if I'm not there."

"You're completely spent, Lily."

"I owe her."

"Why?" Garrick saw his window. "Do you think you're to blame for her disappearance or something?"

Her eyes widened as she looked at him, wondering why he would ask such as thing. Was she acting guilty? Did he know something?

"This is…" She turned away, rushing to the window. "I just know something horrible has happened and…"

Garrick came up behind her, gently placing a hand on each of her shoulders. He had to remind himself that the distraught act was more likely guilt than real pain. "What is it, Lily? Tell me what's upsetting you so much."

The comfort of his hands on her made Lily feel a speck of calm circle within her. She leaned back into him, wishing he would wrap his arms around her. "Oh, Garrick, I can't. Just hold me. Please, just hold me."

As he did as she asked, Garrick couldn't ignore that the gesture came so naturally to him. It was as if they were both shaped to mold into each other. He could feel the tightening of her entire body begin to loosen. The confusion was overwhelming. He knew what he knew, but his instincts told him to protect her, comfort her.

"I'll help you get through this," he whispered into her ear before kissing her cheek. "No matter what, I'll help you in every way I can."

Lily closed her eyes and felt herself begin to float in his arms. If only she could tell him the truth.

No, Lily thought, something is definitely wrong. She had been off kilter all day because of Sabrina but was left with the distinct feeling that Garrick was distant from her.

He was so warm that morning, holding her and promising that he would help her. She hadn't wanted to let him go, but they had to separate so she could handle requests by the many employees who were too distraught to work or wanted to help search for Sabrina.

She felt confident the police were taking the case very seriously. Garrick was quickly back in her office when they came to talk to her. She thought she was going to squeeze the life out of his hands as she answered their questions. Her answers went well until she was asked about the last time she had seen Sabrina.

She hadn't lied exactly. The last she had seen Sabrina was at work, but when she told this to the detective, she began to hyperventilate. He seemed to interpret it as stress and decided to end the interview and reschedule for another time.

Lily, racked with guilt, had turned to Garrick, hoping for the sympathy she knew she didn't deserve, but he was distant. Despite his promise earlier that day, Garrick suddenly seemed

to be anywhere but with her. He had forgotten a lunch interview and had personal business to attend to in the afternoon.
He promised to pick her up for the ball that night and rushed
out of her office as if it was on fire.

Lily was confused, but her state of emotions didn't have the
ability to go further and try to clarify. Brody's words were tor-
turing her, and everywhere she went she felt afraid. There was
no good turn. If her suspicions were true that whatever
happened to Sabrina was because of what she'd asked her to
find, then what was wrong at Wolfe Realty was far beyond
anything that had happened before or she could have imagined.

And Brody was right. It would all lead to her father, and if
she told what she knew, they would come right after him. It
would kill him. Every time she tried to think of a way to tell the
truth, she ran into a brick wall. It was all she could do to try to
make it through the day and pray Sabrina would be found.

The last thing she wanted or needed was to smile and look
pretty for a crowd, who, thanks to the six o'clock news, all
probably knew about the young woman missing, with scenes
of foul play at her apartment, who happened to work at
Wolfe Realty.

She was numb as she prepped for the evening, until Garrick
showed up. He was the only comfort she sought, but he was
still distant. She was paranoid even though she knew he
couldn't possibly know anything. It wouldn't be hard to
believe he was jarred by the news, but he barely knew Sabrina.

The silence in the car on the way to the Four Seasons Hotel,
which continued once there, was too much for her to take.

"Garrick, tell me what's wrong," she pleaded as they sat
down at the reserved table at the front of the ballroom.

"Please stop asking," Garrick said. "Nothing is wrong. I'm
just tired. The lunch didn't go as I'd planned and I've been
running around all afternoon."

Although he'd had enough of her questioning, Garrick knew he needed to straighten it up. He'd had to get away from her after she'd squandered her last chance to tell the truth when she'd held back from the detective. It had made him so angry; at her for what her withholding meant, and at himself for wanting to believe in her even up to that last moment.

He spent time psyching himself up for tonight, knowing that he couldn't give up. He had more reason than ever to make this case, now that violence was a part of it. No matter what he was feeling, which wasn't even clear to him at this point, he had to go on. He had to ignore the disgust he felt when he thought of her, as well as the desire he felt when he saw her.

"But you've been this way since before you left the office." She slid her chair closer to him for more intimacy, but he barely looked at her.

"I don't know what you're talking about," he said. "I'm fine, Lily. Please stop asking…"

"I'm being too needy, I know that. It's just that I'm so anxious right now."

He felt his teeth grinding together as he looked at her, the downturn of her eyes pleading for understanding he couldn't give. "I understand. Everyone is. It's so tragic. If only the police could get a clue."

"They won't tell us anything."

He gripped the napkin in his hand. "They don't have anything to go on. Someone has to be able to give them some clue that they can work with."

Lily swallowed hard, lowering her head. She bit her lip to hold back the tears she had no right to cry. When Garrick reached out and took her hands in his, she looked up at him, wishing for so much.

"I know you care about her," he said, trying to get past the feelings of sympathy that, unbelievably, were somehow still inside of him. "You've done everything you could. You've told the police everything you know, so you shouldn't feel bad."

Lily felt a silent gasp escape her as she pulled her hands away. "Garrick, I—"

"Glad to see you could get her here." Brody looked down at both of them, his arms folded across his chest. "It's extremely important."

Garrick was fuming. He was certain Lily had been about to open up to him. "We're having a private conversation, Brody."

"I just stopped by to say hel—"

"Excuse me." Unable to stand it, Lily got up and rushed away, feeling as if she was going to suffocate. She heard Garrick call her name but couldn't stomach turning to face him.

Garrick stood up, coming face-to-face with Brody, who appeared ready for the challenge. "What is going on?"

"What do you mean?" Brody asked.

"She can't stand to be near you," Garrick said. "That's what I mean."

Brody's expression went flat. "You need to mind your own business."

"She *is* my business."

"If she was, then she would have told you." He smiled. "You're not as important to her as you think."

"Just stay away from her."

Brody laughed. "I only tolerate her for her father. I'd prefer not to deal with her at all."

After Brody walked away, Garrick found it hard to convince himself to go after Lily. He was wound too tight and didn't trust himself. He knew he needed to build on what he thought might be some sort of a confession before Brody had interrupted, but he wasn't sure he could stand it if it turned into another lie.

"You're the new guy, aren't you?"

A woman, caramel brown, short-haired, in her sixties and

dressed as if she'd had money all her life, stood before him with her similarly styled lady friend at her side. They were both smiling widely as they looked Garrick up and down.

"The new guy?" Garrick smiled, not finding it difficult to muster charm for older women, all of whom generally treated him like the son they wished they had. "I guess that's me."

"Allow me to introduce myself." She held her jeweled hand out to him. "I'm Lois Albers and this is my friend, Mrs. Reva Jackson. We know everyone in Atlanta."

"Well, I'm new, Mrs. Albers." Garrick shook her hand although he got the feeling she had expected him to kiss it. "So I don't know anyone."

"My daughter works at Wolfe Realty," she said. "So, from what I hear, you certainly do know a certain someone."

Garrick smiled. "Are you attempting to make me uncomfortable, Mrs. Albers?"

Her head fell back, laughing as she seemed to enjoy the indulgence. "I just love that little Lily. I knew her when she was born. Her mother was a lovely woman, wasn't she?"

Mrs. Jackson silently, but effectively, nodded her agreement.

"Absolute paragon of virtue in this society," Mrs. Albers continued. "And that little Lily has taken after her so well, hasn't she?"

Mrs. Jackson nodded again, this time with a tenderhearted smile.

"Ms. Wolfe is a fine woman," Garrick said, trying to hide his smirk.

"Oh, she certainly is." Mrs. Albers reached out, grabbing his hand. She squeezed it in hers. "She has certainly suffered from the sins of her father and the death of her sweet, sweet mother. It was all so hard on her, because she simply never deserved any of it."

"If you'll excuse me…" Garrick was eager to go, but Mrs. Albers tightened her grip on his hand. When he looked at her again, her face held no pretense.

"She is a good girl," she said. "That's why she left. No matter what you hear around here, believe me when I tell you, she is a good girl. I was best friends with her mother and I know everything."

"Why are you telling me this?" Garrick asked.

"Because we need young women like Lily Wolfe in Atlanta," she said. "Young women we can be proud of. Now, I know why she's come back, but he won't keep her here. Not after the way he has betrayed her. You… I think you could be why she stays."

"I don't listen to rumors," Garrick said. "You can count on that. I only go on fact."

The pretense and smile returned. "That's good to hear, Mr.…"

"Pratt," Garrick said. "My name is Garrick Pratt."

Making his way through the ballroom of beautiful people, Garrick felt a headache setting in. Just when he had made up his mind… Never before had something he was so sure of been called into question by something as flighty as a casual comment by an old lady. It was because, no matter what he knew, he still wanted to believe Lily was innocent. But she couldn't be. It wasn't possible that her reason for not telling the detective she had been to Sabrina's house that night had just been the basic gut reaction of fear.

But what would she have to fear if she was innocent? Maybe, he thought, having the last name Wolfe made her fear everything. After all, it was her last name that made Garrick believe she was guilty in the first place.

Stepping onto the fifth-floor terrace of the hotel, Lily took a deep breath, but what helped clear her lungs failed to clear her mind. Lily felt like a cold, selfish fool for holding back. Sabrina needed her. Nothing that she felt for her father or herself meant more than helping Sabrina right now. If what she knew could help the police find her, then she had to tell them.

"Don't do it."

Lily jumped, her hand coming to her chest as Brody joined her on the terrace. Her antenna hit the tilt and she moved away. "Stay away from me."

"Whatever you're thinking," Brody said in a warning tone. "Don't do it. You'd be making a terrible mistake."

"You're threatening me, aren't you?"

"You are a supreme idiot, Lily." His exasperated, impatient tone was almost childlike. "I'm not threatening you. I'm trying to protect you, protect your father, myself and the company."

"I don't care about the company," she said.

"That's always been your problem, little flower."

"Don't call me that!" Lily didn't care that she spoke loud enough to garner a few stares. Brody knew that he was pushing her buttons.

"Only Daddy can call you that," he mocked. "The daddy that you claim to love."

"I don't have to answer to you," she said. "No matter what I feel about Dad, I'm not going to let you get away with murder."

"None of us murdered anyone." He was speaking through gritted teeth. "You don't even know if she's dead."

"I won't keep quiet."

"You will," he said. "You wouldn't do this to your father."

"If he didn't do anything, he has nothing to fear."

Brody's expression was taut. "Don't waste our time with stupid comments like that. You know better."

"I can't live with this."

"What exactly are you living with? You haven't done anything."

"It could have been my fault that she—"

"Just stay the hell out of it, Lily."

Looking at him, the anxiety on his face opened Lily's eyes. "What are you doing?"

"Nothing for you to worry about," he said. "But I'm going to find out what happened."

"Why won't you just tell the police?"

"Because I have nothing to tell them that won't hurt your father and Wolfe Realty."

"Are you trying to doctor evidence or something?"

With a disgusted frown, he said, "I'm done with you."

"Wait!" Surprising herself, Lily grabbed him by the arm to prevent him from leaving. "Tell me what you're doing!"

"I'm finding out the truth." He jerked his arm away. "Only, unlike you, I'm doing it with your father in mind."

"What do you think I've been doing? The only reason I haven't spoken up is Dad, but we have to think of Sabrina now."

"Just stay out of it," he repeated. "Think of your own safety; your own life."

"I can't protect myself from something I don't know."

"I know," he said. "If you stay out of it, you'll be safe."

"They'll track her cell-phone records," Lily said. "They'll know she called us. You have a voice mail you can share with…"

"It's gone," he said flatly.

"Then I'll…"

"Don't you dare," he warned.

"I won't sit back and do nothing," she said. "I've already done too much of that. You say it wasn't Wolfe Realty. Then, it was someone from AFC who didn't want her to find out the truth."

"I'm handling it, Lily. Stay away from the police, focus on your nice new romance and pay a visit to your father every now and then."

She called after him, but he stormed off the balcony and did not turn around. She couldn't believe him or a word he said. She had to go to the police and prepare herself for the truth.

As he stepped onto the terrace, Garrick was struck by the pain he felt at the sight of Lily in such despair. Seeing Brody appear from the balcony with a disjointed expression, he knew he would find Lily there.

He approached her and, hiding his apprehension, he reached out to her. It was almost painful to touch her. When she turned to him, tears in her eyes, his instinct hit him clearly and he wrapped his arms around her.

"We should leave," he said. "This is too much for you."

"Garrick." Lily buried her head in his chest, wanting to drown in him. She wanted the strength of his arms, the clean smell of his cologne to engulf her. "I can't keep this in anymore."

His nature kicking in, Garrick couldn't help but feel excited. "Let's go somewhere private."

He led her to a smaller meeting room just down the hall and closed the door behind them. It was dimly lit and empty, so they both went to the edge of the elevated stage and sat down.

"Tell me, Lily." He took her trembling hands in his. She looked terrified and he had to admit, guilty. "I'll make it better."

"You can't, Garrick." Lily felt nauseous. "I've messed up too much."

"Tell me everything."

"It's all my fault. Sabrina could be dead because of me."

Garrick knew not to say a word, but just listen. He should have worn a wire.

"Since I've been back, I've been suspicious that things were… You know my father's history with the law."

He nodded.

"I was just being paranoid," she said. "Or at least I thought I was. Brody was acting suspiciously."

"How?" He cringed. He had to control the eagerness.

"He's so secretive," she answered. "He always has been, but he was particularly secretive about this company I have questions about, AFC. I saw some financial papers on our business dealings with them that made me curious. I should have investigated myself, but…"

"You let Sabrina do it."

She nodded. "I got a call from her and I knew something was very, very wrong. I went over to her house. I…I saw the place and it was a mess. Brody was there."

"Do you think he did something to her?"

"I don't…I honestly don't know." She pulled her hands away and began wringing them together. "I thought he did, but then he said she left him a message to help her and he seemed… He isn't a killer. He told me about the blood. There was blood all over her bedroom."

"Did you tell the detective this?" he asked.

Shame made her barely able to look at him. "I can't."

"What are you afraid of?"

"What if her disappearance didn't have anything to do with me? What if it's really about her boyfriend or some random violence and the police go after my father?"

"I don't think you're contemplating that," he said. "I think you know what it's about."

"I don't want to turn on my father," Lily said. "But I can't just shut up while Sabrina is missing. What can I do?"

He believed her. He wasn't thinking with his heart or any other part of his body. He was thinking with everything he was and he believed her. He wanted to help her.

"You have to get that document," he said.

"What?"

"The one you saw that made you suspicious. You have access to it, don't you?"

"I might." She buried her hands in the thickness of her hair. "I think whoever hurt Sabrina is from AFC."

"Your business partner?"

The lights switched on and they both turned to a uniform-clad older gentleman who gave them a scornful stare. "There's no messing around in here."

"We're just talking," Garrick said.

"I ain't going for it, young man." He gestured toward the door. "Let's go."

Lily looked down at her watch. "I have to get ready to present."

"You don't have to do this," Garrick said.

"I do." She smiled, reaching out to place her hand gently on his cheek. "Thank you for listening. I know I can trust you."

Feeling a sting of pain inside, Garrick took her hand in his and kissed the inside of her palm. "You can trust me, Lily. I'll get you out of this."

"Let's move!" the old man urged.

As he led her out of the small room, Garrick felt Lily squeeze his hand tight. He squeezed back, feeling better than he had in a long time. Yes, he knew he was fooling himself to think he could have a life with Lily, but he could still save her.

"Sit down." Lily directed Garrick to the sofa in the living room as they entered her condo. "I'll make us a drink. What do you want?"

"Nothing." Sitting down, Garrick knew alcohol was the last thing he needed.

Earlier that evening, after her confession, Lily had gone to the bathroom to freshen up and Garrick had called Jamarr, who was resistant to his defense of Lily's innocence but glad she was beginning to talk.

As he sat at the table, watching Lily soldier on through the event, Garrick was working everything through his head. He was proud of her for holding her head up high and getting through this, but at the same time angry with her for still not agreeing to tell the police. He understood her pain because the truth could, and probably did, lead to her father. But if her father had betrayed her before, why would she try to defend him now? And at the expense of another woman's life.

It was that last thought that made him do what he was doing now. The second she was out of sight, he took the miniature bugging device out of his pocket and tagged it underneath the mahogany-colored wooden coffee table.

"You're not doing anything wrong," he whispered to himself. "You're doing your job. This is right."

As he sat back on the sofa, a manila folder on the table caught his attention. Without touching anything, he leaned forward and tilted his head to read the label: Tony Sund.

"He's our CFO," Lily said as she entered the room with a glass of wine in her hand.

Garrick leaned back as she joined him on the sofa. All he could think of was how much he wanted to touch her.

He waited for Lily to retrieve the folder and hand it to him. "Do you think he had something to do with this?"

"Not for sure. I know Sabrina spoke to him from her phone call, but Tony just isn't the kind to hurt a fly."

"They say that about a lot of people." He looked through the files, which contained basic employee information. "You got this from HR?"

"Before I left today."

"Have you spoken with him since?"

She shook her head. "I threw up at the thought of confronting him even though I don't think he'd hurt Sabrina. Tony is a follower. He would never take the initiative in something like this. Besides, his was the note I saw on the financial documents."

"Note?"

"He was worried about all the checks Wolfe Realty was writing to AFC. He wanted to talk to Brody."

"The police need to talk to him."

She put her glass of wine down and tried to study his face. "You think I'm a bad person, don't you?"

He looked up. "No, Lily, I—"

"You'd be right," she answered. "I'm a coward. I run from reality and resolution. I always have."

"I'm not going to say it's okay to keep this information from the police. I can't do that, but I don't think it makes you a bad person. I know you're scared of what it might mean for your father, but if he is behind Sabrina's disappearance, then he has betrayed you again."

"What?" Lily blinked, unsure of what she'd heard. "Betrayed me again?"

"That's what it was, wasn't it?" he asked, going on auto-pilot now. "When he got in trouble, he was lying to you. He was using you and he pulled you in without telling you. You're his daughter, he should have kept you as far away as possible."

"He was never convicted."

"Don't do that, Lily." He reached out and placed his hand firmly on her thigh. "There's too much to deal with now to go backward. Your father got lucky, but he did do what he was accused of."

Her head fell into her hands and she began weeping. Garrick slid over to her and wrapped his arms around her. She leaned into his chest and he knew he could get her to turn. Her father had broken their bond.

"I've been running from it all these years," she cried. "I'm so angry at him, but I...I still love him and I can't turn on him."

"You'll kill yourself trying to look away from this. It will never happen." He grabbed her by the shoulders, making her

look up at him. "You're a good person, Lily. You wouldn't be
in this much pain if you weren't. Look at what you're doing
for your cousin."

"But he's my father, Garrick. If I turn on him, then I'll
be...I'll be all alone. I'll have no one in this world."

"No, you won't," Garrick said, his voice full of emotion.
"You'll have me."

When she looked up at him, her quivering lips called to
Garrick and he couldn't stop himself. His lips took hers and
he immediately felt carried away by the passion that was a
constant while in her presence.

When he grabbed her by the arms, pulling her to him, Lily
felt a relief from the prolonged anticipation of his affection,
his lips. She pressed against him, feeling the heat of desire
take her over. She wanted him so desperately, to take away
her pain and give her body what it needed. Most of all, she
wanted to feel his hands everywhere.

"Garrick," she whispered his name as their lips separated
and his mouth came to her neck. The fire of his lips against
her flesh was delightfully unbearable. "Yes."

Boldly, Garrick followed the power his passion for her had
over him and reached for the straps of her dress. Flipping them
down, he grasped the soft flesh of her arms, loving the creamy
feel of her silky clean. He wanted her desperately and the
moan emitting from his body told her so.

Lily was grabbing at him, frantically pulling his jacket off.
When his lips returned to hers, she felt an overwhelming
desire to please him, to show him how much she had wanted
him since the first moment she saw him.

As his tongue explored her mouth, his craving for her
reached a fever pitch. His pulse was pounding as currents
of hot lava flowed through him. He wanted to taste every
inch of her.

Taken over by the smoldering flame inside her, Lily leaned back to allow him to position himself on top of her. She wanted desperately to feel the pressure of his commanding body over hers.

As his lips left hers, Garrick breathlessly and eagerly kissed her chest, the whiff of her perfume only increasing his drunkenness with her. As he reached up and pulled her dress down, her delicate yet full breasts were exposed. When his tongue circled her left nipple, he felt her body shudder and the effect was volcanic for him.

The tingling sensation Lily was feeling all over her body turned into frantic vibrating as his mouth took in one breast while his hand gently teased the nipple of the other. She dug her hands into his shoulders and groaned her pleasure. She was floating in the air, surrounded by fire that intensified with every circle of his tongue.

Garrick's tongue trailed up her chest, her chin, before his mouth reclaimed hers. He was buried in carnal madness as he heard Lily let out a groan and fiercely meet his demand. He pressed his hands against the sofa, lifting himself up enough for her hands to reach his pants button. As she undid his zipper and pushed his pants down, her hands cupped his rear and she squeezed.

He responded by kissing harder, searching farther with his tongue. He wanted her to feel him; to feel how hard she was making him. He wanted to feel her too; to touch inside of her and know what he was doing to her.

"Garrick." Her voice was barely audible above her labored breathing. In her haze, she reached for the last sense of mind she had. "Do you have protection?"

Her words brought Garrick back to earth as reality took its last breath. He was going to make love to her and it was what he wanted more than anything. Thank God he didn't have protection because it, not his sense of professionalism or right or wrong, was the only thing that made him separate from her.

"No," he said, his voice laden with shame.

Lily sat up, leaning toward him, trying to comprehend his expression through her clouded passion. Despite pulling her dress up, she wasn't ready to give up. "Is it at your place? We can go there."

"No, Lily." He stood up, reaching down for his pants.

Lily felt the chill rush over her in a split second as he seemed unable to even look at her. She couldn't believe he could be that offended that she wanted him to use protection. "What's wrong?"

"We can't do this." He looked at her and felt physical pain at the thought of not being able to make love to her. He hated everything right now. "It's wrong."

"It can't be," she protested. Nothing in her life had ever felt so right. "What have I done?"

"Nothing." He grabbed his shirt and moved toward the door.

"Are you leaving?" She felt too much passion to focus on the stinging rejection. In her mind raced the only thought that she couldn't have been mistaken about how much he wanted her.

"I have to." Garrick knew she wouldn't understand the battle that his sexual urges were waging with every part of him. He had to get away from her. "I won't make the right choice if I stay."

She rushed to the door as he stood in the doorway. "Garrick!"

He turned back to her. The bewildered and injured expression on her face killed him inside. "Lily, you know it's not right. You're too emotional, scared."

"All I know," she pleaded, "is that I don't want to be alone."

"I can't be with you tonight and not make love to you. I... We would both regret it." If only she could understand how much. "I will help you through this, Lily. But right now, I have to go. Good night."

She slammed the door behind him and dropped to her knees. Through her humiliated tears and sobs, Lily couldn't listen to the words he'd just said. She could only believe that his rejection was more than his wanting to be a gentleman. To resist such a heated encounter would take much more for a man. It was the look of shame on his face before his hasty flight that told Lily why he left.

He didn't respect her. No matter what he said, Garrick was a highly moral person and he couldn't get past her refusal to help the police find Sabrina. He was right. She knew she was horrible and she was all alone; exactly as she deserved to be.

Chapter 7

The first thing Lily noticed as she stepped out of her car was the public phone only a few feet from where she'd parked. Pay phones were not common anymore now that everyone was using cell phones, but that wasn't why this one in particular caught her eye.

Feeling more alone than ever after Garrick deserted her, Lily thought of calling the police several times. As the morning came and she readied for her weekly visit to Courtney at the rehabilitation center, making an anonymous call to the detective on Sabrina's case seemed like the obvious solution.

She couldn't sit by anymore, but she couldn't live with her father knowing she was the one who'd implicated him. She knew the FBI was bloodthirsty for him, and even if someone at AFC was alone in what happened to Sabrina, they would find a way to blame Ward for the relationship, which was clearly illegal somehow. What Lily feared most was that they wouldn't have to find a way; it would be there waiting for them.

A pay-phone call would not be traced back to her, so they wouldn't come after her with more questions; questions she wasn't able or ready to answer.

Only, just as she reached inside the partially covered phone booth, a car, pulling alongside the street across from her, caught her eye. At first she thought she was simply nervous, and she was, but there was something about the car and the two men inside that made her uncomfortable.

Using the shield of the booth, Lily could see that both men, white and in their mid thirties, were looking in her direction. They made no attempt to get out of the car, instead choosing to roll down their windows. Lily couldn't break the feeling that something…something was wrong.

Then she remembered. It was more of a flashback than a memory and it left a very unsettling feeling in her stomach. A simple Chevy parked on the curb.

They were following her. As her heart began to beat rapidly, Lily leaned against the phone and tried to imagine every step she had taken. Had she remembered seeing that car anyplace other than her father's house on the first day she returned to Atlanta?

As she suddenly recalled it, the vision seemed as clear as day. The car had been outside of Wolfe Realty's offices, probably more than once. Lily's hand was shaking as she placed the phone back on the hook.

She assumed the car was there to keep an eye on her father. If they had been following her since she returned to Atlanta, then they might have been following her when she arrived at Sabrina's! Was it FBI or the police? Were they working together? Had the detective known about this when he questioned her?

Lily fought off the panic, knowing there was not much she

could do now but walk inside and visit her cousin. She was grateful she hadn't made the call, since it would certainly be traced back to her.

With uneasy legs she hoped wouldn't give out on her, Lily made her way across the street, pretending the car wasn't even there. She felt their eyes on her but didn't look. For some reason, her mind only went to Garrick and his promise to help her through this.

How could he help her when he seemed unable to stand being with her?

Despite all that was going on, Lily couldn't help but smile at the sight of her cousin, Courtney Harris. She was getting her beauty, her glow, her spirit back. Once a stunning, long-legged vision, Courtney's downfall began with smoking weed during lunch in high school. Lunch turned to hours after school, which bled into the weekends, when she would meet the boyfriend who introduced her to meth.

Methamphetamine was generally referred to as the white man's drug, but it showed no preference in its damage and quick, easy addiction. Soon, Courtney dropped out of Spelman, left her mother's house and followed her boyfriend/pusher around the country. At some point, he'd left her in the middle of the night, a night when she was almost attacked by a group of fellow addicts. The incident shocked her enough to come home, but only lasted a few months before she ran off again.

No one heard from her for a year. Then a friend of the family happened to spot her while vacationing in Paris. Courtney's mother called Lily, begging for help. How she recognized Courtney was a surprise to Lily because she was only a fraction of the little girl she had grown up with. Drugs had taken its toll.

It hadn't been easy, chasing Courtney from club to club, getting her to clean up only to watch her get caught up again.

After an intensive rehab at an exclusive clinic paid for by Ward, Courtney was doing better than before. Lily wasn't willing to leave her behind when she got the call after her father's attack. Fortunately, the clinic in Paris had a connection to the Dunwoody Center in Atlanta and Courtney was able to complete her rehabilitation near family.

"You look good." Lily joined her on one of the flowery sofas in the sitting room. They hugged and kissed and Lily felt glad she'd come despite the way she was feeling that morning.

"I feel good." Courtney ran a nervous hand over her short, wavy cut. She had large brown eyes and eyelashes a mile long. She wasn't wearing any makeup on her petite features and despite having gained weight, she was still drowning in her T-shirt. "But you, I don't know."

"Thanks a lot." Lily knew that she wasn't going to win any beauty prize today.

"Seriously, cuz, what's wrong?"

"It's early."

"It's ten-thirty."

"It takes an hour to drive out here."

"Trust me," Courtney said. "I'm not eager to hear it for the drama. This place provides enough."

"But you're doing good, right?"

"Don't try to turn this back on me," she said. "I'm doing great. What's up with you?"

"A lot has been happening at work and… What the hell, okay, there is this guy."

"Ohhh, the good stuff." Courtney rubbed her hands together. "Give the vitals."

Lily told Courtney everything. She hadn't intended to, but once she got started, she couldn't stop. Courtney seemed to take it all in stride while the silence between them, once she was finished, was driving Lily crazy.

"Well?" she asked.

Courtney shrugged. "I've been through worse."

"I know you have," Lily said, suddenly feeling selfish for even letting Courtney know she had problems. "Sorry to bother you with…"

"I'm just kidding, girl." Courtney reached out and grabbed her hands in hers. "This is pretty deep. Do you think he was lying when he said he would help?"

Lily didn't expect the smile that came to her lips at that moment. "I don't think he lies."

"Everybody lies," she said.

"Well, I think he meant it."

"So why are you worried?"

"He turned down sex, Courtney."

"That is a little weird." Courtney frowned, confused. "But you said he was a gentleman."

"It was about more than that."

"A man isn't going to let a little thing like suspicion of murder get in the way of getting some," Courtney said. "You're just feeling paranoid."

"Well something is going on," Lily said.

"Uncle Ward just wouldn't get into this again. I know 'cause of what Mama told me. You know how close our mothers were. They talked about everything."

Lily nodded. "What did Aunt Jonelle tell you?"

"It wasn't anything in particular. It was just… Aunt Jesse was so disappointed in Uncle Ward."

"I remember how it was around the house," Lily lamented. "So cold and quiet, like a space of miles was between them. But she never let it show outside."

"Because she was a good wife and she took her vows seriously. Also, she didn't completely blame Uncle Ward. She said Brody forced him into it."

Lily's brows centered, expressing her doubt. "As much as I would like to believe that, I can't. Brody worships my father and would follow him to the ends of the earth. It is clear who is in charge."

"The impression I got from Mom was that Aunt Jesse thought it was all Brody's idea and he convinced Uncle Ward to take a chance."

"So what about now?" Lily asked.

"Listen to me, Lily. Even if you thought for a second that he was doing bad business again, you know your daddy is not going to be involved in murder or kidnapping or whatever it is you think happened to Sabrina."

Lily found comfort in hearing someone else saying it. "But what about Brody?"

Courtney shrugged. "Don't know him that well and I don't like him. He used to look down on me."

"When?" Lily asked. As far as she remembered, Courtney and Brody rarely crossed paths.

"When I got back here." Courtney cleared her throat to pass the awkward moment. "You know, after that—"

"I know."

"Well, I used to hang out with some friends down in Sweet Auburn. I know it's what got me in trouble, but that was the disease."

"What does that have to do with Brody?"

"I used to see him hanging out around there. Don't ask me what he was up to, but he was up to something. Then, whenever we crossed each other's path among family and friends in respectable neighborhoods, he would look down on me like he forgot I knew he hung out in Sweet Auburn."

"That's just the way he treats everybody," Lily said. "Everyone but Dad."

"Then why was he going to quit?"

Lily's lower lip dropped. "Quit?"

"That's what I heard."

"Brody would never leave Dad. Especially not after they got away with…after everything was over."

Courtney leaned back, looking down at her nails. "All I know is Connie Taylor told my mother he had given her husband his résumé right about the time I got back home."

Lily didn't know what to make of this information, or whether or not to make anything of it at all. She wanted it to mean something but it didn't yet. She would have to figure out a way to make it mean something. If Brody was operating separately from her father, she could protect him if she acted fast enough.

She could only hope that her father would trust her more than he trusted Brody and she wasn't too optimistic about that.

The news was good.

As Lily waited for her father to settle with the doctor's office, she felt confident he could take what she was going to ask him.

Following a TIA, various kinds of tests were recommended, especially for someone who was a possible candidate for surgery. Today's test was a second catheter angiography of his head and neck and a blood pressure check. These tests would go a long way to determine whether or not surgery was required, and Lily could tell her father was anxious.

"You ready, little flower?"

"I'm ready." Lily put the magazine down and jumped up from her seat. "This is good, right?"

"I've avoided the butcher's knife for now."

"Don't say that, Dad."

When they stepped outside, Ward took a deep breath as if he hadn't smelled fresh air in a long time. "It's coming, you know."

"Surgery?" she asked. "If it's unavoidable, then…"

"Not surgery," he said, turning to her at the bottom of the steps. "The stroke."

Lily stopped as the pain touched her stomach. "I know what the doctor said, but…"

"I just have to be ready for it." He reached out and gently touched her cheek. "I don't want to be a burden to you. If I can't take care of myself, I have made arrangements, so—"

"Stop." She removed his hand, stepping closer to him. "It doesn't have to happen."

He smiled affectionately. "We'll go for ice cream."

Lily sighed. "It's not good for you."

"What is it?"

"It's high in fat and—"

"No, Lily. What's upsetting you?"

Lily sighed, her shoulders slumping. "We should go."

"Tell me here." Taking her hand, Ward led Lily to the wooden bench at the edge of the sidewalk. "It's a nice day. I want to stay outside for a while."

"Dad…I…" Lily bit her lower lip, looking down at the ground. She watched a squirrel rush by and fought off changing her mind. "I think Brody is behind Sabrina's disappearance and I think he's doing something illegal at the company."

Ward blinked, smiled and finally nodded.

Lily didn't know how to react. "You're taking this well."

Ward slapped his hand on her knee. "Brody told me you suspected him of this. It's complete nonsense, Lily."

"It isn't. Let me tell you what I know."

"No." He held his hand up to stop her. "Let me tell you what *I* know. Brody is not a perfect character, but he would not physically hurt anyone, especially not a woman."

"Maybe he didn't hurt her," she said. "But whatever relationship he brought to Wolfe Realty through AFC caused her disappearance. I know that."

"You don't know that. Lily, baby, you've been here for a few weeks. You don't know what Sabrina has been up to. She could be dealing with someone you don't know about. She had this secretive boyfriend, and—"

"Did Brody tell you this?"

Ward's eyes lit up with excitement. "These changes I'm making are going to be great for Wolfe Realty. Brody's been there with me through it all. Even when he found out he wasn't going to get the company, he—"

"Wait! What are you talking about?" A long time ago, it was made clear to everyone that Brody would succeed Ward when he chose to retire. "You're not thinking about…"

"Giving it to you?" Ward laughed out loud. "Oh God, no. I think you've suffered enough."

"Then who?" she asked.

"It will all be revealed soon," he answered.

"Dad, please stop with the mystery. I just don't think we have the luxury of it anymore."

He rolled his eyes, clearly deflated by Lily's refusal to share his enthusiasm. "Brody will be in charge after I leave, but… Things will be different. What's important is that I changed his future and he supported me."

"I'm not so sure of that," Lily said. "His secrecy is different from yours. Yours is hopeful. His is…I don't know. It's just that he's different and this whole thing with AFC…"

"AFC is playing a big role in the change of this company. It is costing us a great deal of money, but there is nothing illegal going on."

"This company doesn't exist, Dad. I've checked."

"I don't know what checking you've done, but I have approved of this relationship. I've met Ann Raines and the transactions are very basic."

"I need to see those records."

Ward's brows centered in obvious frustration. "You don't need to worry about this. It's a small company in Sweet Auburn that is focused on the community."

"But I..." Lily blinked, leaning back. Everything was separate but connected. She remembered where she had heard about Sweet Auburn, Atlanta's oldest black business district. "Where in Sweet Auburn?"

Ward stood up. "A converted two-flat, I guess. She came to my office when I met her. Look, let's go get some ice cream now."

Lily stood up, her mind elsewhere. "Okay, I'll...I'll get the car."

"I'll get the car." He held his hand out to her.

"No, Dad. You aren't driving."

"Allow me some dignity, kid. Just from the parking garage to here, okay? Keys."

Without protest, she handed him the keys.

Standing alone, Lily felt both a sense of relief and anxiety. Relief that she could believe her father was telling the truth and anxiety over what Brody was really doing. If he was going against her father, something she couldn't imagine him doing, there was no telling how far he was willing to go.

Lily glanced around the corner in search of her father. She was certain he would take his own sweet time. Deciding to wait patiently and not worry, she leaned against a nearby tree to take in the ever-expanding Perimeter Center. She hadn't gotten beyond a block before being shocked by what she saw.

Was it him or did she just have Garrick on the brain?

She took several steps to her left, stood behind another tree and squinted her eyes to see more clearly. Yes, it was him.

Garrick was directly across the street, standing in front of a nondescript building with the woman he had introduced to her as Annette. The woman who was supposed to have only been a business acquaintance at a job he'd lost over two weeks ago. Lily was certain their closeness, not to mention Annette's hand placed firmly on Garrick's arm, meant she was more than that.

Lily couldn't fight the jealousy she felt as she watched Annette's hand move up and down Garrick's arm. While his expression seemed somber, the smile on Annette's face was tender and affectionate.

"Business acquaintance my ass," Lily said to herself. Had he been lying about their relationship? She didn't take him for a liar, but what could explain what she was seeing?

As her father pulled up, Lily felt panic set in at the thought of Garrick catching her spying on him. She rushed to the car and asked her confused father to drive.

"I thought you didn't want—"

"Just drive, Dad."

Carolyn removed her hand from Garrick's arm as he looked around. "What's wrong? Getting paranoid?"

"No." Garrick couldn't shake the feeling that someone was watching him. "I guess I am. Hey, thanks, but I don't need comforting."

Despite his better judgment, Garrick told Carolyn about last night with Lily. He had intended only to report that the bug was in place, but her questions had him revealing a lot more, including his guilt.

"You did the right thing," Carolyn said as they started for the garage. "You stopped it."

"But I didn't want to, Carolyn." Garrick could still feel the heat and intensity of being with Lily and all he could think of was that he wanted her again. "That's just it. I was willing to risk everything just to be with her like that."

"Good thing the right head won over the wrong one."

Garrick offered a quick, weak smile. "You're intent on making me laugh, aren't you?"

"You've been tempted before," she said. "You've never given in."

"This is different." Garrick had never been this tempted. "It's beyond temptation. It's like instinct or…fate."

After he left Lily's place last night and took a cold shower, Garrick could not dampen his desire for her. While going for a long walk to calm his body down, he thought about what he was doing and tried to reason with himself.

He was being insane to think there was a chance between him and Lily. He tried to talk himself out of the possibility, knowing that no matter how innocent she might be, he was here to send her father to jail and subsequently ruin the company he had spent the last thirty years building. Aside from the awkward family gatherings, there was that whole thing about him lying to her about everything he was.

As soon as he convinced himself he was crazy, he became depressed and carried it through to this morning. Jamarr hadn't seen past anything but the bug and Lily getting the financial records tying Wolfe Realty to a bogus company. Carolyn, on the other hand, saw something more. She saw Garrick's torment.

"I just want this to be over," Garrick said as they reached his car.

Carolyn's phone rang and she reached for it. From the look on her face, he knew this wasn't her husband calling to ask about dinner tonight. She looked at him as she said goodbye.

"That was Jamarr," she said. "They found Sabrina Dunkle's car in Sweet Auburn and not the good part."

"No Sabrina?"

She shook her head. "But more blood. It's at CSI now. They're dusting for prints, DNA, anything."

Garrick found his resolve. "And here I was feeling sorry for myself. This isn't about me or Lily. No matter what happens with us, I've got to focus on this case and only this case."

Garrick was worried.

Yesterday, after leaving the office, he arrived at Wolfe Realty only to find out Lily had taken the day off. When he tried her cell phone, she wouldn't answer. After contacting Jamarr, he was linked to the car that was trailing her and found out she was at her father's place. There was no way for him to go there because he wasn't supposed to know where her father lived or that she was there. He could only try to keep calling her, but she never answered. It was midnight before he gave up, realizing that she wasn't going to come back to their building.

He didn't have the ego to believe his decision not to make love to her would have such an effect, so Garrick tried to figure out what it could be. All he cared about was her safety, so when he heard that she had left her father's home for the office, he was relieved that at least she was okay.

He was eager to see her for reasons more personal than professional that morning when he walked into her office, but she wasn't there. Instead, Ward Wolfe was standing behind his desk feeding documents into a shredder. The sight kicked Garrick's adrenaline into high gear.

"Who are you?" Ward asked, seemingly annoyed at his abrupt entrance.

"Hello, Mr. Wolfe." Garrick approached with his hand extended. He was going to try for a quick glance at the documents, but Ward promptly set them aside and out of Garrick's line of sight. "I'm Garrick Pratt."

Ward's suspicious frown turned to a somewhat less suspicious smile. "Is that so? I've been waiting to get a load of you."

"Lily has told you about me?" Garrick shook his head, careful not to press too hard. The man was clearly still physically weak.

"I know about you," he offered. "My daughter currently fancies you."

"Fancies me?" Garrick smiled. "You're an old-fashioned man."

"In every way." This was clearly a warning.

Garrick nodded respectfully. "I understand, sir. I care about your daughter very much."

"You got a nice little consulting gig out of it."

"It isn't what you think." For a moment, Garrick wondered what it would be like if he wasn't an FBI agent and he meant every word he'd said. Then again, he thought, he did mean it all and that was the problem.

He stood before this man, a man he was certain was a criminal, and still he felt unworthy because of his feelings for this man's daughter. It was ridiculous. He wasn't the bad guy here. He wasn't the one who had taken advantage of all those poor single mothers, hardworking men, and gotten away with it.

"It's only temporary," he said. "I'm looking for something."

"I've heard." Ward's eyes roamed his desk as if searching for something lost. "Let's hope you find it soon. I don't like this arrangement."

Garrick nodded respectfully. "Is Lily here?"

"She's around," he answered. "Take a seat."

"Sir, if you don't mind my asking… Aren't you supposed to be at home?"

Ward frowned. "Actually, I do mind."

"I'm sorry." Garrick walked to the other end of the desk, wanting to get a peek at the papers Ward had out, but the man's eyes wouldn't leave him. "I just know that Lily is worried about you getting enough rest."

"Lily knows I'm here. We came in together."

When Lily entered the office and saw Garrick standing across from her father, she froze for a second. Quickly studying her own reaction to seeing Garrick after having spotted him with the blonde yesterday and receiving his endless phone calls, she didn't know how to talk to him or what to say. He said he wanted to help her, but she made the decision to handle this herself.

"Lily." Garrick, confused by the blank expression on her face, started for her. He was eager to reach his arms out to her, but got a breeze of freezing air as she looked at him with an icy smile and kept walking toward her father.

"You've met Garrick." Lily directed her attention at her father, who was making a mess of his desk.

"We've met." Ward laughed. "I don't want you going around telling people I'm an invalid."

"I didn't."

"Lily." Garrick approached her, feeling her rejection loud and clear. "I've been trying to reach you."

"I've been busy." She turned to look at him as she spoke but quickly turned away to hide the emotion in her face.

"Busy keeping an eye on me," Ward said. He reached for a folder on the desk and offered it to Lily. "This is what you want. It isn't a lot but…"

"Thanks." Lily snatched the folder and slid it into the portfolio under her arm. "We can talk about business later."

Garrick's antennae shot up. She deliberately didn't want him to hear whatever Ward was about to tell her. Even after she knew he wanted to help her. If he needed any more confirmation her cold shoulder wasn't just about his leaving last night, this was it.

Was she on to him? Garrick knew it made no sense, but he had made slipups because she was such a distraction to him. Had he seemed too eager?

"Lily." Garrick didn't back down even though he could hear the pounding in his head. "Can I speak to you?"

"Actually, I need to have a private conversation with my father." She held the portfolio tight to her chest. "Can we schedule something for later?"

He blinked, noticing the bulge in her neck as she swallowed hard. He'd been in this situation before and he knew how to pay it cool. "Sure thing. I'll come back later."

After he left, Lily felt her body relax and the electricity that danced around at his very presence begin to weaken. She turned to her father, who was staring directly at her. His eyes lowered to her hands.

"You're going to break that planner if you squeeze any tighter."

Lily let go, reaching inside the portfolio to pull out the folder he had just given her. "What do you have here?"

"Do you wanna tell me what that was about?" He returned to his shredding.

"First," she said, pointing, "what is this about?"

"Don't get worried." He held up a few sheets so she could see. They were old interoffice memos, nothing important. "I needed to come in to get you that file, so I thought I'd make up a reason to stay a little longer. Now, what about that boy?"

Lily sighed. "I'm not in the mood to talk about him."

"Not working out?"

"Not much is these days."

"Things will take a turn for the better soon."

"If you aren't going to tell how then just zip it." She opened the folder.

Ward laughed. "You are your mother's daughter with that mouth."

Inside the folder, Lily glanced at the brochures for AFC Corporation and read the standard brokerage line. She read the letters of recommendation from community leaders and other clients. "This is all you have?"

"Brody's file has all the serious stuff, but his office is locked."

"But you say you met her? Ann Raines."

He nodded, sitting comfortably in his chair. "She's an older woman, close to my age. Salt-and-pepper hair, runs the small business out of a two-flat all by herself. I saw nothing suspicious about her."

A sense of comfort enveloped Lily at the sight of her father sitting in his chair with a wide smile on his face. She remembered the better days before everything turned their lives on a head. "You look happy."

He leaned back. "I am, little flower. At least for this second."

"What does that mean?"

A serious expression took hold. "I don't know why I let you make me worry, but I do."

"About Brody?"

"I trust him with my life," Ward said. "But I'm worried. If what happened to Sabrina is somehow connected to AFC, then Brody has been lied to."

"That's possible," Lily said. "But how can you explain that I couldn't find any records for AFC in the finance files just now?"

"Is that where you went?"

She nodded. "I made Tony Sund unlock all the drawers. He seemed just as surprised as I was. They're all gone. Tony said that Brody hasn't let him work on any of the AFC invoices or transactions. He's been doing it himself. Isn't that weird? Tony's the CFO, but he's been kept completely out of the loop on a major relationship costing Wolfe Realty hundreds of thousands of dollars."

As he leaned forward and grimaced, Lily rushed to him.

"What is it?" she asked, panicking. "Are you having an attack?"

"Just a little dizziness." He held her away. "I'm okay, Lily. Really, I know there is an explanation for this."

"And I'll find it." She was on her cell phone, dialing his nurse. "Where is your nurse?"

"She's downstairs in the car. I didn't want to walk in here with a nurse at my side."

"Well, she needs to come up here."

"Hey." Ward grabbed the cell phone from Lily and closed it. "I don't want my employees to see a nurse come here for me."

Lily wanted to respect his need to remain a figure of leadership and strength, but weighed against his health, it wasn't going to work. "Then, you have to go to her."

"Fine." Slowly he stood up, handing her back her cell phone. "Do me a favor, okay? Let me walk out of here on my own. It was embarrassing enough walking up here with your hand under my arm like I was an invalid."

"As long as you go down to the car."

"I'll see you for dinner?" he asked, leaning forward.

She kissed his cheek. "Dinner."

After he was gone, Lily had to lean against the desk. The second of panic that had rushed over her at the sight of him leaning over was too much. The stress of police detectives raiding Wolfe Realty and the embarrassment of the media connecting him to a missing woman would be too much.

Glancing down at the sparse folder on AFC, Lily decided she would have to make it enough to start. And it would have to be a start without Garrick.

"Lily!"

Just before she reached her car in the garage, Lily turned to see Garrick rushing toward her. She felt a confrontation coming on and already ached for it. She wanted to pretend he didn't exist for just one moment so she could concentrate on more important things, but that seemed impossible.

"Where are you going?" Garrick asked, noticing the folder her father had given her in her hand.

She was so attracted to him that his just standing there made her want to jump into him and have his strong arms wrap around her. She wanted him to kiss her and make things better in a way only his kiss could.

"What are you doing out here?"

Garrick decided to tell the truth for once. "I followed you. You're acting weird and I want to know what's going on."

"I don't have to answer to you," she said coldly.

"Lily, please." He reached out to her, but she backed away and it stung him enough to make him pause. "About the other night, I—"

"I have to go, Garrick." She wanted to turn and leave, but the dejected look on his face made her stay.

"I was trying to do the right thing," he said. "I wasn't rejecting you."

"You were," she said. "For whatever reason you say is fine, but you did reject me."

Swiftly, Garrick stepped to her and wrapped his hands around her waist. He leaned in and planted a strong, hard kiss on her lips. In a rush, she pushed against him, but he wouldn't budge. The pressure of his lips against hers, igniting a fire, quickly urged her to give in, but Lily was defiant. No matter how good it felt, she wanted to deny her body.

When he leaned away, instead of the smile he expected to see, Garrick was met with a quick slap across the face. He let Lily go and stepped back, bringing his hand to his cheek.

"You don't think I know, do you?" she asked, her anger fueled by her body's betrayal of her mind.

Garrick kept his cool. "I don't understand what you're talking about."

"I'm not a fool, Garrick. And I'm not a criminal."

"I've never accused you of being either." In the back of his mind, he kept telling himself she couldn't know, but he had to admit he was getting a little nervous. "Where is this coming from?"

"A redbrick building in Perimeter Center." She felt a surge of vindictive victory as his eyes widened. "Yeah, I think you get it now."

"Lily, I need to tell you…"

"Spare me your excuses," she said. "Either you rejected me because you think I'm a horrible person for trying to protect my father or because you're sleeping with someone else. I don't know which, but—"

"You're wrong, Lily."

"Don't!" She raised her voice loud enough for it to echo around the garage. "Don't try to tell me that you were having some post-firing follow-up meeting with that woman, because I won't buy it."

Confused, Garrick only shook his head.

"I saw her touching you," Lily said. "I saw the way she was looking at you."

After a second, Garrick sighed in relief. "No, Lily. What were you doing out there?"

She placed her hands on her hips and looked him up and down. "Is that your response?"

Garrick smiled. "No, I just meant…"

"Save it."

"There is nothing going on between me and Car—" Garrick stopped as he realized he had forgotten what name he had used for her when Lily first met her. "She's just a friend. She's been helping me find a—"

"I don't have time to hear this," Lily said. She was afraid she would be too quick to believe any excuse he gave her because she so desperately wanted to. "I have to go."

"I thought we agreed I would help you with that." He pointed to the folder. "Now you seem to want to keep it from me. All because you think I'm seeing someone else."

"I don't care if you are or aren't," she lied. "I don't need your help. This is a family matter."

"This is a criminal matter, Lily." Garrick knew he'd just insulted her, but she had to be made to understand. "You're pulling yourself further and further into it by whatever action you plan on taking on your own here."

"You don't know what this is," Lily said. "Just stay out of it."

"What about the records we agreed you would get from Sund's office?"

"We didn't agree on anything," she asserted. "You told me what to do. I've decided to do something different."

As she turned to leave, he grabbed her by the arm and pulled her back to him. "Listen to me!"

"Stop!" She tried to wrestle free, but he wouldn't let her go. She was confused by the anger, excitement and fear that intermingled inside her. She just loved being close to him, even at a time when she couldn't stand him.

"You can't let yourself get caught up in what your father and Brody are doing," he warned. "The more you decide to go off on your own, the more involved you'll look. I won't be able to help you."

"You can't help me anyway." She reluctantly pulled away. "My father is innocent in all of this."

"If that's true then—"

"It is!" She turned and headed for her car.

Garrick followed. "Then an investigation will bring that to light, Lily."

"I can't risk that." Reaching her car, she turned to him one last time. "How long would an investigation take? How much damage before the truth is found out, if you even have faith that it will? They are after my father and they'll do whatever they can to make him guilty, whether he is or isn't."

"I'm worried about you."

"I'm not," she said. "I'm worried about my father. An investigation will destroy his reputation, which he has tried so hard to rebuild, in ways he could never repair. It would destroy his dreams for the future of Wolfe Realty. His health won't take it."

"How do you think Sabrina's health is faring?" The look on Lily's face in response made Garrick regret his words immediately.

"How dare you?" Anger seethed through her every pore. "I know I'm to blame for this, so don't bother…"

"I'm not blaming you for anything," Garrick said. "I'm just telling you to let the law take care of this. It's about doing what's right despite the consequences."

"Just stay away from me." The words came out like liquid fire. "I wouldn't want to get any of my oh-so-imperfect stink on you."

As she slammed the car door, Garrick was already headed toward his car. Whatever she was about to do, he had a feeling it would end in disaster if he let her go it alone. Yes, she wanted him to stay away from her, but that had become an impossibility a long time ago.

Chapter 8

Garrick was beginning to wonder if the woman had gone crazy. They had driven around for what seemed like forever before she slid her car along the curb on a converted business street in a black neighborhood. For a while there, he thought she'd caught him trailing her, because she circled the same block a few times. Then he deduced that she was lost and continued to follow her.

He pulled alongside the curb less than a block away from her, surveying the area for threats. It was a generally quiet street, farther away from the big business and companies they had passed to get here. Mostly small two-flats converted into a series of businesses such as hair salons and BBQ joints. He noticed the sign that said Sweet Auburn Chicken to Go. There were a few people milling about, no one looking dangerous, but Garrick still wasn't happy she was here.

He flipped on his cell phone just as a call from Jamarr came through.

"I was just calling you," Garrick said.

"What in the hell do you think you're doing?" Jamarr asked in a highly irritated tone.

Lily checked the folder to make sure she had the right address: 1251 Clairmont Road. A converted two-flat, just as her father described.

There was a voice in the back of Lily's head that told her she was a fool as she rang the doorbell, but she didn't care. She'd made the decision at some point that, ridiculously, she could fix everything, and she was going to do that, even if she had no idea how.

After an impatient moment, Lily rang the doorbell again and followed with a quick knock. Nervously, she looked around and found no evidence of the plain Chevy that had been following her recently. She was happy not to see it outside the office that morning because she had been half tempted to confront the two men. It would have been stupid, but stupid wasn't fazing her too much these days.

After not getting a response, Lily walked over to the window off the porch, but was unable to see through the blinds. She wasn't about to give up. Stepping off the porch, she started down the side of the house next to the empty driveway.

Okay, Garrick thought, that was it. Now he couldn't even see her. "I have to go, Jamarr."

"Wait a second," Jamarr said. "I have my guys there."

"But she's disappeared around the house." Garrick was out of the car and starting down the street already. "You're telling me this is near the area where Sabrina's car was found, then that means she's in danger."

"You'll blow your cover."

"No, I won't. We got into an argument. I'll just tell her I followed her like any insane, stalking boyfriend would."

He hung up while Jamarr was in the middle of a sentence, and picked up the pace. He was getting a bad feeling.

The side window shade was partially open and Lily, ignoring the dirt on the siding that would smear her business suit, leaned against the window to look in. The place was practically empty, with only the bare essentials: a desk, fax machine, phone and an old cabinet. She could barely make out a sofa on the other side, but what she could make out piqued her curiosity.

At the foot of the old, fake-leather sofa were two unmarked file boxes. The bottom one was closed, but the top was half-open, and she could see that the folders sticking out were lime green—one of Wolfe Realty's signature financial-file colors, thanks to Sabrina. Someone had taken the files Lily had been looking for that morning and brought them to AFC.

Lily's adrenaline kicked into high gear. So much for thinking that AFC was acting alone in this. Someone at Wolfe Realty had to be helping Ann Raines and her company and there was no turning back from that fact now.

Looking against the wall, Lily could see an expensive portable DVD player next to a box set of DVDs from a popular action show on MTV. It struck her as curious that it all belonged to a woman whom her father had described as a female around his age who worked alone. Most women in their mid sixties weren't carrying around portable DVD players and weren't too interested in watching episodes that several critics basically billed as an hour-long rap video in television format.

Leaning back, Lily tried to lift the window, but couldn't. Not only was it locked, it was nailed shut from the inside. There had to be some way she could get inside.

Around the back of the house, she spotted another window and a door. She tried the window first, but it was shut tight. When she reached the door, her hand was on the knob before she heard the rustling of rocks behind her. Before she could turn, she felt a hard, piercing thump on her head and everything went black.

As he heard the tires screeching off in the alley behind the houses, Garrick's quick strides turned to a sprint. When he reached the back of the house, the dust from the alley concealed the identity of the car speeding away. Garrick's instinct was to go after it, but something made him turn around.

The sight of Lily lying on the ground sent waves of rage through him. Garrick ran to her, kneeling on the ground.

"Lily!" He wanted to shake her, but he knew not to. Looking her over, he couldn't see an injury anywhere and she was breathing. "Lily, wake up."

Reaching inside his jacket, Garrick pulled out his phone to dial 911. He was so filled with fury, he could barely focus to dial. He knew enough to share his agent number to make sure the ambulance knew he was FBI. He yelled his location into the phone and ordered them to hurry as if a cop was down.

When he heard footsteps around the side of the house, Garrick shot up. He reached inside his jacket for his gun and held it up to the two men in black and gray suits who appeared. Both men immediately went for their guns with one hand while showing their badges with the other, while yelling out, "FBI."

Garrick replaced his gun and returned to Lily. He took her hand and gripped it tightly between his. "The ambulance is on the way."

"We have her," the man in the gray suit said. "You aren't supposed to be following her. That's our job."

"Good job you did," Garrick asserted. "She was hit over the head by someone who…"

For the first time, he noticed that the back door was open. Both men noticed as well and raised their guns. Garrick nodded to them to enter. He wasn't going to leave Lily.

Impatiently, Garrick rubbed Lily's hand, looking down at her as he said her name over and over again. He loved her, it was completely clear to him now. How that happened, he wasn't so sure, but he was sure of how he felt. Seeing her lying there filled him with such pain and rage, he could barely think. Someone was going to pay for this.

"There's no one in there," one of the men offered as they both came back outside. "You have to go."

"I'm not leaving her," Garrick said. "Go out on the street. Look for the ambulance."

"You have to go," the man repeated. "If she comes to, your cover will be blown."

"I don't give a damn." He would give anything for her to open her eyes. She had to be okay. "She's been hit in the head."

"This case has obviously escalated." The man shoved his gun back into its holster. "We need you inside more than ever."

Garrick didn't respond, only squeezing Lily's hand tighter.

"You're an agent of the FBI!" the man yelled. "Get yourself together and get the hell out of here. Don't ruin this case. We'll take care of—"

"Shut up!" Garrick shouted.

Taking a deep breath, he slowly, reluctantly, let Lily's hand go. He refused any help from the men as he stood up. He looked at the man whom he hated for telling the truth squarely in the eyes.

"I know what I am," he said. "I'm the man who drove her to this."

He was able to take a few steps away before turning back to her. It made him ill to see her lying there. No matter what he knew to be right, to be his job, it was completely unnatural for him to walk away from the woman he loved as she lay unconscious on the ground.

"I'll be in my car," he said as more of a warning than a note of fact.

In a daze of anger and self-loathing, Garrick focused enough to follow the ambulance to the hospital and was able to breathe again at the sight of Lily moving her arms while on the gurney as they rolled it into the emergency room. At least she was okay.

"What do you want?" Garrick asked Jamarr as he answered the phone.

"We're on the scene," he said. "Do you want to come back?"

"I need to find out…"

"Garrick, she'll be fine. Her father is going to show up and you can't let them see you. Come back to the scene. You can help her from here."

The first thing Lily felt was pain. Still lying on her back, she lifted her arm to touch the back of her head, but a string attached to her finger prevented her from reaching it. It was then she thought to open her eyes. Everything around her was white and bright enough to hurt her eyes.

She heard herself moan instead of speak the words she intended to say.

"Lily?" It was her father's voice, but she couldn't see him. She moaned again.

He was leaning over her now, smiling down at her. "She finally awakes."

Lily tried to smile, but it hurt too much. "Wha… Wha…"

"You're in the hospital," he said. "You were attacked. Someone hit you over the head pretty bad."

She tried to reach again. "I…I can't…"

"They have your finger attached to a monitor," he said. "You don't need to touch your head. It's bandaged up. Good thing they didn't have to shave your head. I know how you are about your hair."

"Sit...up."

"Here." Ward pressed a button.

Lily felt her upper body lifting slowly until she was sitting up. This was much better. Gingerly, she moved her head to look at him. "Who?"

Ward frowned and in a deep dark voice, said, "They don't know yet, but when they do I'm going to kill him."

"Don't say that." She reached out to him, but her hand fell flat. She had to be on something. "Drugs?"

"For the pain," he answered. "You have a concussion and they have to keep you overnight so they can wake you up regularly."

"The...files," she said. "Did they find..."

"Find what?"

"Police."

"Yeah, the police are outside and they wanted to talk to you as soon as you woke up, but I thought I would give you a minute."

She swallowed hard, trying to find her voice. "What did they find?"

"There was no one there, from what I heard. What were you doing in Sweet Auburn?"

"I wanted to...meet Ann Raines...face-to-face. I wanted... answers."

"I should have never given you that information. Where is it now?"

She tried to shrug, but every movement hurt her head. "Something was...very wrong, Dad. We have to... We have to tell..."

"You're getting upset," he said, placing a gentle hand on her arm. "That's enough."

"I saw the files," she said. "Dad, I...I saw our files there."

"The missing AFC files?" His expression stilled. "How in the hell did they get there?"

"Brody put them there."

"You don't know it was Brody. I saw him on my way out of the building this morning and we…"

"Dad, you…you have to at least consider the possibility."

"It could be someone else," he said. "He isn't the only person who had access to those files and he has the least motive to bring this company down again."

"I know, but…" She placed her hand over his. "I just have a feeling."

"He wouldn't hurt you, Lily. No matter what he thinks of you, he cares too much for me to hurt the only thing I love."

Her pain was tempered with feelings of tender joy at his words. Lily closed her eyes as he leaned forward and kissed her softly on the forehead. "Dad, I…I don't want to believe this because I love you, but if your belief in his loyalty is misplaced then the premise for all your beliefs in him is unfounded."

"I know." He lowered his head. "I'm going to get to the bottom of this."

"Dad, your health. You can't exert yourself. Stress will cause—"

"You're in no better condition than I am," he insisted. "And after this incident, there is no way in hell I'm going to let you continue to be involved. Let me do what I have to do. If it destroys the foundation, then…"

"What foundation?"

Ward sighed with a resigned smile on his face. "My big secret. My big promise to your mother. Oh, Lily, it was all going to be so perfect. It was all going to work and it still might if I can take care of this."

"What can you look for if you don't even believe what I tell you?"

"Just let me do what I have to do," he answered. "I've given Brody power over everything, but I haven't been completely ignorant of my company. I know how to find out what I should."

"Are you prepared…for the truth even if it makes everything you already thought a lie?" she asked.

"There is nothing I can find out that would be worse than seeing my baby girl in a hospital bed."

His words gave Lily a sense of hope about their relationship that she never thought was possible. "Dad, I wish I could—"

She was interrupted by a hard knock on the door. The detective outside didn't wait for permission to enter. With his partner in tow, he approached the bed on the other side of Lily with a completely stony expression on his face.

"Ms. Wolfe, it's good to see you're awake."

Lily wasn't fooled by his words. The entire demeanor of this middle-aged Italian with distinguished gray temples told her that she had to stay alert with him. She hoped she was up to it.

"You remember me, don't you?"

"Detective Rego," she said with a slow nod. "You're working on Sabrina's case."

"Good," he replied. "I need a few moments of your time."

"I was going to call you," Ward said.

"It's okay," he replied without looking at Ward. "We heard the voices, Ms. Wolfe. I'm going to be in charge of your case. I need you to tell me everything that happened so we can catch the person who did this to you."

Trying to nod, Lily winced in pain at the same time. "I don't know how much I can tell you but I'll try."

"First, I want to know what you were doing there."

"She wasn't doing anything wrong," Ward interjected.

"I wasn't accusing her of anything," Detective Rego said defensively.

"Your tone," Ward warned.

The detective ignored him. "Ms. Wolfe?"

Lily squeezed her father's hand in hers. "I was visiting a business partner."

"And who would that be?" He looked down at his notes. "That office hasn't been occupied for several months."

Lily looked at her father, whose complexion went at least two shades lighter. She quickly turned back to the detective. "I don't know what you mean."

"Who occupies that building?" he asked. "The neighbors say no one ever comes and goes there. At least not through the front door."

"It's… I thought it was the office of a business partner of ours. I guess I had the wrong address in my file."

"Can I see that file?"

"I don't have it anymore."

He wrote on his notepad. "Did you have that file on you when you went to the address?"

She nodded.

"Nothing was found on you or in your car," he said. "The person who hit you must have taken it off of you."

"I guess, but…there were other files. Boxes of them in the office. I saw them through the window. Someone was obviously working…"

"There were no files," he answered curtly. "Just a few newspapers, medical books and office supplies that weren't being used."

"I don't know what to tell you." Lily realized someone must have known she was coming.

"Just tell me everything," Detective Rego said. "From beginning to end, tell me everything, Ms. Wolfe."

Lily felt confident that she told Detective Rego and his partner all she could, all she remembered at that point. Of course, there was one lie.

"Why did you have business with this person?"

"We are planning on restructuring the company," Ward spoke up. "It means we'll be cutting off some of our partnerships that we no longer have a strategic need for. Lily believed it would be better to do this in person with all the local companies."

Detective Rego stared Ward down for a second before turning back to Lily. "Ms. Wolfe, the question was for you."

Lily cleared her throat. "My father is right. I just wanted to pay them a visit. We haven't done business in a while."

The detective didn't bother to hide his lack of satisfaction at her response. "I'll need as much information as you can give me on this company. If you've done business with them, I'm sure you have extensive files."

"I'll do whatever I can," Ward chimed in. "Now, if you don't mind, my daughter is recovering from a very serious injury."

Detective Rego, who appeared annoyed with Ward's mere existence the entire time, suddenly smiled in his direction. "Mr. Wolfe, you wouldn't by any chance have anything to tell us to help shed light on this incident?"

Ward shot up from his seat. "What are you implying?"

"No." Lily reached out to her visibly angry father. "Your health, Dad."

"It's just a question." Detective Rego folded his notebook closed.

"My father wasn't there," Lily said. "He had nothing to do with…"

"Well, it's just curious to us that he doesn't know about a business housed in an office he owns."

"What?" both Ward and Lily asked at the same time.

"The building." The detective's victorious smile was cheek to cheek. "It's owned by Wolfe Realty. You bought it two years ago."

Lily turned to her father, who looked just as surprised as she.

"I buy a lot of office buildings and homes." Ward's tone gave away how much he was caught off guard. "I don't make the purchases personally."

"It's just all very curious," the detective said before returning his attention to Lily. "I'll be following up with you, Ms. Wolfe."

As he reached the door, letting his partner pass, the detective stopped and turned back. "You didn't ask about your friend."

"Sabrina?" Lily asked. "What? Is there news?"

"Her car was found abandoned," he said, "just a few blocks from where you were attacked."

Lily's chest tightened. "You mean…"

"There was blood on the steering wheel." He spoke as nonchalantly as if he was ordering from a menu. "Her purse was there, including her medicine."

"She needs her medicine," Lily said. "What is she going to do without it?"

"Your friend needs a lot of things, Ms. Wolfe." Detective Rego tapped the wall with his pen. "Mostly she needs your help. You give me a call if you can think of anything else."

After he was gone, Ward sat back down. "Damn."

"Do you doubt it's all connected now?" Lily asked, not fighting the tears that streaked her face. "Sabrina has hepatitis C. She'll die without her medicine. That is, if she's alive at all. We have to do something."

"I will," he said, standing up. "I'll do it now."

"What are you planning?" she asked. "I want to help."

"You're out of this from now on." His expression softened as he leaned over her bed. "The boy. Do you want me to call him?"

"The boy?" she asked.

"You know, the boy."

"Garrick." Lily smiled at the familiar name her father used for every boyfriend she'd ever had. "No, I…I don't want to deal with him right now."

After her father was gone, Lily couldn't get Garrick off her mind. She was thinking of their argument, their last kiss, but mostly the feeling she couldn't shake that she had heard his voice while she was at that house. Was it before or after she was hit? Or did she just have Garrick on the brain as well as in her heart?

Seeing Carolyn shake her head as she sat across the desk from him, Garrick knew what her response would be. He hadn't much cared what anyone else would think, but he hoped she would be on his side because he'd come to respect Carolyn over the last several weeks.

"He won't let you bring her in yet," Carolyn said. "I know you think it's the best idea right now, but maybe you're thinking too much with your heart than your head."

Garrick leaned back, running his hand over his hair. "It was messed up, Carolyn. Seeing her lying there unconscious… I've never been so angry."

"You're a good agent," she said. "You have to reach inside and find—"

"I'm trying, Carolyn." Garrick's voice made clear his sense of urgency. "I'm trying to recall every bit of experience I have to bring perspective to what I'm doing, but I've never felt this way about a woman during a case or in my real life. I feel…"

"Responsible," Carolyn offered. "You old-fashioned men. Your outdated paternal instincts toward the women you love can really get in the way."

"It isn't that I think she can't take care of herself," he said. "I just feel like I should because…"

"What about doing the right thing?" Carolyn asked. "I'm sorry, but if this woman is the great person you seem to think she is, she would come to us."

"It isn't that simple," he said. "You know that. This is her father."

"Isn't Sabrina her friend?"

"Barely," Garrick said. "And nothing trumps blood. Would you pick my well-being over that of your husband?"

"Fine," she said. "But think about what you're doing this for."

"To protect her."

"She doesn't want to be protected. This is all about you wanting to be her savior because you hope it will mean something to her." Carolyn sighed, leaning forward. "We've discussed this. You're going to lose her either way."

Garrick didn't want to hear that. "She'll hate me for a while, but…"

"You're going to send her ailing father to prison," Carolyn said. "Last I checked, there isn't anything in the Tiffany catalog that can make nice after that."

Garrick wasn't so sure he hadn't already lost Lily. He expected a call from her or someone at the office that knew about their romance, but no one bothered. He had to ring the office and ask for her before he could be told what happened, so he would have an excuse for knowing. When he arrived at the hospital, he was turned away. She had spent the following day at her father's house, not returning his calls.

The sense of desperation overcoming Garrick was completely unfamiliar, but he was trying to deal with it the best he could. "I'll figure out something."

"That's not good enough," Jamarr said as he entered the office. Standing at the end of the desk, he was clearly unhappy. "You can't build an FBI case on *figuring out* something."

"You can't build one on old grudges either." Garrick met Jamarr's cold stare with one of his own.

"You promised me records," Jamarr said. "You promised me documentation. Where is it?"

"It's possible to—"

"I don't want possible," Jamarr said. "Whatever has been going on between you and this girl has hurt this case; the exact opposite of what she was supposed to do. We have nothing now."

"We could have her," Garrick said.

Jamarr placed his hands flat on the desk. "Don't even talk to me about bringing her in to flip her. Unless you're hiding something from me, everything you've said equals out to the fact that she won't turn on her father."

"That's because she believes he's innocent," Garrick argued. "If we can prove he's guilty…"

"She already knows about the documents," Jamarr said. "Her friend is missing, likely dead because she asked her to investigate. Not to mention, she was just hit over the damn head. She knows this is connected to her father. His being guilty doesn't seem to make a difference to her."

"And she doesn't trust you anymore," Carolyn added. "So you don't have that leverage."

"Thanks," Garrick said.

Carolyn shrugged. "The case comes first. You know that."

"There's something else," Garrick said. "There has to be."

"You can bring her in," Jamarr said. "As soon as you have something on her or—"

Garrick slammed his fist on the desk. "She's innocent, Jamarr! I've told you that."

"Not if she keeps information from the police. You threaten her with jail time for what she's withholding."

Garrick stood up and came face-to-face with Jamarr. "She is not going down on this."

"She will if she has to," Jamarr said.

"Wait." Carolyn stood up, coming to stand between the two of them. "There is another way."

"What?" Garrick asked, trying to calm down.

"If we can find hard evidence against her father," she said, "we can call her in and turn her. Not with a deal for her, but with a deal for her father. If she helps us, we'll reduce the charges. If not, he gets the book. She's worried about his health, and if we can convince her he's going down either way, she'll do whatever it takes to lessen the pain."

"But we don't have the evidence," Jamarr said. "We don't have anything now because you've screwed—"

"Enough!" Garrick yelled. "I've had enough of you and this damn case. It was too weak in the beginning and you want me to bail your ass out. Well, to hell with you and the whole thing!"

Garrick heard Jamarr yell out his real name as he stormed off, but he didn't look back. He'd had enough of all of this. Lily was the only thing on his mind and he was going to go crazy if he didn't see her. And Jamarr would have hell to pay if he thought he could hurt her.

When the banging on her front door began, Lily dropped the ice cream in her hand and the bowl shattered into pieces on the kitchen floor. She was frozen in place, wondering if she should have agreed to her father's suggestion she hire a bodyguard.

She couldn't move and only thought of Garrick, wondering if he was a few doors down, as she had been all morning since returning to her place.

"Lily! Lily, open up."

The voice was angry, but it was clearly Garrick, and Lily allowed herself to feel relief. She hesitated, feeling the uncertainty of the moment before walking to the door. Seeing him through the peephole, she could tell he was not happy and she felt a little sense of satisfaction at it all.

She opened the door, keeping the latch on. "What do you want?"

Garrick had to hide the fact that he was just so happy to see her again. He was mad at the world and he would blow up in a second if she didn't open that door. "Let me in."

"No," she said. "What do you—"

He reached out and placed his hand between the door and the wall. "Lily. I'm sick of this."

"You're sick of this?" she asked. "Move your hand. I'm closing the door."

"Lily." His voice was dark and deep. "Open this damn door."

Despite the roll of her eyes, Lily felt a sense of excitement at the strength of his insistence. Stepping aside, she felt a rush of heat flow through her at the way he stormed into her living room.

Garrick turned to her, slamming the door behind him. He noticed right away that she was wearing a long, button-down tailored man's shirt, a pair of socks and nothing else. It turned him on like crazy. "You have company?"

"Why?" she asked.

"That shirt isn't your size."

She shrugged. "You're not the only man to step foot in this condo."

"The way you're treating me, Lily, it's foul, real foul."

"Thanks for the lecture," she said. "But if you don't mind, I've had a stressful few days, so…"

"I do mind." He refused to let her frigid response deter him. "That you could let some misunderstanding about a coworker of mine get between us when you're lying in a hospital bed is simply ridiculous."

"Don't flatter yourself," she said. "And it's *ex*-coworker, isn't it?"

"Sit down." He pointed to the sofa.

Lily placed her hands firmly on her hips. "It would appear I'm not the only one who's been hit over the head."

The viperous look on his face made Lily sit down as quickly as if her father had told her to do it. It didn't escape her that she couldn't have pushed him as far as she had right now if he didn't care for her. But what good was his caring if it was tainted with disdain for her or if she was just one of many women he cared about?

Garrick sat down next to her. "Tell me what's going on."

Lily sighed, her shoulders falling. "I don't know anymore."

"You know."

She pressed her lips together, her eyes squinting in anger. "Don't call me a liar."

"I'm not…" He grabbed her by the shoulders and looked squarely into her eyes. "Will you stop trying to protect yourself from me?"

Lily hadn't expected the tears that were coming. "I don't know what else to do. I'm confused and I'm scared and angry and…"

She fell into his chest so easily, and as he wrapped his arms around her, Lily felt like she was home. There was no point trying to talk herself out of this. She wanted to be with this man no matter who he was, what he thought of her or what else he was doing.

"Garrick." Her arms went around his waist as she slid the rest of her body to his. "Someone tried to kill me. I really don't know what to think or who to believe."

"We were supposed to be doing this together." Garrick could feel his affection for her taking over every inch of him, reason and mind be damned.

"I couldn't trust you."

"Because of Annette?" He held her tighter. "Whatever you saw, it wasn't what you think. She's a friend of mine, a good friend now. She's helped me get through what I'm…I'm going through now, but it is a purely professional relationship. I have no feelings or attraction to her at all. She's happily married with children and…"

"It's not that," Lily said, realizing it just as she was speaking. "It wasn't just her. I know you're not the cheating kind and I know you're not a player. I tried to make myself believe that it was her so I could blame this on you and be done with it."

"What is it?"

"It's what it's always been from the moment I met you. From the moment I invited you in here and you wanted to be such a gentleman and do things the right way. You're a good, honest person and—"

"Stop, Lily." Garrick couldn't stand it. "I'm not what you think."

"You *are* what I think," she said, lifting up. She looked into his eyes, touched by the tender pain on his face. "You're a good person and I couldn't stand your thinking less of me. I've been living with the shame of my family for years now and I let myself forget it by leaving for Europe, but it hasn't gone away."

"I'm not judging you by what your father did," Garrick said.

"But what about by what I do?" she asked. "I know you don't like the way I've handled things since Sabrina went missing. You say comforting words, but your eyes tell me what you think."

Garrick's hand went to her face and his fingers lifted her chin. "Lily, I could never think less of you. I…. When I saw…when I heard you were hurt, my heart ripped into a million pieces. I was consumed with so much anger, pain and fear. How could I judge you when I love you as much as I do?"

Lily gasped the second she heard the word love. "You… you love me?"

Garrick smiled. "God help me but I do. And I won't ever judge you, Lily. I just want to help you. You can't shut me out and—"

When her lips came to his, the longing in her soul sent a storm of desire rushing toward her. The taste of him made her want more and more. There was no buildup for Lily; her body seared with desire for him in that second.

There was no contemplation for Garrick as his arms wrapped around, pulling her body to his. His lips responded with tormented demand as his emotions of anger and lust collided into rapturous passion for the woman he loved.

As their lips explored each other's mouths, hungry hands searched for flesh to touch, to hold and make theirs.

Lily gasped as Garrick grabbed her shirt and ripped it apart, the buttons flying every which way. The fire in his eyes as they raked over her exposed flesh created a smoldering lust inside her. He wanted her as much as she wanted him.

Everything inside of him leaped to life at the sight of her naked breasts. They were so beautiful, so enticing; so perfect. Taking her by the waist, he lifted her body and brought her breast to his face. She wrapped her legs around his waist and held on as his mouth and tongue explored her flesh.

Shivers rushed through her as the agony of intense pleasure increased with every touch. She moaned as she lowered her head, and he looked up to take her mouth with his. The world erased as she felt wrapped in an erotic web. The ecstasy of feeling her insanity build with his tormenting kisses delighted her beyond words.

He was going crazy and he loved every second of it. The touch, the taste of her silky, firm skin, the seduction of her eager, full lips was leading his desire to a fever pitch. As she reached and frantically pulled at his polo shirt, he let go of her only long enough to get it off.

The kinetic energy of their bodies so close to each other made them feel as if they would light on fire at any moment. As he caressed her hips, she left sizzling kisses everywhere, taking a moment to bite his ear before whispering about protection. He didn't hesitate to respond in the positive this time before drinking in the sweetness of her lips again.

As he eased her back onto the sofa, Lily reached out and tossed all the pillows around the room before reaching her arms up to receive him. He steadied himself over her to lessen the weight, but Lily wanted to feel him. She wanted the pressure of his strong, incredible body on top of hers.

He seized her mouth again, groaning as her hands stroked his chest. His mouth greedily took possession of everything it touched, stopping at her breasts again. They were so supple, so enticing, he couldn't get enough. Garrick forced himself to try to stay sane long enough to make sure Lily was pleased. He wanted to enter her now but knew she deserved more than that. He wanted to make her scream for him.

Lily called to him as a savage thirst began to take her over. Her trembling fingers dug into the expanse over his shoulders, her body shivering as she felt his hand travel down her stomach and reach her deepest point. She opened her legs wider as his fingers slowly circled the edges of her center. When they finally entered, Lily's entire body felt a jolt rip through it. He stroked her gently, moving slowly in and out, but the effect was anything but gentle. Lily was becoming manic.

When he lowered his head, his tongue replacing his fingers, Lily's body began to squirm and her moans were becoming louder and louder. Her arousal made him wild and he stoked the fire by stroking the outside of her thighs harder and faster. He was grateful to hear her pleading for him, because he couldn't take it anymore. He had to have her; to be inside of her.

When she welcomed him to her, a pure explosion ripped through her entire body. He filled her with his formidable hardness with a savage intensity and her body was throbbing with ecstasy. She grimaced at the agonizing pressure as she wrapped her womanhood around him tightly.

Their bodies quickly found a rhythm and Garrick felt himself drowning in soul-drenching excitement. His head was spinning and the world was turning around him. He was crazed as her center held him tight. As the crescendo of desire rose to ungodly levels, he picked up the pace, losing himself in the sensual music their bodies made. Whenever he thought it would be too much, more than he could take, his body asked for more.

The more he demanded, the more Lily gave. As she spiraled further and further in a world of raw, flooding, ravishing passion, nothing in the world made sense. She had never felt this aching, fiery pleasure in her life and she never wanted it to end. As his thrusts came faster, she arched her body to meet him. When she felt the gusts of desire building and climbing within her, her legs came up and wrapped around his thighs.

Her fingers dug into his back and she screamed his name loudly as her body climaxed, exploding with a burst of unreal pleasure. She was shuddering all over, reveling in the titillation from her head to the tips of her toes.

Her climax spurred his own eruption and, with a carnal moan, Garrick gave in to the pleasure that raged through him, twisting him into heaven and flushing him with a cool breeze of complete satisfaction.

Chapter 9

"This looks much better." Garrick sat up on the sofa. Lily was walking toward him with two teacups of ice cream. She was wearing his shirt this time. "You can burn the other one."

"Burn it?" Lily laughed, sitting down as she handed him his cup and spoon. She snuggled up to him, loving the feel of his warm body against hers. "This shirt has some good memories for me. You're not one of those guys who want to pretend their girl was a virgin before he met her, are you?"

"What guy isn't?" He leaned forward and kissed her, getting a quick whiff of her hair, which smelled like fresh pomegranates. "You know I'm kidding, right?"

"You better be," she said. "If you ever want to see what's underneath this shirt again."

"I do. Again and again and again and…"

She leaned up and kissed him. "I love you."

Garrick blinked, looking down at her adoring face, so full of love and trust. The words jarred him. "I... You do?"

She nodded, turning her whole body to him. "And it feels so good. I've forgotten what love really felt like. My life has been so...empty for so long. I feel stronger and smarter and sexier and..."

"You're really inflating my ego." Garrick put the ice cream down, suddenly not hungry. "You should stop."

Lily recognized a change in his tone. He wasn't too happy right now. "I'm sorry. Am I scaring you?"

"No," he said. "You know that I love you, Lily. I couldn't be happier to hear that you feel the same."

"You certainly don't look like it." She didn't want to feel anxious about his sudden turn in mood. She wanted to believe she was just being insecure. "I'm not the clinging type. You don't have to worry about that."

"I don't think you're clinging at all." He gently touched her cheek with the back of his hand. She was more beautiful than ever before and it only made the reality more and more painful each time he looked at her. "And if you were, it wouldn't matter. I love you, Lily."

Lily smiled, still confused by the sadness in his eyes. "Do you trust me, Garrick?"

Garrick swallowed, maintaining a smile. "Yes, why?"

"Because I trust you completely." Lily took his hand in hers and brought it to press against her chest. "I hope you'll forgive me for keeping things from you, for pushing you out. I know you'd never hurt me and now I know you'd never judge me."

"Lily." Garrick took his hand away, feeling the guilt wash over him, threatening to suffocate him. "You don't—"

"No," she said, stopping him. If she hesitated, she might chicken out. "I want to tell you everything. I need to bare my soul and con—"

"No!" Garrick saw the shock on her face at his tone. "Lily, you don't have to."

After a moment's hesitation, Lily said, "I know, Garrick. You don't want me to think I have to, but I don't. I want to. You deserve to know everything. You've been nothing but good…"

Lily reached out to him as he dropped his head and slammed his fist on the sofa. "What? What's wrong?"

Garrick looked up at her. "I love you, Lily. You have to know that."

"I do." Lily was starting to get frightened.

"And I want to help you," he said. "No matter what you tell me and no matter what happens, I will help you in every way I can."

She smiled, her hand coming to his cheek. "I know you will, baby. I finally get that and it's why I'm going to tell you everything."

As she went step by step through everything that had happened since she returned to Atlanta, Garrick felt his gut caving in. He would have to report this; he would have to tell. Or would he? He was hating himself for even thinking of withholding the truth from Jamarr, but even more so for giving in to his desire for Lily.

Sleeping with a mark was not unheard of. It happened a lot. Not as much as one would think from cop shows on television or in movies, but there were people whose job it was to get as close to the mark as possible. It was up to them to decide how far they wanted to go. Sleeping with them was considered unethical, but everyone knew it was done.

Before he'd even had the chance, Garrick decided he would never go all the way. It went against everything he believed about sex and professionalism and was highly discouraged by the brass. Sex complicated things, compromised priorities and skewed values. It jeopardized cases, and sometimes, broke innocent hearts.

What had he done?

"You can't quit," Carolyn said.

Garrick turned to her, sitting on his left as they both sat across from Jamarr at his desk. "I'm not quitting the FBI. I'm quitting this case."

"You can't quit." Carolyn threw her hands in the air. "You just don't quit a case."

"I've never done it before," Garrick said, "but there aren't many more choices."

"Cut the crap," Jamarr said. "You're not quitting."

"I think it's my choice," Garrick said. "I wasn't assigned to this case. You asked for me and I was looking for a change of scenery. I don't work for you."

"The FBI isn't just a name outside of buildings in various cities and states," Jamarr said. "It's an entity, and in that entity I outrank you. So, you *do* work for me."

"We'll see what Chicago has to say about that."

"You'll be sorry," Jamarr said.

Garrick leaned forward. "Are you threatening me?"

"Hold on, boys." Carolyn stood up. "Let's keep the testosterone under control."

"If you quit this," Jamarr warned, "you are quitting the FBI."

"Like I said," Garrick said, "we'll see. Once Chicago knows the case is dead…"

"Why would you say dead?"

"You don't have anything," Garrick said.

Jamarr laughed. "I beg your pardon?"

"I know what's going on," he said. "She's told me everything and she's completely innocent. She believes her father is completely innocent and I believe—"

"After two hours of great ass, I'd believe anything, too."

The second Garrick jumped up from his seat, Jamarr pushed away from his desk. As he went for him, Garrick could see real fear in Jamarr's eyes and he wanted it there. He was ready to rip the man apart until he realized what Jamarr was really saying.

Jamarr calmed down as Garrick was frozen in horror. "You forgot, didn't you?"

Garrick turned to Carolyn who lowered her head as if ashamed. "We turned it off when you started... Well, you know."

Garrick had a hard time catching his breath as he leaned against the wall. He had placed the bug under the coffee table and completely forgotten about it.

"We tried to give you your privacy," Jamarr said, still backing up a little, "but an hour went by and then another and... Well, damn. You sure know how to make a brother jealous."

Garrick's fierce glare erased the smile from Jamarr's face. "You had no right."

"Say that into the mirror," Jamarr said. "No one told you to lay the pipe to her."

Jamarr straightened up as he saw Garrick's hands form into fists at his sides.

"We turned it back on right before she told you everything," Carolyn said.

Garrick's mouth opened but nothing came out. This couldn't be happening.

"We can bring her in on that tape alone," Jamarr said. "We'll charge her with obstructing justice and go from there."

"That's bull," Garrick said. "Those are empty charges that won't stick."

"They'll get her in here," Jamarr said. "And once she hears the tape and knows what you've done, she'll be too messed up to think straight. We'll take advantage and push. She'll give up something."

Garrick groaned as he took another step toward a cautious Jamarr. He wanted to kill him but he knew this was all his doing.

"Give me time," he said. "I'm asking for time."

"I thought you quit," Jamarr said.

"Hey!" Carolyn shot Jamarr a warning glance. "That's enough. How much time?"

"Forty-eight hours." Garrick was trying desperately to find the humility through his anger.

"Fine." Carolyn nodded.

Jamarr was shaking his head vigorously. "Carolyn, you don't have the authority to—"

"He's got forty-eight hours, Jamarr." She stood her ground, not flinching. "You owe me."

Jamarr looked like a child ready to throw a tantrum. "Just know, I'm getting Ward Wolfe no matter how I have to do it."

Without a word, Garrick grabbed his keys and walked out of the room. He felt like he was in the twilight zone. Everything had gone wrong from the beginning with this case and now he was in a full-blown disaster. He wasn't sure what he was going to do, but he had to figure something out. He would have to accept that Lily would find out who he really was and he might lose her. He would try hard as hell not to, but he might.

But not this; the tape was too much. He could never, ever let her know about it. He didn't care what he had to do, legal or otherwise. He only knew that Lily would never, ever hear that tape of her pouring out her soul to him after they made love.

Telling the truth was the most liberating experience in the world. Lily felt like things could finally be resolved, now that she had bared everything to Garrick. She was initially confused by his reluctance to hear her confession, but his comfort made her feel as though everything was going to be okay. She loved him for his patience and understanding. He made her believe it was okay to need someone when life was getting a little hard.

It seemed so simple, the way he explained how this would go, but she had been too caught up in the issues between her and her father to see it all. No one would win this. No matter what Lily thought she could do, everyone touched by this was going to get hurt. Some would get even worse.

He'd tried to ease her guilt about Sabrina, but that would never go away. Lily knew there was no excusing what she had gotten Sabrina into. All she could do was whatever it took to make sure whoever was behind this paid for what they'd done.

There was nothing Garrick could say that would ease her mind about her father either, which was why the first place she went after she and Garrick parted ways was to his home. She was going to tell him everything that she and Garrick were up to including going to Detective Rego. She knew her father wouldn't like it, but she would explain it all to him the same way Garrick explained it to her.

She lamented the fact that she would probably have to sacrifice any hopes at a real, meaningful relationship with her father. Recent interactions with him made her hopeful, but she knew she was in no place to make demands. She would tell him the truth and promise to fight for him. She only hoped she wouldn't have to fight him, which was what she thought as she pulled into her father's driveway and saw Brody's car. This could be where she paid the price for waiting too long to repair their relationship. If it came down to a choice between her and Brody, who would her father pick?

When she entered the living room, she saw them sitting casually on the sofa, talking just above a whisper. When they turned to her, she could see the animosity in Brody's eyes instantly and she wondered if she was safe.

"What are you doing here?" Ward asked, looking worried as she rushed in. "You promised you would rest if I let you go home."

"I'm fine," she said, turning to Brody. "I'm all rested out. There's too much to do."

"You're not doing anything," Ward said. "It's my turn to play doctor."

"Where have you been?" Lily asked Brody as she sat in the love seat across from them.

"I don't answer to you." Brody's eyes never left hers. He didn't blink and he didn't look away.

"Let's not get into it," Ward said. "Lily, Brody and I are getting to the bottom of this."

"Is that so?" she asked, hating that she was the first to turn away, but she couldn't stand Brody's serial-killer stare any longer.

"You don't think that's possible," Brody said. "Considering you believe I'm at the bottom of this."

"Brody has been investigating what happened to the files," Ward said. "I'm trying to find out more about the sale of that house in Sweet Auburn."

"What have you found out?" She sat back, folding her arms across her chest.

Brody spoke first. "It was just part of—"

"I'm asking my father," Lily said.

Brody smirked and rolled his eyes.

"It was part of a big buy-up before the changes. There seems to be a few details missing."

"Don't you find that convenient?"

"Look, Lily." Brody leaned forward. "No one is denying that there is someone inside involved, but unfortunately for you, it isn't me."

"We believe that Sabrina might have been involved in

something," Ward said. "We are reviewing her appointment book. It was downloaded from her computer. She has several visits to AFC's office listed."

"She's conveniently not here to defend herself." Lily wasn't going to let Brody get away with pinning this on Sabrina. "Who did the downloading, Brody? Was it you?"

"I don't know how to do that." He cracked a thin smile. "Jason in IT did it for me and he made it clear that if anyone had gone in and changed it, the revisions would be dated in the code and they weren't."

Lily was silent for a moment, contemplating what it meant if Brody was telling the truth. "She didn't know anything about AFC except Ann Raines's name."

"That's what she told you," Ward said.

"If she was in on it," Lily said, "then why would she get hurt?"

"Someone obviously felt she was the weak link," Brody answered.

Lily was shaking her head vigorously. "No, no, this doesn't make sense. Something is missing."

"You're the one with the new boyfriend," Brody said.

"This has nothing to do with Garrick!"

"Look, Lily." Her father placed his hands on his hips, a gesture he always made before trying to reason. "Don't you find it odd that this has all been happening since he showed up in your life?"

"He lives down the hall from me," Lily said. "He was there before I got back."

"And he conveniently has the skills that would give him access to financial records," Brody said.

"You vetted him yourself," Lily said. "You said he was clean."

"Vetted?" Brody frowned, seeming confused. "Why would you use that word?"

"What difference does it make?" Ward asked. "The point is, anyone who is new in our lives is suspicious."

"Garrick is new to Atlanta," Lily said. "This thing with AFC has been going on for almost two years."

Ward turned to Brody who was still staring, confused. "Well?"

"Vetted?" Brody asked again.

Lily rolled her eyes. "It means—"

"I know what it means," Brody said. "I have experience with the FBI, remember."

"Dad." Lily took a deep breath. "Garrick and I have been talking."

"How much of this have you told him?" Brody asked.

"Can I speak to my father alone?" she asked, irritated.

"I'm in this," Brody argued. "I'm trying to find out what the hell is going on and who is trying to destroy everything your father has worked for. So, no, you can't."

"It's okay." Ward nodded to Brody, who sighed in disbelief. "Just for a moment."

After Brody was gone, Lily joined her father on the sofa. "I don't trust him, Dad. I don't think you should either."

"Tell me about your boyfriend," he said.

"I'm serious, Dad. You can't give this to Brody. He'll—"

"I don't have the strength to do it," he said. "I'm not letting you get involved in any of this anymore. There's no one else I can trust."

"There's Garrick," she said.

"I don't even know your boyfriend."

"I do." She smiled wide, leaning into her father. She kissed him on the cheek. "And I trust him completely."

Lily began with a hopeful explanation of everything she and Garrick had decided, but hope soon turned away as her father's reaction grew colder and colder.

"No," he said. "We can't do that yet."

"We have to," Lily urged. "Dad, Sabrina is out there."

"If I thought you had something that could help find her, I would make an anonymous call, but nothing that you have is useful."

"Not that we know, but there could be something in the police investigation that seems useless to us but they're just waiting to put the pieces together."

"It would ruin everything." Ward slowly stood and began pacing the floor with his hands wrung together. "Everything that I've been working for these past years for Jesse wouldn't have a chance if…"

"Do you really believe that Mom would want us to keep these secrets?" Lily was beginning to worry about his building frustration.

"Your mother cared about the community very much," he said. "I broke her heart when I did what I did. I knew I would too, but the opportunity was there and in a moment of selfishness, I believed I could make it all work."

"You broke my heart too," Lily said. "But hearts mend. Mom's did and so did mine."

He stopped pacing and smiled tenderly. "Let's tell the truth, little flower. Your heart has not mended quite yet."

"I love you," she said. "I know that. I also know that right is right and even if it hurts, you have to do it. I need you to understand and I need you to come with us."

"To the police?" he asked. "Wouldn't Pruitt just love that?"

"No, he wouldn't. He would hate to see you coming to the police because that would make you look innocent."

"You're naive Lily." He laughed, placing his hands at his sides. "Nothing will ever make me anything but guilty as hell in that man's—"

"Dad!"

Lily lurched from the sofa toward her father as he made a whimpering sound and grabbed his left arm. She caught him just as he was about to fall back, but he was too big for her to hold up and they both fell onto the sofa.

"Help!" she yelled out. "Someone, please help! Dad, please. No."

Brody rushed into the room in a panic. "What did you say to him?"

"Brody, please help." Panicked, Lily wasn't sure what to do. "Where is his nurse?"

"Dammit, Lily!" He was already dialing his cell. "She's off today. What have you done?"

"I'm sorry," was all she could say as she felt her father grip her arm tightly, his eyes squeezed shut. He was whimpering, trying hard to breathe, and Lily couldn't even comprehend the fear she felt. "I'm sorry. I'm so sorry."

Garrick could hear the woman standing behind the desk at the emergency room of the hospital call to him, but he wasn't listening. All he could think about was the tearful, frantic message Lily had left on his voice mail.

He didn't have time to kick himself for being unavailable when she called. He wanted to clear his head after the reality of the debacle he'd created settled. So he went to ESPN Zone, his favorite sports bar for a few beers and a rerun of last night's basketball playoff game. It allowed him to escape for just a moment.

He would lose Lily for sure; all logic told him that, but his heart wasn't willing to accept it. As his head pounded and the noise around him faded away, Garrick imagined the tender, and some not-so-tender, words he and Lily had spoken to each other as they made love twice on the sofa. Their souls had connected and it went beyond any of the secrets they were keeping from each other.

He'd made so many mistakes with women in the past, partly because of his job, but mostly because of him not caring enough to make it work. This was different. He would do anything to make it work with Lily, and the irony was that all his efforts would do no good.

He reached a point so low that he could see himself willing to let a criminal get away with his crime just to have her. All those years he'd spent believing that nothing mattered more than what was right and just were wasted. All he could think of now was the look on Lily's face if Jamarr made her listen to the tape of her baring her soul to him after making love.

He had been too caught up in himself to hear his cell phone ring, so it wasn't until he left the club that he checked his voice mail and got the frantic call from Lily telling him that her father had suffered another attack and was at the hospital. Despite aching for her, Garrick also knew that this would only make things worse for everyone. Even though much earlier that day he'd told Lily that there would be no winners here it was only now that he really believed it.

Then he saw her.

Sitting on the cushioned bench against the wall, hunched over with her face in her hands, she looked like a lost soul, and Garrick couldn't get to her fast enough.

"Lily." He opened his arms as she turned to him and fell into them. Her tear-stained face looking almost surprised to see him. "I'm so sorry."

"Where have you been?" she asked, unable to comprehend the relief at being in his arms.

"I've been thinking," he said. "I didn't hear the call. I'm so sorry, baby. Is he…"

She leaned back, shaking her head. With the torn-up tissue in her hand, she wiped her face. "No, but he's had a minor stroke. He's in there now and they won't let me see him."

"What does minor mean?"

"What difference does it make?" she asked. "It's all my fault. I tried to tell him, but he—"

"Sir." The nurse from the front counter loomed over them. "You can't come in here. This area is for family only."

"He's family," Lily said, squeezing his hand. "He's my family."

Garrick only lowered his head, waiting for the nurse to leave. It kept getting worse. "Thank you."

"I want to see him," she cried.

"They'll let you in when they can," he said. "But you can't blame yourself. You told me his condition was on edge."

"And I knew he couldn't take the stress of this situation," she said. "I can't go through with it. We have to think of something else."

"Lily." His fingers came to her chin, lifting her face to his. "There is nothing else."

"You don't know that," she said.

"I do."

She leaned away, trying to examine his strained expression. "How?"

Garrick blinked, wishing he could find the words to make her feel better, but they didn't exist. "God, Lily. I...I just wanted to protect you."

"I don't care about me," she said. "He could be paralyzed or brain damaged, Garrick. You have to understand that I don't care..."

"What are you doing here?"

Garrick looked up as Brody approached them. He stood, knowing that face-to-face was the only way to deal with this man. "Lily called for me."

"This is for family only," he said, looking down at Lily. "You know that."

"So why are *you* here?" Garrick asked.

As Brody took a step closer to Garrick, he lifted his chin and braced himself.

Lily jumped up to come between them. "I can't believe you would think of this right now."

"I'm sorry." Garrick turned to her, rubbing her arm. "I'm sorry, baby. I know you're upset. I—"

"Michael?"

They all turned to the long-legged, caramel-skinned beauty standing before them in a sienna wrap dress. Her long hair was pulled tightly into a bun, adding to the stern look on her face. She was focused on Garrick and when Lily turned her head to him, the look on his face made it glaringly clear that he knew her well.

Garrick's mouth opened but nothing came out. He blinked, wondering if he was going nuts or...no, he had to be going nuts. This couldn't be happening was all he was saying to himself. This was impossible.

"Michael," Melinda repeated in a more impatient tone. "What are you doing here and who is she?"

"No," was all he could say as he held his hand out to her. "No."

"Who is this?" Lily asked. "Why is she calling you..."

"Lily." He turned to her, feeling rage and fear at the same time. "Don't think... Look, I can explain..."

"Michael, I want to talk—"

"No!" He was loud enough for everyone within a good distance to hear. "Melinda, you can't... What are you doing here?"

"I followed you from the Sports Zone," she said. "I knew you'd be there. I've been driving by every day for two weeks. What are you doing with this woman? Michael, is this what you—"

"Stop." He rushed to her, still telling himself that this couldn't be happening. "Go outside and I'll talk to you."

"I need to talk to you now." She pulled at his shirt with pleading eyes before he pushed her hands away. "What are you doing?"

"Garrick?" Lily took one step forward before Brody grabbed her by the arm and pulled her back.

When Garrick turned to her, the look of complete bewilderment on her face was pitiful. He hadn't thought it could get worse, but there was no end to the hurt he was causing her.

"Who is Garrick?" Melinda asked as she grabbed his arm. "Michael?"

Garrick jerked his arm free of her and returned to Lily. He reached out to her but she stepped back and the gesture alone was worse than a knife to his gut. "Lily, please."

"What…" Lily was shaking her head in disbelief as she backed away from him again. "Who is she? Who…are you?"

"She's an ex-girlfriend," he explained. "Just please, let me handle her and I'll be back and explain everything."

"But you…" Before she could finish, Brody stepped between them.

"Get the hell out of here," he said, "before I have you and your girlfriend thrown out."

Garrick couldn't look him in the face because with all the anger he felt now, he knew he would hit Brody and make things worse on a completely other level. Violence was the last thing this moment needed.

"Move out of my way," he grumbled.

"Haven't you done enough?" Brody leaned forward. "Michael."

Garrick was ready to blow, when the nurse returned, this time with a security guard at her side.

"Now," she said, "who exactly is family here?"

"They are not," Brody said. "They have to leave."

Garrick was ready to protest, but catching a glimpse of Lily looking like a broken child as she peeked behind the safety of Brody, he didn't have the strength.

Instead, he stared into Brody's eyes and said, "I'm coming back."

Lily held on to Brody to keep standing. She felt nauseous and dizzy at the same time. "I… What just happened?"

"I told you that you couldn't trust him." Brody led her back to the bench.

She looked up in time to catch a last glimpse of Garrick turning the corner, gripping the woman's arm in a harsh movement. Then they were gone and Lily was completely stunned.

"She called him Michael."

"He isn't who he says he is." Brody gestured for the nurse. "Whatever you think you knew about him, you were wrong."

Lily couldn't believe that. How could it be true? How could he have fooled her? What had he fooled her about? "Who is Michael?"

"He is." Brody turned to the nurse as she arrived. "That man does not get back in here. Tell security. He's her ex-boyfriend and he's a threat to the health of the patient."

As the nurse nodded and rushed away, Brody turned back to Lily, who was looking up at him as if she was wishing he could answer all her questions.

"Thanks to you, he's a threat to everything," Brody said before turning and walking down the hallway.

Garrick, still floored by his encounter with Melinda, returned to the emergency room at the hospital only to be met with a security guard who refused to let him back him. Having already decided that Melinda's surprise arrival meant that God had it in for him, several thoughts went through his head, but he knew they would end with him going to jail. He wanted to fight someone and would fight anyone, even the man who was clearly seventy-five pounds heavier than him and at least three inches taller.

He was tempted to show his badge because he didn't give a damn at that point if the whole world knew he was FBI. Only Lily, thoughts of Lily, kept him from going crazy, and it was thoughts of Jamarr coming after her that made him determined to reach her.

It took some time, but he was able to find his way back in, only to find that Lily was nowhere to be found and Ward had been transferred to the intensive care unit, which made getting into the emergency room seem like a piece of cake.

Brody was the only one Garrick could find and the two came to verbal blows immediately.

Lily watched from the protection of a room at the end of the hall where she had been allowed to rest. It was a room used by the staff when they needed to catch a ten-minute nap, and after the scene with Garrick and that woman, Lily needed it. Her head was spinning as she prayed for God to let her wake up from the nightmare.

There was a part of her that wanted Garrick to come back and tell her anything that could explain her doubts. She wanted to believe she was being unreasonable, but she knew she would have to be crazy to think that.

So it was better that he not come back. That was what Lily decided. It was just a coincidence that she would spot him in the hallway arguing with Brody when she decided to give up on trying to sleep and try to get in to see her father again.

Lily couldn't hear what they were saying, but she was too afraid of a possible confrontation with Garrick to step outside. She watched with her broken, confused heart as the man she believed to be honest and decent argued with the man she thought could possibly be a killer. Could she have gotten them mixed up? She doubted everything at this point.

Garrick finally left under the urging of two security guards and Lily couldn't help herself. She had to know what had been said even though she knew it wouldn't soothe her mind. She hated him for making her think of her heart when she should only be thinking of her father.

Maybe Brody could tell her something, anything that could tell her she wasn't crazy.

She called his name, but Brody had already made his way down the end of the hallway and was quickly out the double glass doors. Lily made sure that Garrick, who had been taken the other way, was clearly out of the way, before going after Brody.

After thinking she lost him, she finally found him in the courtyard, talking on his cell phone. He was clearly still angry and something told her to approach with caution. Something also told her she wanted to hear what he was saying. Leaning against the wall, she scooted closer to the edge until his voice was clear.

"No, he isn't going to die," Brody said in an annoyed tone. "It's a stroke, not a heart attack, and it's minor… Yes, he'll be okay… Because he has to be… Listen, baby, just…"

Lily scooted closer.

"Don't second-guess me," he ordered. "It was the only thing to do… Nothing is falling apart. If you'll just… Well, she's fine so don't worry… I had no choice. Ward gave her the address… I didn't even know he had it. I thought I took everything."

Lily felt her chest constricting as she put his words together.

Brody sighed impatiently. "So, what does he know? I got rid of the files. I burned them. You…. No, babe, you are the one who left all your shit in the office."

He was talking to Ann Raines! The fear Lily felt told her she should run, get as far away from Brody as possible, but she couldn't move.

"You should have taken it with you when…" He sighed heavily. "I was going to torch the place, but Lily showed up and now the cops are there… I thought she would give up after… Fine, but we can't go back to that."

Lily couldn't listen to any more. She was too disgusted and too afraid to stay and risk getting caught. Tiptoeing out of earshot, she ran back into the hospital. She wasn't thinking at his point, just doing. She couldn't feel or care, she had become too numb for all of that. She just did.

Learning over the front desk at the ICU, she asked again when she would be able to see her father. She was told he would be moved in the next two hours and she would be able to see him then.

Lily hoped she could be back in time.

It was such bitter irony to say such a thing, but Lily felt like something was wrong.

She looked down at her watch and realized that she only had a half hour. After arriving at the police station and asking for Detective Rego, she was made to sit and wait. Sit and wait while she contemplated what she was about to do. Sit and wait while not knowing what state her father was in. Yes, the doctor had said minor stroke; six months' recovery, but the guilt she felt kept it from meaning anything.

Would her course of action make things worse?

She remembered what her mother had told her after her father was been arrested years ago. *Sometimes things have to get worse before you can make them better. Sometimes, Lily, it's the only way to ever get better.*

When she was finally able to see Detective Rego, Lily had

stipulations she would stick to, but she knew she couldn't keep this from her father for long. What was important was that she had evidence, firsthand proof that whatever Brody was up to didn't include her father.

She told him everything she had overheard Brody saying on the phone and he took studious notes on the computer at his desk. He seemed pleased that she was there but distracted by a woman in a poorly fitting green skirt suit who kept coming over to his desk and whispering into his ear. After Lily was finished, he thanked her for her information and told her he would be right back.

When he returned, the look on his face told Lily that despite her not believing things could get worse, they were about to.

"What's wrong?" she asked. "I have to get back to my father."

"I know you do." He leaned back in his chair and entwined his hands behind his head. "Only there's a little glitch and trust me, it isn't my choice."

"What do you mean?"

"Well," he said, "when I heard you were waiting for me, I looked up my cases and…"

Lily turned around as his attention moved to something behind her. The same woman in the badly fitting suit nodded to him. When Lily turned back around, Detective Rego nodded back. He stood up, grabbing his keys off his desk.

"What's going on?" Lily braced herself, gripping the edges of the desk with her left hand.

"Someone is here to see you," he said. "Follow me."

"Who are you talking about?" Lily followed him through a door and into a hallway.

"Who do you think?"

"Thinking hasn't been my strong point recently, so indulge me."

"I'm just a lowly detective, sweetheart." He motioned for

her to turn a corner he seemed uninterested in taking himself. "They want you not me."

Lily paused for a second before slowly making her way around the corner. She gasped at what she saw and didn't know if she was angry, frightened or happy.

"What are you doing here?" she asked, taking a few very cautious steps toward him.

Standing next to a closed door, Garrick could barely look at her. "I…Lily, I want you to understand something."

"No more understanding," she said. "I don't know what you're up to, but I don't care anymore."

"I want to—"

"No, Garrick. Or Michael or whatever your name is. Your games mean nothing to me now."

"I have to warn you."

She laughed. "Warn me? Please, brother. Let me guess, you're trying to help me, right? And that woman is…another ex–coworker who is helping you through this difficult time. Oh yes, and she called you Michael because… Don't waste your time."

He reached out and grabbed her, shaking her once. "Listen to me, Lily. This is no joke. You have to make some decisions before you walk into that room and I—"

The door opened and Lily gasped as Jamarr Pruitt stood in the doorway with a smirk on his face as he looked from her to Garrick.

"I've think we've made Ms. Wolfe wait long enough, agent. Why don't you let her in."

Jamarr opened the door wide, revealing a table and chairs, one of which Lily noticed was occupied by Annette.

"What is…" Lily turned to Garrick. "Agent? You…"

Garrick nodded. "Yes, Lily. I'm an FBI agent. My name is Michael Monroe."

"Nice to meet you again, Ms. Wolfe." Jamarr held his hand out to shake.

Lily didn't divert her gaze from Michael. She felt her knees weaken. "Go to hell, Pruitt."

"Ouch." Jamarr held his hand back. "I thought you said she was nice."

"Shut up," Garrick growled. "Lily, I…"

"How…could…you…" Lily felt the hallway begin to sway back and forth before she heard Garrick yell her name and the world went black.

Chapter 10

When Lily came to, the first thing she saw was Annette, leaning toward her. The first thing she heard was Garrick and Jamarr arguing. So it hadn't been a nightmare.

"Where…" She looked around and realized she was in the office now, sitting at the table.

"Look at her!" Jamarr pointed to Lily. "She's fine now. There's no need for the hospital."

Garrick rushed to Lily's side, kneeling to meet her face-to-face. "Are you okay? Do you want to go to the hos—"

The slap across his face was loud and stung like a wasp. He saw sparks and light and the pain shot through him to the tips of his fingers. If he hadn't been holding on to the table, he would have fallen back.

When his vision steadied again, he could see nothing but pure, white-hot hatred in her eyes. "Lily, I want to explain."

"There's no time for that." Jamarr took a seat on the other side of the table.

"No!" Garrick grabbed a seat and pulled it up to Lily's. "I'm an agent with the FBI and I was brought in to investigate your father."

"No." Lily tried to get up, but her head began to swirl and she fell back into the seat.

"Forget this," Garrick said. "She's not feeling well. We can't do this now."

"How could you do this to me?" Lily found the words despite reeling from the deceit that she was yet to fully comprehend.

Garrick sighed. "It's my job, Lily. But I promise you I meant it when I said I would help you."

"By destroying my father?" Lily didn't want to cry in front of them all, so she dug her nails into the palms of her hands to keep from giving in to her emotions.

"Your father is a criminal," Jamarr said. "As far as I'm concerned, so are you."

Seeing nothing near her but her purse on the desk, Lily grabbed it and tossed it at Jamarr. It hit him in the head before dropping to the floor.

"That's a felony!" Jamarr yelled.

"Lily." Garrick recaptured her attention. Her lower lip was quivering, but Garrick had to keep his mind together. If there was anything to save from this disaster, now was his only chance to do so. "I need you to help me if I'm going to help you."

Lily tried to concentrate but it was impossible. All she could think of was how everything had been a lie. "The way we met? You planned this? You…"

"Hearts break," Jamarr said. "Then they heal. Let's get down to business."

Garrick slammed his fist on the desk. "Jamarr, I'm not going to tell you again."

"You sons of bitches." Lily made sure to make eye contact with all three of them, but settled on Jamarr. "I knew you were bitter about losing your sorry case, but to go this far."

Jamarr leaned forward. "No one told you to hop into bed with the first guy who looked your way after getting back on American soil."

Lily gasped, turning to Garrick. The way he lowered his head told her everything. How much did they know?

"Did you get a good laugh?" she asked, unable to stop the tears now. Her humiliation was too much. "You sleazy bastard."

Lily couldn't look at him anymore. She felt as if she could throw up right now, trying to hold on to her sanity. What in God's name had she done to her father?

"You don't have to go to jail," Jamarr said. "If you help us."

"I haven't done anything," Lily snapped. "And you know I won't help you."

"Your father is in a hospital bed right now," Jamarr said. "I suggest you get over your hurt feelings and start thinking about what is best for him."

"Oh yes," Lily said. "I'm sure finding out that the FBI sent a whore to seduce his daughter will make him feel fantastic."

Garrick stood and turned away from her. He didn't want her to see the anger on his face because he knew her insults were the least of what he deserved.

Jamarr laughed. "If we arrest you and—"

"We're not arresting her," Garrick said.

Jamarr grumbled under his breath. "She withheld information from the police."

"Go to hell," Lily said. "I don't have to listen to this."

"You do," Carolyn said. "We're not local cops, Ms. Wolfe. We're FBI."

"And who would you be?" Lily wiped her tears with the back of her hand. "Annette, the helpful coworker, right?"

"Carolyn is my partner," Garrick answered.

"I wasn't talking to you." Lily shot him a deadly look. "I don't want to hear anything from you."

"You came to the police," Garrick argued. "You told Detective Rego that you overheard Brody saying. You know this is drastic and I can help you…"

"Would you stop saying that?" Feeling strength from her fury, Lily shot up from the chair. "Stop saying you'll help me when all you've done is try to destroy what I love."

"Someone attacked you," Garrick said.

"It wasn't my father," she answered back. "So, he's the only person I can trust now. Pruitt, all you care about is making amends for your complete and utter idiotic, colossal failure six years ago."

If she wasn't so obliterated, Lily thought she might get a moment's joy out of the dark, furious expression that came over Jamarr's face.

"You little…"

"Jamarr," Garrick warned.

"Do you trust me, Garrick?" Jamarr mocked. In a lower tone, he said, "Yes, why?"

Lily looked at him confused, wondering what he was doing.

"Because I trust you completely." Jamarr blinked his eyes. "I hope you'll forgive me for keeping things from you, for pushing you out. I know you'd never hurt me and now I know you'd never judge me."

"That's it!" Garrick rushed for Jamarr and both men began struggling with each other.

Lily felt all the blood rush to her head as she realized what Jamarr was doing. He was repeating the same words she had said to Garrick at her…just after…

"Oh my God." Lily's hand went to her chest, which felt as if it was about to cave in. The blow of reality was so hard she stumbled backward. "You…no, you can't… You couldn't."

Jamarr pushed Garrick off of him, but before Garrick could come back, Carolyn stood in between them.

"Stop it!" she ordered as she held up both her hands. "You're both acting crazy."

Jamarr turned to Lily. "That's right, Lily. We have you on tape and it's enough to get a warrant. You have a choice."

Carolyn grabbed for Garrick, but he jerked her arm away. Approaching Lily, he put his hands in the air to let her know he wasn't going to touch her. "Listen, Lily. It's not what you think. That wasn't part of it. I forgot that I'd put the bug…"

"You put it there?" Lily was so horrified, she could barely breathe. "You put it there and they listened to us…"

Lily rushed for the door.

"Wait!" Garrick turned back to Jamarr, who was smiling victoriously despite the bloody lip. "I'll kill you for this."

"You're just breaking all kinds of laws today, aren't you?" Jamarr asked.

"Go after her," Carolyn said.

Lily had to hold on to the wall as she tried to make her way down the hallway. When Garrick reached her, he grabbed her and turned her to him.

"Lily, you have to listen to me." Garrick knew he would be dead if looks could kill. "If you help us with the investigation, Jamarr promises to wait until your father is better to prosecute."

"My father hasn't done anything!"

"Maybe he hasn't. If what you overheard Brody saying is true, you might be able to avoid that altogether, but not before Jamarr learns the truth. I know you hate me and I deserve it, but—"

"Hate would be putting it mildly," she said. "If I could, I'd kill you now."

Garrick felt the sting and let it go. "If you walk away from this, Jamarr is going to act on the tape and he'll go after your father. Don't let this happen."

"I didn't let it happen, Michael." She placed her hand on her hip. "That is your real name, isn't it? Michael."

He nodded. "Lily, you have to think past you and me."

"There is no you and me," she said. "Isn't that the point? I thought there was, but it was only you trying to destroy my life!"

She turned to leave again and Garrick tried to grab her. "Don't leave, Lily."

She struggled free, yelling for him to let her go. By this time, they had garnered enough attention for a uniformed officer to make his way to them. He tried to reach in and break them up.

"Please," he said. "If you two will just—"

"Get off of me." Lily pushed the officer away.

"Stop!" Garrick could see where this was going. "That's an officer, Lily. You can't hit him."

"Just stay away from me!" Lily was manic, with only a mind to turn and run.

"Let her go!" Carolyn called after Garrick, who had started to give chase.

Garrick turned to her. "She's unhinged. I can't…"

"You'll only get her into more trouble," Carolyn said. "She's not going to help us. You have to face that fact right now so you can decide what you have to do next to help her."

Garrick sighed, trying to calm himself. He could barely think.

"I'll follow her to make sure she's all right." He noted Carolyn's doubtful expression. "I won't stop her. I won't bother her. I just want to make sure she gets back to the hospital all right. I'll come right back."

"Hopefully you'll have a job to come back to," she said. That was the last thing Garrick was concerned about.

Lily thanked the doctor for updating her after telling him for the third time that she didn't need any help. It was easy for the doctor to ask. Despite doing her best to pull herself together on the drive back, she looked like a train wreck.

Garrick's betrayal was too overwhelming to grasp, so Lily tried desperately to focus on what was good for her father. She couldn't find anything. This was a complete and utter disaster and her heart was in irreparable pieces. Even through she fought them, images of every scene between her and Garrick kept flashing before her eyes. The smiles, the laughs, the touches and the promises all threatened to make her break down.

She imagined him laughing with Pruitt as they listened to the tape of him making love to her and it made her so sick she had to pull over. She was too miserable to laugh at the irony of her thinking that he was too good for her because he was such an honest person. It would have been better if he'd just spat in her face and walked away, but his attempts to play the regretful lover to save the case made the situation all the more humiliating.

If she could have, she would have burrowed into a dark corner and rocked back and forth until everything disappeared. But she couldn't, because of her father, the father she was probably going to put in a grave when she told him what she had done. He needed her, so she would have to delay dealing with her own nightmare.

"Don't be so upset," Ward said in a barely audible voice as Lily sat next to his bed. "It's just some numbness down my left side. The doctor said there doesn't appear to be any brain damage, at least not any more than before."

Lily knew he was trying to make her laugh but she couldn't. "Dad, I…"

"I'll be in a wheelchair for a while," he said, "but the feeling should come back. I'll have the surgery and it will be fine. So please stop looking as if you have to leave here to plan my wake."

"Dad," she said, unable to look him in the eye. "I'm so sorry for all of this."

"It's not your fault." He sighed as if merely speaking was exhausting. "The doctor said it was just bound to happen, even if I had been eating perfectly, exercising every day and feeling completely relaxed. None of which I was doing, by the way."

She took a deep breath and tried her hardest to complete a sentence. "I've made a horrible mistake with everything about Sabrina, AFC and…"

"You haven't," Ward said. "You were right. Your mother wouldn't have wanted me to protect myself for anything, not even for her memory, if it meant someone else would get hurt or could die. No matter what the risk to Wolfe Realty and its future, we should have gone to the police for Sabrina."

"You don't understand," Lily said. "They want to destroy you and blame you for everything."

"They think I'm up to something, but they'll understand. You see, the surprise I had is that for the past two years I've been restructuring everything in the company to liquidate all our assets, pay off all of our debts."

"Why?"

"Wolfe Realty's future is not in the real estate business," he said. "I was turning the company into a foundation, a foundation focused on providing housing for the poor and the working class."

"But…" Lily wasn't sure she understood. "Why? How?"

"It's too complicated to get into," Ward said, "but Brody and I have been secretly making this happen. I was doing it in your mother's name. I was going to call it the Jessica Wolfe Foundation."

Lily let out a tearful sigh, full of emotion at the thought of how proud her mother would be. As her father's weak, shaky hand slowly reached out, she leaned in and kissed his palm. She missed her mother now more than ever.

"She would be so happy," Lily said. "A foundation named after her is so fitting."

"I know." Ward looked straight ahead, appearing to be lost in a memory. "They think my secrecy is about being up to something, and with these horrible events happening, they assume they are related. I can't blame them and I can't hate them."

"You can," Lily said. She certainly did.

"No, Lily." He turned back to her. "You see, they were right. I was wrong. I saw an opportunity and I took it. I ignored everything that I believed in and—"

She held her hand up. "Don't talk, Dad. This room could be bugged."

He smiled. "Don't be so paranoid."

"I'm not being paranoid," she said. "That's what I have to tell you. Garrick isn't what I thought he was. Dad, he…"

Lily's face fell into her hands as she began to cry uncontrollably.

"Lily, what's wrong?"

"I'm sorry." She looked up and reached out to him. "I know I've ruined everything, but I didn't know Garrick was an FBI agent. I didn't know…"

Lily jumped halfway out of her seat when the door opened. She expected Jamarr Pruitt with his guns blazing. Instead, it was Brody and she was suddenly reminded of why she'd gone to the police in the first place. She was so stunned and devastated by Garrick's betrayal and fearful for her father, the biggest danger had slipped her mind. Brody was the one who'd attacked her and most likely murdered Sabrina.

"Where have you been?" Brody asked. "The last thing he needs right now is to worry about your whereabouts."

"I could think of worse things," Lily said with a threatening stare. "I want to be alone with my father."

"You didn't answer my question," Brody said.

"Wait a second," Ward interjected. "What did you just say, Lily?"

"Not now, Dad." Lily turned to him, shaking her head vigorously.

He was ignoring her. "Garrick is an FBI agent?"

"What?" Brody rushed to the bed.

"Dad, I need to speak to you alone."

"How do you know this?" Brody asked, not bothering to hide the panic on his face. "Did he tell you?"

Lily glared at Brody. "I'm not telling you anything, Brody."

"Jesus!" Brody's hand flew into the air. "This is not the time for your childish suspicions."

"Tell me, Lily," Ward said.

"I'll tell you," Lily answered. "Only you."

"Do you know what this can do to us?" Brody asked. "I am the only one who can protect Wolfe Realty."

"Or the only one who can destroy it," Lily said.

Brody leaned back, a look of curiosity appearing briefly on his face. "Ward?"

"Call our lawyers, Brody," Ward demanded. "Do it now. We'll figure out what we have to do."

"I want to know everything," Brody said.

"You will," Ward said. "But first, get the lawyers."

Reluctantly, Brody left the room and Lily felt herself relax a little bit.

"You can't trust him, Dad."

"I've heard enough of that."

"No, you haven't." She sat back down in her chair. "You haven't heard the half of it."

It was then that Lily told her father everything. She paused as it seemed the information was more than he could take, especially after she relayed Brody's telephone conversation she had eavesdropped on and Jamarr Pruitt's threats. After she was finished, she sat silently as her father took his time taking it all in. All the while, she kept an eye on the monitors tracing his blood pressure and heartbeat.

After a while, he turned to her and smiled flatly. "It's not as bad as you think, little flower."

"It's horrible, Dad."

"You're thinking with a broken heart," he said. "When we've been betrayed by the one we love, the apocalypse seems upon us."

"I'm not thinking about Garrick," she said, even though she knew it was a lie. No matter what else was going on, Lily couldn't stop thinking of his lies, his deceits or his kisses. "Jamarr has bloodlust for you, Dad. He'll try to find a way to make what Brody did your fault."

Ward was shaking his head. "I'm not willing to accept Brody's betrayal."

"After everything I've told you?" Lily knew it was painful, but she had to let him see who Brody really was.

"I know what I know," Ward said. "I know that Wolfe Realty is in trouble, Sabrina is missing, my daughter was attacked and that Garrick, Michael or whatever his name is will pay for what he's done to you. But it's possible you misunderstood what you heard Brody saying. He wouldn't betray me to this degree."

"You love him like a son," Lily said. "But you have to think of yourself. Pruitt is going to come after you with everything he has."

"Which isn't very much," Ward added.

"It's enough to cause you pain, which you can't use right now."

"I don't think so," Ward said. "Think about it, Lily. What happened the last time he came after me?"

Lily wondered if her father's stroke had affected his memory. "You almost lost everything and went to jail. If it wasn't for the missing evidence, which…"

"I did not steal that evidence," Ward said. "I mean that. With all that I did do, that is one thing I didn't."

Lily felt confident that Brody was behind the missing evidence, but that didn't matter now. "So, whatever happened to the evidence, it was the only thing that kept you from going to trial."

"No, it wasn't," Ward said. "It was a public relations game from the beginning. I've just had a stroke. I'm half-paralyzed and due for surgery. He won't come after me now."

"I don't think he gives a damn," Lily said. "As a matter of fact, I think he just wants to hurt you whether he has a case or not."

"What I…" He smiled at her. "What *we* have to do is make it too painful for him to be able to do so."

"What about Brody?"

Ward sighed again, looking terribly uncertain. "I'll deal with him."

"Dad, please."

"Don't worry." He nodded as if he werefinally resigned to whatever it was he'd decided to do. "I'll make sure he thinks I believe everything he's told me."

Somehow, Lily didn't think that would be enough.

As they stepped outside, in front of his building, Garrick was disappointed that the cab wasn't there. He needed to move on from this moment so he could get back to Lily. He knew it was wrong to treat Melinda this harshly, but he seemed only capable of anger for everyone right now.

He wanted to blame her for showing up in Atlanta and ruining things, but he knew it was misplaced. Not that he was forgiving her for all she had done, which frankly made him wonder how sane she was, but no one was to blame for the position he'd allowed himself to get into.

"You don't have to stay and wait with me," Melinda said. "I know you can't get rid of me fast enough."

"What do you expect?" he asked. "You break into my brother's home and—"

"That could have all been avoided if you had just said goodbye."

"I said goodbye, Melinda. In two million ways."

Melinda's hands went to her hips as she took an accusatory stance. "You blew me off, Michael. You tossed me aside like I was trash. Do you know how that feels?"

Garrick looked away, wishing he could yell to the world to get off his back.

"You don't even want to look at me," she said. "Not because of what I've done, which I'll admit is a little crazy, but because of what you've done."

"What did you want, Melinda? A little sitdown over dinner where I'd go through a list of why it's me not you?"

"How about a simple I'm sorry."

Garrick took in the emotion on her face, her almond-shaped eyes filling up. "Don't cry, Melinda."

"I'm beyond crying," she said. "I've humiliated myself, turning into a stalker over a man who never gave a damn about me."

"That isn't true, Melinda."

"Then why not a simple I'm sorry?" she asked. "You were

so eager to get rid of me. Why couldn't you at least show some regret that we didn't work?"

Garrick lowered his head. "I'm sorry, Melinda. You're right. I'm sorry."

She sighed, shaking her head. "You love her, don't you?"

Garrick looked up, not certain of what to say. He thought it would be best to say no, but he didn't think he would be able to pull that off.

"Yes, I do."

"But you've lost her."

The cab pulled up. "Your ride is here."

"I could be happy," she said. "But I'm not. Because I really am sorry we didn't work."

It was hard for Garrick to feel much of anything now but regret. Still, he had enough room in his heart to realize this failed relationship was also his fault.

"I'm sorry," he repeated, holding his arms out to her. He hugged her tightly. "And thank you for not being happy I've lost Lily."

Lily had been too busy trying to get money out of her purse to see Garrick and Melinda standing right in front of her, but the second she paid the cabbie and hopped out of the cab, they all came face-to-face. She almost felt herself falling back at the sight of him releasing from an embrace with the woman who had interrupted them at the hospital. She was too spent to do anything but laugh even though she wanted to scream to high hell.

Garrick was hit more by his relief at seeing Lily than by the horror of her seeing him embracing Melinda. She looked a complete mess yet was still beautiful to him. He felt like his chest was flattened by a brick wall as she laughed. She attempted to walk by him, but he grabbed her by the arm.

Lily swung around and slapped Garrick across the face. He

backed off, letting her go, and her pain was lightened for only a moment by any pain she might have briefly caused him. "If you touch me again, I'll kill you."

"Lily, I wish you would listen to me for one second."

"I need you to listen to me," she said. "Can you do that?"

Garrick nodded, grateful she was even talking to him. "I want to do anything…"

"Shut up," she demanded. "I want you to first understand that I wish you were dead for what you've done to me and my father."

"So do I," he said barely above a whisper.

Lily was halted by his words and the deeply honest look of pain on his face. She had to remind herself this was all about him trying to save the case, get her to cooperate. She would be damned is she let him make her feel any pity for him. "The truth is, I was looking for you. I want to make a deal."

"Anything." He reached out to her, but she backed away.

"You help me protect my father," she said.

Garrick hesitated. "He needs to come in."

"He can't and you know that. Garrick…Michael or whoever you are, I need you to hold Pruitt off until he's better. His medical condition is dire. He's going in for surgery. He's paralyzed on one side."

"Lily, I'm so sorry." Garrick had to take another step back just to fight the urge to hold her. He wanted so badly for things to rewind, feeling as if he would give his life to see that tender smile he had so quickly become accustomed to.

"I don't need you to pity me or my father," she said. "I need you to get your ass to the FBI and push this weak case back."

"I'll do what I can."

"No," she said, and in a threatening tone, added, "you'll do better than that. You make it happen or else I come after you."

"I'm going to help you, Lily."

"I know you will," she answered. "Because I don't think

you want to be dragged through the lawsuit I'm going to slap on you."

"Lawsuit?"

Lily nodded, feeling empty inside despite hoping this would feel good. "I haven't had time to check, but I'm calling a lawyer first thing in the morning. What you did to me has to be illegal. Deceiving and lying is part of the job, but you had no right to seduce me."

"I know," Garrick said. "I wanted to fight it, but I fell in love with you."

"Stop." Lily wasn't prepared for the emotion that hit her in response to his confession. He was a liar and a user. She couldn't possibly believe a word he said. "The fact that you know it was wrong makes it even worse. If I can't get you fired for this, I can at least use it to hurt your case against my father. Personally, if I'm able to destroy you even half as much you've destroyed me, I'll be in heaven."

"Lily!" he called after her as she turned and walked away.

She didn't turn around because she didn't want him to see the tears streaming down her face. Her threat was an empty one. She didn't have the stomach to relive Garrick's seduction, illegal or not. She could only hope he didn't know that.

"Damn."

Garrick turned to see Melinda standing behind him with a stunned look on her face. He had forgotten she was there.

"I thought you did me wrong," she said. "I feel like I got off easy."

Chapter 11

Michael had done his best, but from the cold look on Lily's face as he entered the hospital room that looked more like a hotel room, it wasn't going to make any difference.

It was almost a month since that horrible day and Michael hadn't seen Lily since, at least not face-to-face. Taking up the role of a stalker, he parked outside Wolfe Realty to catch a glimpse of her driving into the garage. It was all he had considering she'd moved out of the condo and into her father's house. She gave orders to Jamarr not to allow Michael near her home and Jamarr, eager to stick it to Michael any way he could, happily obliged.

Michael wouldn't have gone there anyway. He didn't want her to see him. He could handle the pain he felt at the sight of her, but the look in her eyes right now was why he didn't want to push it. She hated him and a bullet couldn't have hurt more.

Everyone looked up at Michael as he joined them at the

table set against the wall in the well-adorned hospital room where wealthier patients had the luxury of recovering from surgery.

"What is he doing here?" Lily asked with an angry scowl.

The fact that her heart leaped the second she'd seen him walk in made her even angrier. What would it take to get this man out of her heart? All of these weeks, she'd suffered in silence while trying to be strong for her father. His surgery went perfectly, according to the doctors, and that was the only thing she found comfort in.

Constantly her thoughts went to Michael's betrayal and her humiliation. She replayed every second of their time together and saw how he'd played her, teased her and pulled her along. She woke up in the middle of the night, drenched in sweat from nightmares of Michael and Jamarr laughing as they listened to the tape of *Garrick* making love to her in her condo.

She hated him with everything she could muster and she refused to believe that he hadn't meant it. How could someone do what he'd done even feel true remorse? He was too deliberate, too smooth. He convinced her he was falling for her. Lily refused to give him any credit for keeping Jamarr at bay so her father could have time to recover. She would hate him forever for not being able to forget him, for turning her around in so many circles that she couldn't trust herself.

Ward, sitting in his wheelchair next to Lily, reached out and grabbed her hand. "My daughter requested he not be here."

"This is my case," Michael said. He looked at Jamarr, who simply rolled his eyes. Since Michael had used his influence in Chicago to keep Jamarr from acting fast on the case while Ward's condition was still severe, Jamarr tried to keep the progress of the case from him. It was Chicago that informed him of this meeting and he rushed back to Atlanta to be a part of it. Nothing could keep him away. He had to see Lily and this was his only escape.

"Ignore him," Jamarr said.

Lily slapped her hand to the table, ignoring Michael's gaze set on her. "I told you…"

"I've made enough concessions for you," Jamarr snapped. "Michael is just an observer. He isn't going to say anything."

Michael ignored him, concentrating on Lily. He waited for her to look at him, but she refused and his anger grew. He craved her attention.

"No more games," Jamarr said. "We need some answers."

"No one has been playing games with you," Ward said. "I've agreed to talk to you. I've told you everything I know."

Jamarr looked down at the open folder in front of him. "Brody Saunders has been missing for almost a month now and I think you know where he is."

Lily turned to her father as he lowered her hand. To add insult to injury, Brody left to "call the lawyers" and never came back. At the worst time possible, Ward had to face the truth about Brody and he hadn't taken it well.

"My father doesn't know where Brody is," Lily argued. "You know that, Jamarr."

Jamarr shrugged, shaking his head. "You're hiding something from us, Ward."

"I had nothing to do with—"

Lily stopped him. "You have nothing on my father and you know it. You're fishing."

"You don't know what I know." Jamarr leaned back with a satisfied look on his face.

Michael grabbed the folder. "Let's see if we can do anything about that."

Everyone, especially Jamarr, seemed surprised by Michael's actions.

"He's been stealing from you, Mr. Wolfe." Michael scanned the sheets, deciding in an instant what he could and couldn't share. "All of those property sales and investments he's been liquidating have gone through AFC, a company that doesn't exist."

"Dammit!" Jamarr grabbed the folder back. "I'll have you fired for this."

"No, you won't. I haven't told him anything he doesn't have a right to know."

Lily wasn't sure why Michael was doing this, but when he glanced at her, she felt a rush of energy.

"We believe," Michael said, reluctantly turning from Lily to Ward, "this company created two separate documents. One with a sale price that was higher than the final invoice on record, profiting from the difference. You know what that is?"

Ward nodded. "Brody told me that we needed to sell below market if we wanted to get rid of the investments. So, if he overpriced the sale, the difference could be millions."

"We only have the records he showed you." Michael leaned forward. "The ones doctored by AFC, the company hired to manage the brokering. We need to know where he would keep the real records."

"I don't know."

"Stop it!" Jamarr stood up, offering Michael a seething glare. "This one is love struck. He wants to believe in your innocence to make points with his girlfriend."

Lily turned to Michael, who lowered his head before looking up at her. Their eyes caught but she turned away. She couldn't stand it. What was it inside her that wanted so badly to believe that after all she knew?

Jamarr placed his hands flat on the table, leaning toward Ward. "You haven't given me any reason to believe you weren't in on this. Playing victim works well as the pale stroke victim, but…"

"That's too far," Michael said. "He's not faking a stroke."

"Shut up!" Jamarr slapped the table. "Wolfe, I'll bury you with this. I know you're—"

"All the evidence points to Brody and Ann Raines, both of whom remain at large." Michael pointed to the folder. "I know you want to find him as much as we do, Mr. Wolfe. You have to think…"

"Get out!" Jamarr reached into his jacket pocket and pulled out his cell phone. "I'm calling headquarters, you son of a bitch!"

Michael stood up, raising his arms in surrender. "I just think you should know the deal."

"Thank you."

Lily was shocked to see her father offer Michael a respectful nod. Did he actually believe Michael was helping them?

"Out!" Jamarr pointed to the door, seeming to get even more agitated by Michael's victorious smile.

Michael stood chest to chest with Jamarr, ready for anything.

"Please," Lily said, made completely uneasy by her father's response to Michael. "Just leave."

Michael turned to her, hurt evident in his expression. She hated him so much she didn't even care that he was following through on his promise to help her. He was a fool to keep believing she cared, no matter how many times she professed she didn't. "Lily, I…"

"Just leave," she said.

Michael sighed, turning back to Jamarr. "You need to get someone for this and it looks like Saunders is all you'll have a chance at. Be smarter."

When Michael glanced back at Lily, she was watching him with wide eyes that looked about to cry. He was certain this was all painful for her, but he was going to fulfill his promise. It was the least he could do.

As he turned and headed out, Lily felt her heart tug as if it was begging her to follow him. *Hear him out,* it begged. *Believe them.*

"No," she said, turning away. "No, no."

"What?" With his hand, Ward lifted her chin to face him. "No what?"

"Don't believe them." She was here, looking at her father, but she felt as if part of her had left the room with Michael. Would he always have that power over her? "This could be a game they're playing together to fool us. You can't trust either of them."

"I don't think so," he whispered. "But what do I know about trust?"

"You know you can trust me," she said.

Ward winked and smiled. "You weren't paying attention, baby. He's trying to help…"

"Now, back to business!" Jamarr returned his phone to his pocket. "Tell me where Brody Saunders is!"

Unable to get what he wanted, Jamarr finally left at the nurse's insistence. Lily didn't have the stomach to argue with her father over Michael's honesty. She was the one who'd talked him out of going after Michael for seducing her because of the deal she made. Now, here he was, believing that Michael might be on their side. It was all too much.

Needing some air, Lily made her way to the courtyard, the same courtyard where she'd overheard Brody speaking on the phone to who she was certain was Ann Raines.

Finding a stone bench near the fountain that wasn't running, Lily sat down and took a deep breath. There was a part of her that wished she could believe Michael, because he was telling her what she wanted to hear. But wasn't that what got her in trouble in the first place? Yes, it was. There was no room for trust when it came to Michael…

As she realized she didn't even know his last name, all Lily could do was laugh. So she laughed, loud enough to create an echo in the almost empty courtyard.

"Can I get in on the joke?"

Lily screamed and jumped a foot from her seat as Michael appeared in front of her. Her hand went to her chest as she stumbled over the bench.

"Lily!" Michael reached out and grabbed her by the arm just before she fell backward. With his other hand, he took hold of her waist and pulled her to him.

"Stop!" Lily pushed against him, frantic to be free. Her body felt a rush of heat at his touch and it made her crazy with anger.

"You'll fall if I let you go." Michael grabbed her tighter. "Calm down."

"Let me go!"

When she broke loose from him, Lily felt herself falling back and this time it was she who reached out and grabbed him, pulling at his shirt.

"Calm down," he repeated.

"Don't tell me what to do, Garrick." Finally stabilized, she let go of him and stepped away. She felt ashamed to look at him, considering how her body had betrayed her at his touch.

"My name is Michael." He wished he could touch her again. Unable to leave, he'd been waiting for her to leave the room for two hours.

"I know what your name is, asshole."

"You called me Garrick." Michael wasn't sure why her insult amused him. He loved her feistiness. He only wished it was in jest and not genuine.

"Why don't I just call you what you are?" Lily asked. "Which would you prefer? Bastard, asshole or di—"

"Whoaa!" He held his hand up. "I'd hoped we were past name-calling."

"I'll call you whatever I want." Lily backed up, afraid of what her body would do if she stayed close to him.

"I was trying to help you in there."

Lily gasped. "What are you… Are you here for your thank-you? Well, you sure as hell wasted your time."

"I don't need a thank-you," he said. "I just thought it would help your father's condition to know that Jamarr's case is weak."

"Do you think that's going to stop him?" she asked. "You know he doesn't care about that."

"He doesn't, but the FBI has a short lease for him. They didn't even want this case. He begged for it and they appeased him because he'd just closed down a huge insurance-scam ring."

"I don't care about this,' she said. "I want you to leave."

"This is a public spot."

"Fine, I'll leave."

"Lily." As she passed by him, he grabbed her by the arm and pulled her back to him. "I'm giving you something you can use."

"How?" She jerked free. "It isn't going to stop Jamarr."

"You can make demands," he said. "If you have information on Brody, then you can…"

"Are you really searching for him or are you waiting on my father to tell you?" she asked. "'Cause he doesn't know."

"But he knows something," Michael said. "He knows Brody better than anyone."

"I think Brody just proved him wrong."

"For whatever reason he has done this, beforehand, your father was the person closest to him. He has to know something."

Lily stepped back, folding her arms over her chest. She

focused her attention on the budding garden behind Michael. "If he can figure out something, then…"

"If we find Brody, we can clear your father. As long as Brody is free, there is no one to say your father wasn't in on the racketeering."

"What does the fact that he's still here say?"

"That he had a stroke and couldn't leave."

Lily finally looked up and the earnest look on Michael's face confused her even more. "Why?"

"Why am I doing this?" he asked, wishing to God he could touch her. "Because I love you, Lily."

"No." She couldn't take it.

He took her arm as she tried to leave, swinging her back to face him. "Yes, Lily. I love you to death and I can't help it. I know you'll never forgive me, but I thought I was doing what was right. I never intended for it to get this far."

"How could you not?" she asked. "We were getting so close. You knew what could have happened!"

"I've done this before and I've never fallen in love. I've never slept with anyone on a case. I thought I could control myself like I have a hundred times, but I couldn't."

"Please, don't say any more," Lily begged.

"I couldn't control it." His finger went to her cheek, gently touching her soft skin. She turned away. "Every time I touched you, I—"

"If you want to help me, please stop this." When he let her go, she stood her ground on weak knees. "Stop your whining and pleading and really help me."

"I'll do anything." Michael couldn't hide his desperation.

"I need to get into AFC's offices."

Michael leaned back. "That's all in evidence now. You can't get in there."

"Then leave me the hell alone." She turned and walked away.

"Wait!" he called after her, desperate for her not to go.

Slowly, Lily turned back to him. "I need to see that evidence. You either get me in there or never come near me again."

Michael knew not only would he lose his job over this, but he could go to jail. It was evidence tampering.

"Michael?" Lily stood with her hand on her hip.

"Let's go," he said, not giving it another thought.

It took a long time to get into the highly guarded evidence room at the FBI office, but Michael made it happen.

It was getting dark, so Lily felt against the wall. "Where are the—"

As soon as her hand reached the light switch, she felt Michael's on top. The energy that surged through her made her still as she inhaled. Inside she was screaming to herself to move her hand but she didn't.

"Don't," Michael said. "They can see the light from under the door. I brought this."

She turned to him as he flipped on his flashlight. Her fingers were still burning from his touch as her hand came to her side. "Where is it?"

"Alphabetical by W." He led the way, oddly wondering if he preferred this cold side of her to the emotional side. "There's mounds of stuff here. What are you looking for?"

She was careful to step around him, afraid to brush against him in the tight aisle. "Something that gives me a clue to Sabrina's disappearance."

"Like what?"

"Something she must have known to make Brody or Ann Raines think she had to go." Lily grabbed a box labeled WOLFE REALTY and sat down on the floor. "With all the names I could have for Brody, killer isn't one of them."

Michael sat across from her, positioning the flashlight on

the shelf so it would light both of them. "What makes you think that?"

Lily shook her head, unsure. "The way he sounded on that phone call I overheard."

Michael read the report Lily gave the detective. Nothing about it convinced him Brody wasn't a killer. "He was at her place when you got there."

"Maybe he was trying to clean up after Ann Raines." She pulled out each plastic bag one at a time, surveyed it for significance before setting it aside. "I think Ann Raines is the one who…. Whatever was done to Sabrina, she did it. Is everything here?"

"Everything." Michael watched her as she studied the objects. This was the closest he had been to her without daggers of hate shooting from her eyes and he wanted to savor it. "Let me help. What am I looking for?"

"Look at this." She held up the bag containing the DVD set. "My father said the woman he met was around his age. What woman in her sixties wants to watch this show? It's barely for anyone over twenty-five."

Michael took the bag from her, looking it over. "We're pretty certain that woman was an actress Brody used to fool your father. If the real Ann Raines is the woman he was talking to on the phone, she was probably younger."

Lily nodded. "She was certainly a lover or someone intimate."

Lily set the box aside and reached for another one. " Something in here has to connect Ann Raines to Sab—"

She dropped the box, with a plastic bag in her hand. "This is what I'm looking for."

"Wait." Michael grabbed the bag from her before she could rip it open. "It can't look tampered with."

"Then open it," Lily ordered impatiently.

"Put on the gloves I gave you." Michael waited until she

did as she was told before handing her the appointment book. "We've looked through this. It's empty. Honestly, no one was working at that place. Plan A was to make it look like an office in case someone showed up."

"Plan B." Lily flipped through the pages. "Knock 'em over the head."

"Was that a joke?" Michael asked, smiling.

Lily flipped her head, her hair falling back as she looked up at him. His smile was contagious and she had to react before she could catch herself. It was the joy of the moment that made her realize what she was doing. Her smile quickly faded as she returned her attention to the empty pages.

"Lily." Michael gripped the edges of the box on his lap to keep from reaching out to her. "Look at me."

With a heavy sigh, Lily mustered the courage to look up and stare at him, straight in the eyes. "Don't waste your time. You can help me all you want, but as far as me ever trusting or believing in you again... Well, you're dead to me."

Michael swallowed hard, the severity of her words grabbing at his heart and squeezing to the point he could no longer breathe. "I thought I was doing what was right. That's all I've ever done. Your father had already gotten away with a serious crime before and you were a part of it, willingly or not. I believed you were involved in something again."

"That's what hurts most." Lily stopped at a page full of scribbled notes, trying desperately to keep her wits about her. "You thought I was a criminal. You kissed me, slept with me, thinking I was a criminal."

"No," he said. "When I slept with you—"

"This looks familiar," Lily said, hoping for anything to change the subject.

Cautiously, Michael slid closer to her. "It's just scribbling."

"The handwriting looks familiar."

"It's a woman's," Michael said. "Very round with the letters connecting. Other than that, it's half a grocery list, the other half illegible."

"Initials." Lily tilted her head to the left to avoid his glance. She didn't want him to see how being this close to him affected her. "E.W."

"We checked it against everything else found at the offices, your company and Brody's apartment."

"What did you find out?" Lily was racking her brains trying to think of what E.W. could stand for, but Michael's closeness was too distracting.

"Lily."

She looked up at him. "Don't piss out on me now, Michael. With the work you do, you can't claim to be sensitive."

"It's not that." Michael tried to conceal the anger in his voice. "I can't tell you what…"

"It would be wrong, right?" She exaggerated the sarcasm in her tone.

"We found the same initials on some sticky notes in Sabrina's apartment."

"Where?"

Michael shrugged, trying to remember. "On the kitchen counter. Next to hearts."

"Hearts?" Lily handed him the appointment book. What she was thinking she wasn't so sure she should.

Michael nodded. "We think it was a boyfriend, but there was no one who could tell us she was seeing anyone."

"She was." Lily stood up, recalling everything Sabrina told her about her big secret. "She didn't want to talk about him. I thought maybe he was married or something, but maybe he was telling her to be quiet about him so no one would know who to look into after she went missing."

"Was he using her?" Michael began putting the boxes back

together. After not getting a response, he looked up at Lily, who seemed miles away in thought. "What is it?"

The more Lily couldn't believe what she was thinking, the more she did believe it. It seemed crazy, but she had to find out.

"Lily." Michael stood up. "What's going on?"

Lily looked at him, wondering why she was even considering trusting him. Maybe it was instinctual. He had that look about him—'You can trust me'—but she had learned that wasn't true the hard way. She could trust no one but herself now.

"Nothing," she lied. "I'm just trying to think."

As she reached for another box, Michael held his hand up to stop her just before turning off the flashlight.

"Quiet," he whispered, heading for the door.

Lily tiptoed after him, standing behind him as he leaned against the wall listening. Her stomach tightened as she heard distant voices. If someone caught them, she would get arrested, and the first thought that came to her mind was asking Michael to help her. Why? Why was she still looking to this man for anything?

"I have to get out of here," she said, feeling the walls beginning to close in on her.

"Just wait."

"No," she insisted. "I have to get out of here now, Michael."

Not hearing the voices anymore, Michael decided to chance it. He opened the door slightly and took a peek outside. When he couldn't see anyone, he stepped out farther.

"Hey." Michael was pushed aside by Lily, who stormed out of the room. Fortunately the hallway was clear.

"Lily, wait." He closed the door and locked it. When he turned to her, she was halfway down the hall.

He wanted to go after her, feeling as if he'd earned the right to spend just a few more minutes with her. After all, he'd just risked his job, the only thing he had left, for her. He knew it was better they part ways; her cruel words were angering him and that wasn't going to do any good. He had hoped her hatred for him would have calmed, but he was a fool to think so.

Michael knew that he had to let go of any idea that she wouldn't hate him forever, any idea that they could even be civil with each other. There was no chance to explain it all from beginning to end, to clear up the misunderstandings and set the record straight. Somehow, Michael knew that he would have to get over Lily Wolfe. He just had no idea how he was going to do that.

The thirty-something, redheaded nurse standing at the door had a vacant stare on her face as Michael stood in front of her. Despite his name or picture not appearing in any of the news coverage, she seemed to recognize him.

"Is she here or not?" Michael asked.

She tilted her head to one side. "Do you have a warrant?"

"I'm not here to search anything. I have to talk to Lily."

It had been two days since Lily walked away from the evidence room and Garrick was going crazy. The more he resolved to get over her, the more he needed to see her. He convinced himself if he could force her to sit still while he explained everything from A to Z, he would feel better. It wouldn't resolve anything; it wouldn't make her love him again, but it would be out there. Then maybe he could stop thinking about her every day and dreaming about her every night.

"She's not here."

Michael tried to look behind her, but she tightened the door to her hips, concealing the view. "Why is her car in the driveway?"

The nurse shrugged. "You have a nice day."

"I'll have a nice day when you tell Lily I'm here."

"She isn't here."

Michael recognized Ward's voice by now, but couldn't see him until the nurse reluctantly opened the door wider. He was sitting in his wheelchair in the foyer and the look on his face made Michael hesitate before entering.

"You have a lot of nerve coming here," Ward said. "To my house and to see my daughter."

"I have a lot of explaining to do to you and Lily, sir." Michael humbly lowered his head. "I don't expect either of you to understand or forgive me, but I believed what I was doing was right."

"How can you figure seducing my daughter was right?"

"Not that part." Michael was shaking his head, wishing he could take back his hastily thought words. "I know that was wrong. I made a horrible choice and broke the heart of the woman I love. I'm willing to do anything to make up for that."

From his expression, Michael knew that he'd struck a chord with Ward. He was a man who knew about disappointing the woman he loved.

"Well, she's gone," Ward said. "Thanks to you."

"What do you mean?"

"She up and went off," Ward said. "Without my permission, mind you. She took her passport and everything. She wouldn't say where she was going. She told me not to worry, as if that was possible. She said it was good news. She said it was because of you."

"Because I upset her?"

"Because you gave her some information." He frowned, confused. "You gave her something, didn't you?"

"I guess I did." Michael should have known Lily would be up to something.

As he stepped onto the front steps of the house, Michael was on his cell phone to his office in Chicago demanding a track on Lily's credit cards, cell phone and passport. Lily's stubborn streak was one of the things that attracted her to him, but he was afraid it was about to get her killed.

Chapter 12

Stepping onto the balcony, Lily took in a breath of fresh air. Her hotel room was overlooking the Caribbean coastline from Belize City and the view was simply spectacular. She hadn't been able to enjoy the island because of her purpose for being here, but as darkness fell, the scene compelled her to take a moment and relax.

It only took seconds for the emotion to grab her. The myriad stars in the sky, the reflection of the ocean and the lights coming from the smaller Cay Islands in the distance were getting to her. It didn't help that all she could see from her balcony were couples taking advantage of the romantic surroundings.

She knew that time would heal her wounds. Thinking of the death of her mother, Lily remembered believing she would never get past the pain and anger she felt. This was a different pain, however, and Lily wished she could know how long it would take. She was past feeling sorry for herself. Her father's condition made that necessary, but she knew it wasn't over; it was just waiting for her to take care of other business.

All she wanted was to stop wanting him, to stop missing him. Was that too much to ask?

Hearing a squeaking noise behind her, Lily turned and looked nervously into her room. When Michael appeared, she didn't know how to react. He stood at the edge of her bed, looking at her, dressed in cool, white linen pants and a yellow polo shirt. He looked so casual, so handsome, just perfect for the occasion.

Lily was certain she was imagining him, standing as she would want him to stand, looking as she would want him to look and next to her bed waiting to make love to her in the mind-shocking way only he could. She was exhausted from her second day of searching. She hadn't eaten much and thought maybe the heat was getting to her.

"Hello, Lily."

Michael intended to come storming into the room, which his FBI badge got the manager to open, and reading Lily the riot act. Only, seeing her safe and alive calmed him down and seeing her in a slim-fitting, blood-red summer dress with a slit up the left leg made him want her.

As he began walking toward her, a look of passion in his eyes, Lily wanted to believe this was her imagination, her fantasy, but it couldn't be this real. "Michael?"

He was standing only a foot from her and Lily slowly reached out, expecting her hand to go right through him. When she touched his chest, his hand shot up and took hold of hers. Lowering his head, his mouth came down to kiss it.

Lily tore her hand away and pushed him back. "What are you doing here?"

"I followed you." He regretted that the moment, as unreal as it seemed, had ended. "You're crazy if you think you can do this alone."

"I have no choice," she said. "How did you find me?"

"I tried to help you, Lily. I took you into the evidence room and risked my job for you."

"So?" She stepped farther away, feeling the tingling on her hand where he'd kissed it. "Do you expect gratitude?"

"I expected some trust."

She laughed out loud. "How ironic."

"We know why you're here."

"Do you?" She peeked into her room. "You come alone or did you bring all your girlfriends with you?"

"We're all here," he said. "I came in here alone. You have to leave and I'm going to escort you to the airport."

"Like hell you are."

"You tracked Eric Wilson here," Michael said. "I don't know how you—"

"Is that his name?" she asked.

Michael frowned, confused. "We think so. When I found out you'd come here, we had records on all E.W.'s flying from Atlanta to Belize within the last two months. We found seven people, six of whom we could track and eliminate. One, we can't find anywhere and we're not sure he actually exists."

"It must be Sabrina's boyfriend," she said. "He's here."

"With Brody?" Michael asked. "How did you know Belize?"

Lily decided not to tell him that she remembered Sabrina mentioning her boyfriend would take her here soon. She wasn't going to tell him anything. "I'm here on vacation. I need some time away."

He cursed out loud. "Lily, this is not a game."

"Really?" She threw her hands in the air. "Wow, Michael. Thanks for telling me that, because I thought it was. I've been having so much fun since I came back to Atlanta, how could I have thought anything else?"

"Okay," Michael conceded. "I don't doubt you get this is serious. I don't mean to be harsh, but…"

"Compared to everything else you've done, that's pretty light." She turned her back to him, leaning over the balcony. "I'm not leaving."

"I can make you leave."

"You can't," she said. "Besides, you need me. I saw her."

"Ann Raines?"

She nodded, even though she was lying. She hated herself for feeling guilty about it. After all, Michael had lied to her in the worst ways possible.

"How do you know what she looks like?" he asked.

"I asked Colombo." She turned back to him with a smirk, but he wasn't going to give up. "I've spent the last two days asking around, and some of the locals gave me the same description. I finally saw her, but I couldn't reach her before she got on one of those ferryboats."

"Where?"

Lily laughed. "You're not listening to me. I'm not telling you anything unless I can stay. I don't trust any of you. For all I know, if I walk away now, you'll come back with more seeming evidence against my father."

"I've been the only one helping your father." Michael realized that Lily wasn't budging, and he had to admit, the idea of having another reason to be around her appealed to him. "I'll see what I can do."

"I'll have a bourbon," Lily told the bartender. "On the rocks."

The bartender, talk and dark, leaned back with a skeptical smile. "You don't look like a bourbon kind of lady."

"I've had a bourbon kind of day," Lily said. "As a matter of fact, I've had a bourbon kind of month, so let's go."

"Coming right up."

After Michael left her room, Lily was in desperate need of escape and the bar was the first place she thought of. It was crowded and noisy and she hoped she could lose herself there and get drunk out of her mind.

"Bourbon on the rocks." The bartender slid the glass her way.

Lily didn't hesitate, taking a quick sip. She grabbed her chest and leaned over, letting out a tortured gasp.

"You should stick with vodka."

Gripping the glass, Lily turned to see the woman she now knew as Carolyn helping herself to the seat next to her. She didn't look much like an FBI agent in her banana-yellow sundress with her blond hair in a French braid down her back.

"You should probably sit somewhere that's safer for you," Lily offered.

"It's against the law to threaten an FBI agent." She nodded to the bartender. "Rum and Coke."

"What do you want?"

"Same thing as you apparently." She reached for the bowl of nuts.

"Well I'm here to get drunk." Lily took another sip of bourbon and this time it went down a little easier. "So, you don't want to get in my way."

Carolyn thanked the bartender for her drink. "You got a deal."

One hour and several drinks later, both women were facing each other, talking as if they'd known one another for years.

"You've certainly got him wrapped around your finger," Carolyn said.

"I beg your pardon?"

"Michael," she answered. "He's pulling all kinds of strings for you."

"Am I supposed to be grateful?"

Carolyn shrugged. "He just loves you is all I'm—"

"Don't bother." Lily waved her hand aimlessly in the air.

"All this stuff he's doing is to assuage his guilt 'cause I won't let him forget what an ass he is."

"No," Carolyn protested. "He really loves you. I mean, he's breaking the law right and left and that is not him."

Lily wondered if Carolyn knew about the evidence-room search. Michael took the time to turn off the cameras that recorded everyone going in and out, but he did have to use his code to get into the room.

Carolyn pointed a finger over Lily's shoulder. "Pruitt is so scared of what he'll do, he had the tape of you two at your place hidden."

Lily cringed at the mention of the tape. "You guys are sick to—"

"We didn't listen to you." Carolyn rolled her eyes. "We turned it off right before and didn't turn it on until after."

"You guys have a weird way of thinking what makes right or wrong."

"You should have seen him, Lily. He was so angry when he realized we'd overheard. He genuinely forgot the bug was there. I thought he was going to strangle Pruitt."

Lily paused at the thought, wondering if Carolyn was lying for Michael's sake. "Yeah, so…he's made it clear he regrets it. That isn't enough. What's done is done."

"That's a shame." Carolyn was shaking her head. "Because he's in so much pain over this."

Lily intended to jump out of her seat, but it turned into more of a stumble. She held on to the bar to stay vertical. "That's it! I've heard enough of poor little Michael or Garrick or whoever he is."

"He was falling in love with you from the beginning," she said. "Even when he thought you were guilty. He had a job to do."

"Boo-hoo." Lily was as loud as she could be. "Is there

anything else you want to tell me about the poor baby? I wouldn't want to lose sight of who the real victim is here."

"Forget I said anything." Carolyn swung around in her stool and gestured for the bartender.

"If I could forget," Lily said, "I would. And I'm going to. I'm just gonna have a word with the man you seem to think is the second coming."

Michael was trying to wake up as he made his way to the door. In between the banging, he thought he'd heard Lily's voice but wasn't sure it was because he was just dreaming about her. When he opened the door, Lily didn't waste any time. She pushed him aside and staggered into the room.

"Damn," she said, turning around to him. "I was hoping to interrupt you with someone so I could tell her to check the room for bugs before she drops her drawers."

It had taken a second, but as Michael shut the door behind him and rubbed his eyes, Lily realized he wasn't dressed in anything but a pair of boxers. His taut, muscled body evoked memories of lovemaking and Lily began to feel the heat of the island circle around her.

"It's late, Lily."

"So she left already? I guess I'm too late. Well, since I'm here, we could listen to the tape together." She acknowledged the impatient expression on his tired face. "No tape? Did you film it? That's sexy. Let's watch."

"Stop it, Lily." Michael was awake enough now to get angry. "There is no one here and there's no tape of you and I making love."

"I know," Lily answered.

This woke him up completely. "You..."

"Carolyn told me all about it." Lily helped herself to the

sofa across from his bed. "Oh, poor Michael. He's so in love. Let's all share a moment of silence for his broken heart."

"I've never asked you to feel sorry for me."

"Apparently you were too busy asking everyone else." She patted the sofa with her right hand. "Come sit, Michael. Tell Mama how awful the girl was to you."

"I've never blamed you for anything," he said lazily.

"Well, that's good." She shot up from the sofa and rushed to within inches of him. "'Cause I blame you for everything."

"That's fine," was all Michael said in response.

Lily's eyes widened, as she was without words for a second, somewhat confused by his placid reaction. She wanted to be angry but all she could do was sigh and back up.

"I hate you."

"I know," he said, not certain where his reaction was coming from. Maybe he was too tired to fight, too hopeless to plead. "But I love you."

"Do you think that matters?" she asked, biting her lower lip to stop the tears.

"Obviously not," he answered. "So why are we doing this?"

"We aren't doing anything." Lily pointed in his face but he didn't flinch. "I'm telling you how much I regret ever meeting you."

"Sorry I can't say the same." He walked away, feeling his anger rise at her confrontational gestures.

"You will when I'm done with you," Lily warned. "You're going to wish you never laid eyes on me."

"Never." He kneeled down, opened the mini-bar and pulled out a can of cola before standing and looking into her eyes. "As much of a disaster as this has become, I won't regret it because I could never regret feeling the way you made me feel."

Lily wanted to look away but she couldn't. She hated him for not giving up because she knew it was her only hope of ever getting over him. What was worse…he knew it. He knew it and as he walked toward her taking a sip of cola, she was entranced by the trickle of sweat that rolled off his forehead and fell onto the middle of his chest.

"You son of a bitch." Her voice was deep and threatening. "For you to think you had a chance to get…"

"There's always a chance," he said, offering her the can. "If your heart is open to love and forgiveness."

"Is that what you want?" Lily decided to play his game, taking the can from him. "A second chance?"

Michael leaped on what little hope he had left. "Is that possible?"

Lily took her time sipping the drink. She felt the sweat from the can drip onto her chest. Lowering it, she looked at him with a lazy, seductive grin and saw that he was buying it. Slowly, she leaned into him.

"Would that make you happy?" she asked.

Michael's lips parted, feeling as if he could taste her from her closeness. "You know it would."

She held the can out and let go and Michael reached it just quick enough to catch before too much spilled out. As she turned her back to him, he set the can aside and drew closer to her. Standing behind her, he could feel the heat from her body float through his. Slowly, he raised his hands.

Lily's eyes closed by instinct as his hands came to her bare arms. Everything inside of her wanted to scream out *take me* as his fingers pressed against her flesh. She moved her hips just enough to reach him and heard him sigh. The feeling was torturous to her, but she was going to hold it together long enough to teach him to never try to fool her again.

"You want me," she whispered.

Michael leaned forward, getting high from the familiar

scent of her hair. What was primal inside of him knew he had to have this woman.

"It would be so easy," Lily said, feeling her belly begin to swirl and her temperature heat up. His magnetic energy was taking her over again. "So easy to give in to it."

"Yes." He lowered his head, his lips brushing against her neck as she raised it for him. His fingers pressed harder as his fire ignited.

"I will give in to it," she said, letting her voice trail into a hymn. "Only not with you."

Michael lifted his head, his mind on alert. He released his grip. "Lily?"

"But I'll be thinking of you." She turned around with a hateful smile. "You know, like the song says. Every time I scratch my nails down another man's back, I hope you feel it."

Michael felt as if alcohol had been dripped on an open sore. She was going for the jugular.

Lily's smile faded as she leaned back. "You will never, ever have me again."

Michael's anger flared as he grabbed her to keep her from walking away.

"Let me go." Lily tried to struggle free but his grip was too strong.

Looking into his eyes, she could see'd she hit him right where it counted and she was surprisingly unsatisfied by it. In her haste for revenge, she hadn't thought of the truth in its success. If she could really hurt him then it meant he really cared.

"I've had enough of this," Michael growled. "It ends now."

"You're right a-about th-that." Lily felt her knees weaken as the fire in his eyes sent a bolt from her head to her toes. "This all ends now. No more apologies. No more..."

"No more guilt," he said. "And no more games."

He pulled her to him with a force Lily had never felt before.

When his lips came down on hers, they were ravishing every bit of her and Lily exploded into desire. She wanted this so badly, she almost felt faint at the pleasure it gave her.

Her arms came up to fight him off and when she pushed, he stepped back just a little. She could hear her heavy breathing and as she looked into his eyes, all Lily could think of was how her lips felt starved without his on them.

When she brought her hands back to him, Michael didn't resist as she pushed him against the wall. He reached out to her as she pressed up against him and brought her lips to his. He was crazy at the thought of making love to her again.

There were no tender kisses or caresses this time as they both gave in to their most carnal need, a need that each realized no one would be able to meet but each other. They dropped naked to the floor, rolling around in a heated physical match of erotic sex and possession. Neither had ever been so wild, so loud and so expressive. Neither had ever known what it was like not to care if the world exploded until now.

As Michael found his way to the foyer of the hotel lobby, he sidled up to Carolyn, who looked tired and hungover. After last night, he was in need of a little comfort, but from the look on her face, Carolyn wasn't interested.

"Don't let my presence here fool you," she said. "I'm still in bed, trying to sleep off too many tequilas."

"You were doing a lot of talking last night." Michael waited for her to turn to him with a skeptical frown. "About me."

Carolyn smiled and nodded. "You heard about that. Did she throw a brick through your hotel window?"

"I'm on the twelfth floor," he answered.

Damage had been done to his hotel room but not from any bricks. The lovemaking between him and Lily last night had been the wildest experience of his life. The anger, the passion and the primal need had consumed them both. As their bodies engaged in a battle of desire and power, furniture was broken and flesh had been bruised.

"What happened to you?" Carolyn asked, reaching out to the scratches on his left bicep.

Michael mumbled under his breath and took the sunglasses from on top of his head to his red eyes.

"Are you going to answer me?" she asked.

"It's nothing." Michael looked straight ahead. "Where is our car?"

"It's coming." Carolyn didn't appear to be giving up. "Did she hurt you?"

Michael laughed. "Is that rhetorical?"

"I knew she was mad, but…" Carolyn's eyes widened as a curious grin framed her lips. "Oh my goodness."

"Don't start." Michael couldn't help but smile just at the thought of the explosive moments he and Lily shared last night. He wanted her again so badly.

"Do you think this was wise?" she asked.

"I don't care." And he didn't. Michael didn't give a damn how stupid it was to sleep with Lily. All he knew was that he was happy again, even though he was miserable.

"Love and wisdom," Carolyn said. "Not good bedfellows."

As Lily cleared her throat to signify her presence, they both turned to her. She knew they were talking about her, probably discussing last night.

"We ready to go asearchin'?" She had a smile on her face that warned them not to trust her.

"I'll check on the car," Carolyn said before walking away.

Lily turned to Michael as he removed his glasses. His eyes were earnest and his expression was void of any interest in games. Last night had most definitely backfired on her. She had intended to tell him off and walk away without another thought. Things had changed and she'd figured her best revenge would be to tease him and leave him cold. Things had changed and she'd ended up having the most erotic night of her life.

"Don't give me that look," she said, trying to find the most detached tone she could muster.

Finally pulling herself together, and off the floor, Lily left Michael's room despite his asking her to stay. Back in her own room, she broke down in tears because it became clear to her that she would never, ever get over this man.

"What look?" Michael asked.

"You know what last night was?" she asked, taking a step closer.

"You and I made love," he answered, no longer fazed by her attempt at coldness.

"No, Michael." Lily hated that her body was on fire standing a good three feet from him. It was as if he owned something inside of her. "We had sex and that was all it was."

Michael nodded his compliance. "It was enough."

"Enough for what?"

"Enough to put an end to this madness between us," he said.

Lily laughed even though her stomach was in knots. "You have no chance with me."

"We'll see."

"What in the hell is that supposed to mean?" she asked in a confrontational tone, feeling an odd kind of fear.

"After last night, I know where you live," he said calmly. "That's what the hell it means."

Lily had no tart response, no quick comeback for that one. As he simply looked into her eyes, she felt every defense she had left come down. They came down because she knew what it meant. No man had ever made her want to do the things she'd done last night without even a thought. He did know where she lived, but she could fight it. She would fight it because she could never let him hurt her again.

"I need some water," Carolyn said, pointing to the old colonial-style drugstore coming up on the corner.

Michael pulled the car over and looked into the rearview mirror at Lily, as he had been all morning. "You want something?"

Lily shot him a disagreeable glance, as she had been all morning. "I can get it myself."

"Why don't you just stay..." Michael didn't waste his time, seeing as Lily had already opened the door and hopped out of the Jeep.

"It's just for a second," Carolyn said.

"I'm not angry about stopping." Michael kept an eye on Lily as she walked around the car toward the store. "I think she's lying."

"Funny way to speak of the woman you love."

"One has nothing to do with the other." Michael felt it was unnecessary to argue the truth. "She's changed her description of this Ann Raines twice and I don't think she's looking for what she is telling us to look for."

"I think you need some water, too," Carolyn said. "You're dehydrating."

Michael continued to explain as they walked together. "I've been watching her all morning."

"Tell me about it. I thought we were going to get into an accident twice 'cause of your little fixation."

"She's hiding something," Michael said.

"Can you blame her?"

"Yes," he said. "I can. I've done everything—"

"Talking about me?" Seeming to come out of nowhere, Lily appeared in front of them.

"My cue to leave," said Carolyn.

"This is not about you and me," Michael said.

"There is no you and me," she quickly corrected. "But what are you talking about?"

"I know you're keeping something from me, but I'm here on behalf of the FBI, not myself."

"So you're threatening me?" Lily placed a defiant hand on her hip and tilted her head to the side. "I'm supposed to be scared now?"

Michael waited for two young women to pass before answering. "You want to pull me on a string, go ahead, but not the FBI. You have to remember, your father is still under suspicion."

Lily got angry. "Don't you lecture me about my father's situation. I know better than you what's going on."

"That's the problem," he said. "You need to tell us."

"Tell you what?" Lily made her way down the aisle toward the pharmacy.

"Lily." Rushing ahead, Michael stopped her from going farther. "Put us aside for a second."

"There is no—"

"Stop it." He could tell he had her attention at least. "This is serious. We're talking about serious felonies and dangerous people who have already tried to hurt you. Remember Sabrina?"

Lily grumbled, feeling her fury rise. "She's on my mind constantly."

"Then tell me what you know," he urged. "Because whatever you're thinking about doing isn't going to work the way you think. Just like at AFC's offices, you'll get more than you bargained for and it could mean your life."

"I know…"

He grabbed her by the arm and pulled her to him. With a

desperate look on his face, he said, "I can't let anything happen to you, Lily. I just…can't."

Feeling emotion begin to overwhelm her, Lily broke free of his grip and stepped away. When she looked at him again, the expression was still there. She was desperately trying to fight the voice inside her that told her he was telling the truth. It was too much to risk. But, oh God, how she wanted to believe that.

"Hey, Linda!" the pharmacist behind the counter yelled into the back, gathering everyone's attention.

Lily turned to him, suddenly aware everyone else in the store was caught up in the soap opera she and Michael had created, especially the little delivery boy standing at the edge of the pharmacist's desk with his mouth wide open.

"Did the interferons and ribavirin from Canada come in?" he asked.

Michael watched as Lily's eyes widened and she made her way to the counter. "What is it?"

Lily turned to him, weakened by the feeling of love she seemed unable to let go of. "He said interferons and…ribavirin, right? That's what he… Sir, did you say interferon and ribavirin?"

The older man, dressed in a conservative white coat with Coke-bottle glasses, looked at Lily uneasily. "Who are you?"

"Who is that medicine for?" she asked.

"It's for a customer," he answered with a strong accent, "who is not you."

As he began filling the delivery boy's basket with white bags, an older woman, dressed in a vibrant red and purple native outfit, came from the back with a professionally, very securely wrapped package in her hand and offered it to the pharmacist. Without a word, she turned and left.

Lily turned to Michael. "You need that package."

"Why?" Michael waved Carolyn over.

"Just get it," she ordered. "I'll tell you."

"Sir." Michael stood at the edge of the counter, flashing his badge. "I need to see that package."

Placing the package behind the counter, the man leaned forward, his eyes squinting as he observed the ID. "We ain't in America, man. This is somebody's private stuff."

"Sir, we are here on official FBI business," Michael said. "Your local police authority is aware of us and will vouch for me."

The man didn't seem convinced. "What you need it for?"

Carolyn was getting out her cell phone. "I'll call police headquarters."

Michael pulled Lily aside. "It's time to talk."

"If you get that package," she said, "you'll find the person who took Sabrina."

"Someone has her now?" he asked, wondering how they would get her out of the States.

"I don't think she's dead," Lily answered. "That's her medication."

Lily explained Sabrina's illness and Michael knew they were on to something. It only took a few moments on the phone with the police chief to convince the man to hand over the package.

"It's ordered over the Net," Carolyn said. "It's from Canada and it's going to be hell to track. It comes directly to the store here. No patient name."

"That's on purpose," Michael said, turning to the pharmacist. "Who ordered this?"

He shrugged. "Some woman. She comes and picks it up."

"You have to know who she is," Lily said. "You wouldn't just order this medication for her unless she gave you some information, a prescription."

"Like I said," the man insisted, "this isn't America. She gives me a lot of money and I'll order whatever she wants."

"We'll check your records," Michael said.

"You need more than permission for that." Despite his words, the man appeared nervous.

"Sir?" The little boy held out his basket.

"That's all," the man said. "Go."

Lily reached for Michael. "What if we wait for her to pick it up? Even if he has an address on file, I'm sure it's wrong. We'll waste time looking for records that won't lead us to anything."

Michael looked around. "If anything goes down, there are a lot of people here."

"They aren't expecting us."

"They're fugitives," he said. "They're always going to be expecting us."

"I'll call for backup." Carolyn was already dialing her phone.

"They'll see us," Michael said. "Tell them to stay back."

"When does she come?" Lily asked.

The man shrugged. "She knows when it comes. She'll show up today."

Michael turned to Lily. "You have to wait in the car and point her out when she shows up."

Lily nodded, feeling fear begin to creep up as she realized this could all come to a head. When she stepped outside, the sound of a horn alarmed her. She turned to see it was the delivery boy's bike horn as he hopped on and turned around the side of the store. Lily wasn't sure what it was that made her rush after him but she knew she had to. She ran quickly, calling out to him. He was just getting into a rhythm when he heard her and turned around. He reluctantly stopped his bike, looking suspiciously at her.

"Where are you going?" Lily asked.

Not looking a day over ten with widely innocent eyes and teeth whiter than snow, he answered, "Deliveries."

Lily pointed back to the store. "That package. Do you deliver it?"

The boy just looked at her with a frown on his smooth, dark face and Lily could sense he seemed a little frightened. "He was going to give you that package, wasn't he? That's what you were waiting for."

"No." He started as if he was going to ride off, but Lily stepped in front of the bike.

"Wait!" She reached into her pocket and pulled out a twenty-dollar bill, showing it to him. The smile on his face made her hopeful. "Where do you deliver that package?"

He folded his arms over his chest. "She pays me a lot more than twenty bucks not to tell anyone."

Lily dug deeper, pulling out a total of fifty. "How about this?"

"You're getting closer," he said.

"I don't have any more."

He tugged at his chin, his brows narrowed. "You are prettier."

A little later, as the boy drove off in the opposite direction, Lily studied the map he had drawn for her on the back of a paper bag. The face-to-face confrontation she came to this island for was still in sight. If only she could escape...

"You have got to be the most stubborn, pigheaded woman on the face of this earth," Michael said.

She turned to him, hiding the paper bag behind her. He was leaning casually against the corner wall of the building. "I was looking for the bathroom."

He approached her, his anger at her actions not stronger than his admiration of her determination. Holding his hand out, he said, "How much did it cost you?"

Lily sighed, rolling her eyes. She handed him the paper bag. "Fifty bucks."

"You're pretty," he said. "Otherwise, it would have cost you more. What is this?"

"It's a map," she said. "Ann Raines isn't coming to pick up the prescription. Not yet at least. She usually has it delivered. I'm sure she pays that pharmacist a lot of money to lie."

"She probably also pays him to call her when someone asks about her." He held his hand out to her. "Come on. We have to make sure he doesn't get on the phone."

Without thought, Lily took his hand and allowed him to lead her around the corner back to the store. To touch him in this way felt good. It felt safe. It felt right.

"This is good." Michael pointed to a spot behind three large rocks and a tree. "You can rest here."

Lily sat on the rock, completely exhausted. "I feel like I'm on a military mission. How long have we been walking?"

"According to this," Carolyn said, looking at the map, "we only have about a quarter of a mile to go."

"Why aren't there any people out here?" Lily noticed they'd left civilization more than twenty minutes ago.

"Of course they want to be secluded," Carolyn added.

Michael offered Lily his water. "I told you to stay in the car."

Lily didn't want to go there again.

After local police arrived to confiscate the package and escort the pharmacist and his assistant to the station, Carolyn informed backup of their change in plans and the three of them drove in the direction indicated by the map.

Lily wasn't happy when Michael decided they would park a mile away and walk, but there was only one road going toward the house and they didn't want to be spotted coming.

"I'm not being left behind," Lily exclaimed. "I told you that."

"What do you think? I'm going to hand you a gun so you can join the shoot-out?"

"Who says there's going to be…"

"There won't be," Carolyn said. "We're white-collar crime agents. We don't have shoot-outs."

"What happened to your backup?" Lily asked.

"I'm in contact with them." Carolyn checked her watch. "They know where we are."

"You still need me to ID her."

"The boy gave exact directions for the yellow and green ranch house next to the river," Michael said. "We don't need—"

"What is wrong with you?" Lily asked, letting her anger get the best of her. "You weren't so eager to get rid of me last night."

"I didn't have to," Michael yelled. "You ran off, remember?"

"Shut up!" Carolyn was waving her hand wildly at them both. "You're acting like high-school kids. You're so busy trying to one-up each other, you almost missed this."

They both followed her pointed finger to the main road they'd recently gotten off in just enough time to see Brody Saunders drive by on a red scooter, completely unaware of his audience behind the trees nearby.

In all of her years, Lily had never seen Brody in a T-shirt and shorts. Those, along with the baseball cap and slick sunglasses, made him look like a completely different person, but it was him. Just as she suspected.

"Let's go," Michael said. "Call Pruitt and tell him we've spotted Brody."

It was then that he noticed Lily's calm stare.

"You got something you wanna tell me?" he asked.

Lily stood up, avoiding eye contact. It was all coming together, the one thing she didn't want to believe but realized was the only thing it could all mean. "Let's just go."

* * *

The yellow and green ranch house next to the river, now with a little red scooter leaning against the west wall, was quaint but nothing special. Lily figured it would be perfect to avoid attention, but once the money was safe and secure, they would trade up somewhere much farther from the States.

They could see everything from behind the bushes and wildflowers only a few hundred feet away.

"So what now?" Lily asked.

"We wait for backup," Carolyn said. "They'll be here in a minute."

"Stay out of sight," Michael ordered, motioning for Lily to come closer to him. "Your colors are too bright."

As she slid next to him, even the dirt gathering on her jeans couldn't distract Lily from the energy she felt. He was serious, studying the house in such an intense manner; she found it sexy.

"You're having fun," she said.

He glanced down at her, her eyes seeming wider and more childlike than he'd ever seen them. He had to concentrate despite her closeness. "You should have…"

"Don't start on me again." She tossed over to her side, trying to find the right position. "I can't see from here."

"You don't need to see," he said. "You need to stay safe."

"I want to see!"

Michael leaned down until their faces were only inches from each other. Despite how angry he was with her, he wanted to kiss her more than anything. "I want you safe!"

Their eyes stayed on each other for seconds that seemed to last forever, before Carolyn interrupted.

"Oh, Mary and Joseph," she said. "Look at what we've got here."

Michael tore his eyes from Lily in time to see Brody strolling down the walkway toward the old-fashioned mailbox stand. It was who was trailing after him with her hand stuck in his back pocket as a show of intimacy that blew him away.

Sabrina Dunkle looked healthy and completely alive.

They watched as Brody opened the mailbox and both he and Sabrina peeked in. They weren't happy and Sabrina's arms became very expressive as she spoke to him. He smiled and leaned forward before kissing her passionately. When their lips parted, they were both laughing.

It was clear to Michael that these two were in love, and when he looked back at Lily, who was stealing a glance of her own, it was also clear to him that she was still lying to him.

"You knew about this, too?" he asked.

Lily turned away, sickened by the scene. "I suspected."

"You…" Michael wanted to yell, but he couldn't. "Dammit, Lily. All this time."

"Not all this time. I just figured it out after we left the evi…." She looked over at Carolyn, who was listening steadily. "I remembered little snippets of information that Sabrina told me about her secret man and their plans. She let her guard down and forgot who she was talking to. It was a hunch, but I didn't have anything left."

Michael was shaking his head. "There's nothing I can do, is there?"

"What do you mean?"

"You'll never trust me, will you?"

Lily swallowed hard. "How can I?"

"I betrayed you, Lily. I know that I can't undo that, but deep down inside of you, beyond all the pain, fear and anger, you have to know that I really do love you, that I would fall into fire for you."

Lily inhaled with emotion, feeling her heart pick up its

beating. "That's just it, Michael. All the pain, fear and anger are too deep. I can't see anything beyond it."

"Wait a second." Carolyn was getting her phone again. "He's on the move. Where is that damn backup?"

Michael and Lily both watched as Brody started for the scooter while Sabrina looked around.

"She needs that medication," Lily said. "She's sending him to get it."

"Stay down," Michael ordered.

"They were in this together." Lily was seething at the thought. "Right behind my father's back. Then manufactured her disappearance when I got too nosy."

Michael looked at Carolyn, who was struggling on the phone. "What is it?"

Carolyn shrugged. "I'm only getting static. Damn, the service just went out."

Michael shifted to his feet, still kneeling. "We can't let him go to the store and see it's closed. I'm going to go in."

"Wait for backup," Carolyn ordered, still trying the phone. "They should be here by now."

"He'll see them on the road," Lily urged. "We can't let them separate."

"I'm going in." Michael looked down at Lily. "You stay here. If you move, I'll shoot you myself."

Lily nodded, feeling a pounding sensation in her head. All her senses were heightened as the reality of what was about to happen hit her like a speeding train. This was real and it wasn't going to be some *Knot's Landing* type of confrontation that she so immaturely imagined in her mind.

Michael gestured to Carolyn, giving her instructions. As he got up to leave, Lily felt a crazy desperation rush through her and she grabbed his arm.

"Be careful."

Michael smiled, deciding to enjoy this moment some time later. "Stay here."

Lily watched as Michael moved to the left and Carolyn moved to her right, feeling as if a cloud of darkness was coming over them. Turning to her side, she glanced over the bush and saw Sabrina lean over the side of the scooter to kiss Brody again.

Then she heard a scream to her left and saw Carolyn's arms in the air as she fell down. The ground beneath her had given way. Without thinking, Lily sat up, looking for Michael. What she saw was Brody hopping off the scooter and Sabrina backing up. When she saw Brody reach behind his back, Lily knew what was going to happen and the thought of losing Michael scared the life out of her.

"Get down!" Michael yelled to Lily as he passed. He had to get Carolyn to safety. "Stay down."

For whatever reason she didn't know, Lily screamed as she lay down flat on the ground. Her hands went to her ears as she heard a series of gunshots. Panic was rising inside of her as she heard footsteps coming her way, running her way.

When she looked up, hoping to see Michael, Lily was amazed to see Sabrina rush right past her. There wasn't time to think. Lily pushed herself off the ground and gave chase. With one leap, she was on Sabrina's back.

Sabrina screamed and struggled against Lily, but the pressure of Lily's body on her brought her to her knees. Lily stood ready to use more force, but Sabrina looked weak and unable to fight.

"What are you doing here?" she asked, looking up.

"You know why I'm here," Lily said. "To get back what you and Brody stole from my father."

"This was all Brody's idea." Sabrina was crying now, trying to brush the dirt from her white capri pants. "From step one."

Lily had no sympathy for her. "You didn't look like anyone was holding a gun to your head a few minutes ago. I can't believe I was living with the guilt of thinking someone killed you over me."

"I know it was cruel." Sabrina's tone held sincerity in it. "I didn't want to do it. I wanted to come up with some kind of a dead end, but Brody said it wasn't enough to make you give up. He thought if you saw what investigating had done to me, you would be too afraid to go any further."

"You just left?" Lily asked. "What about the blood? It was yours?"

"It was mine. I have reserves at a blood bank for experimental testing. It's a Centers for Diseases Control program that—"

"I don't care about that," Lily said. "I just can't believe you would steal from my father. That Brody would, after all he had done for him."

"Brody thinks your father betrayed him!" Sabrina's belief in what she was saying was clear from the strength in her voice. "Brody was supposed to get Wolfe Realty, not a damn foundation."

"But you… Dad never did anything to you."

"I love him," Sabrina confessed. "I love Brody. Ward Wolfe means nothing to me."

Lily gasped at the cold tone of Sabrina's last sentence. As the two women stared each other down, they both ducked as they heard two more gunshots. Again, Lily felt manic at the thought of Michael getting shot. She couldn't see anything from the distance she'd chased Sabrina to.

"I didn't want anyone killed," Sabrina offered. "I just wanted to get away."

It was then that Lily heard the sirens down the road, but she feared it was too late.

Epilogue

"You read this?"

Ward Wolfe offered Lily a copy of today's *Atlanta Journal Constitution* as she joined him in the living room.

Lily nodded, inspecting the other papers around him. They looked like office work. "What are you doing?"

Ward sighed. "I'm allowed to do a little work. It's been two months since my surgery, Lily."

She joined him on the sofa. "*Little* being the operative word here. The firm we've hired is being paid a lot of money to take care of everything. I'm seeing to it."

It hadn't been easy, but the decision to sell Wolfe Realty was expedited by a New Canaan, Connecticut, firm's generous bid. After returning from Belize, when the whole truth was revealed, Ward and Lily just wanted to wash their hands of everything. This was easier said than done, of course.

The shoot-out was more bark than bite. Yes, Carolyn was grazed, but she was fine after a couple of stitches. Brody was shot in the leg by Michael, and Sabrina hadn't put up a fight at all for Lily. Once backup arrived, Lily was shuffled away despite wanting to see Michael to make sure he was all right.

Later, she found out he was, but there were too many other issues to be concerned with. Sabrina repeated her confession for the FBI. It was Brody's decision to steal from Wolfe Realty after he'd felt Ward betrayed him by deciding to turn the company into a foundation instead of the million-dollar real estate firm Brody had been spending his lifetime waiting for.

At first, Brody tried to get a job elsewhere, but his reputation was too tarnished for a position as high as COO, so he'd decided to stay at Wolfe Realty and come up with another plan to get what he felt was his right after years of loyal service to Ward, through thick and thin.

When Sabrina returned to Wolfe Realty, their affair began immediately. After her illness was revealed, Brody was there for her through it all and she felt she owed him. She was skeptical at first when he asked her to help him put together a phony brokerage business and use her authority in finance to help with the duplicate documentation, but when he showed her how much they could make, her greed got the best of her. After all, her medical expenses were very high.

When Brody realized that Sabrina had told the real story, he filled in the rest. He claimed to be filled with remorse for turning on Ward and convinced the FBI that his former boss had nothing to do with the scheme and was tricked from the beginning. Brody had used the old man's trust to swindle him out of more than two million dollars.

The confessions were made, the stolen money was found

and the FBI had an altogether different case. It was rumored that Jamarr offered Brody a deal if he would confess to the crimes from six years ago, but Brody didn't budge. Ward respected him for that, but Lily couldn't find it in her heart to appreciate him for anything.

"In big bright headlines." Ward held the paper up. "'Local Businessman Exonerated Again,'" he quoted.

"Is that really accurate?" Lily asked, unable to find joy in much of anything today.

Ward shrugged. "It was your boyfriend who did it, you know."

Lily didn't want to talk about Michael. She hadn't seen him since the shoot-out in Belize and her heart was still aching as if it was yesterday. The last month had been a whirlwind of so many legal, business and medical issues to deal with, there was barely one moment of peace. But every now and then, things would calm and Lily's mind would wander to Michael, to the man she knew as Garrick.

She tried to convince herself their affair was too brief to matter so much. When that didn't work, she tried to convince herself it was his utter betrayal that made her hold on to the thought. When that didn't work, she just admitted that she had fallen head over heels in love with the wrong man.

"What are you working on?" she asked.

"He used his pull in Chicago despite that damn Pruitt trying to keep me mired in this," Ward said, not answering her question. He shook his head, setting the paper down on the coffee table. "You speak to him at all?"

Lily somberly shook her head as well. She wouldn't have returned his calls, if he'd ever called. She would have refused any flowers or gifts, if he'd ever sent any. She would have walked away, if he'd ever approached her, but he hadn't. He left Atlanta for Chicago and never looked back. Despite all his professions of love, Michael had given up on her. She'd convinced him there was no chance, even though she hadn't been convinced herself. That was what hurt the most.

"Can we please not talk about him?"

"It's hard not to," Ward said. "You walk around like a zombie. Believe me, baby, I know firsthand that a man can break a woman's heart even though he loves her. A man can be sorry and really mean it."

Lily fought back tears. "Don't compare what he did to you. You were married to Mom for twenty-eight years before you started in all that mess. You were honest about her with who you were, what you wanted from her. You earned her forgiveness."

"What difference does it make if it's twenty-eight years or twenty-eight days?" he asked. "A heart is either broken or not. An apology is either true repentance or not. What's the same is that if there is true love there, forgiveness has to be there, too."

The doorbell rang.

"You expecting someone?" Lily asked, praying to get off the subject.

He shook his head. "Probably some lawyers with more paperwork. I'm glad as hell you decided to stay with me, little flower."

Lily placed her hand over his with a tender smile. "This is home."

The new live-in nurse arrived under the archway to the living room with a confused look on her face. "The FBI?"

Almost before Michael appeared behind her, Lily felt her heart jump. When she saw him, it practically leaped out of her chest. It seemed like a year had passed since he told her he would fall into fire for her. Lily had accepted she would probably never see him again, considering there would be no trial. He looked incredible in casual khaki pants and a ruby-red polo shirt that hung on him perfectly.

"Hello, Mr. Wolfe." Michael did the polite thing and addressed the man of the house first despite every inch of him being focused on Lily.

She looked like a seventeen-year-old, in a pair of jeans, a Braves T-shirt and a bouncy ponytail. Even without makeup, she was the most beautiful woman in the world to him. His entire body ached at the sight of her; he wanted to rush across the room and take those lips with his own.

"Hello, Lily."

Lily was speechless as she managed to stand up from the sofa.

"What brings you here?" Ward asked. "Our business with the FBI is over."

"I know, sir." Realizing that Ward could not get up from the sofa, Michael walked around to face him. "I apologize for intruding and coming unannounced but I'll only be in Atlanta for today and I…I wanted to speak to your daughter."

Ward looked at Lily but she looked away.

Michael added, "If that's okay with you, of course."

"Why are you asking him?" Lily asked. "I'm thirty years old."

"I'm sorry," Michael said. "I guess I'm old-fashioned."

"As am I," Ward said. "But ultimately, it's up to—"

"What do you want?" Lily asked in a cold tone. She was trying to deal with the emotions knocking her around. The only one that was clear was that she was happy to see him.

Michael smiled, not having expected the same. "It's private, Lily. If you don't want to…"

"Let's go." She gestured for him to head back to the foyer.

"Keep it together," Ward told her as she stepped past him.

"Why is he here?" she asked, taking her hand to her belly as if to quell the butterflies.

He shrugged. "Remember what I said. Where there is true love, forgiveness must also be."

Michael could feel the nerves in his stomach as Lily approached him in the foyer. It had been so long since he'd seen her and he would tell no one how hard it was not to park himself outside of her home and scream up at the windows for her to take him back.

"Redecorating?" he asked, looking around.

"Yes." It was a stipulation Lily made her father agree to. They had to move on. "The whole house. I'm in charge of it all."

"You live here now?" he asked, deciding to play it safe for now.

Lily nodded. "While my father is recuperating from surgery."

"Then you'll be going back to Paris?"

"No." Lily felt like it was torture standing two feet from him talking small talk when all she wanted was for him to touch her. "What did you come…"

"You're selling Wolfe Realty?" he asked.

"And my father and I are starting a foundation together, but that's in all the papers." She snapped her fingers. "Oh yes, that's right. It's only in the local papers and you're off in Chicago."

"You can't seriously be standing here acting as if you're mad I left." Her attitude made Michael feel hopeful.

Lily was angered by her own admission of feelings. "My father needs me, Michael. I don't have time for polite conversation with you."

"I'm not here for polite conversation, Lily. I'm here to see you. This last month…"

"I know what you've done for my father," she said. "So if

you want a thank-you, then thank you. You won't get more than that."

"Is that why you think I'm here?" He laughed. "They had nothing against your father. It was no big deal."

"But Pruitt was doing everything he could to drag my father into this. I know you had to ruffle some feathers."

"I got a promotion out of it."

Lily couldn't hide the smile on her face. Was she actually happy he was promoted for all the pain he'd caused her? "Yippie for you."

"It's a big deal, Lily. I would be second in command at the Chicago office. A lot more money and no more undercover."

"So you won't have to lie unless you want to."

Michael smiled. "I've missed your sharp tongue."

"I'm sure there are plenty of sharp-tongued women in Chicago."

"That there are," he said. "But none of them are you."

Lily wondered if he was playing games with her. "Yippie for me. Have fun in Chicago."

"I turned it down."

She looked into his eyes, searching for meaning, and it was laid out plainly for her. "Why?"

"Because I don't belong in Chicago anymore," he said. "My heart is in Atlanta."

"No." Lily turned to run away from everything her heart was screaming for, but he took her by the arm and brought her to him. "Michael, don't say this."

"Don't walk away," he ordered, loosening his grip. "I'm taking an agent job in Atlanta, working under Pruitt's replacement."

"Pruitt was fired?"

"He quit."

"Why are you telling me this?" She was almost near tears at the happiness she felt at knowing he would be close. Why would she be happy when she knew it would be torturous?

"Because I took the job for you. I love you, Lily, and I'm coming back to Atlanta to win you…"

"You can't." She pulled free of him.

"I can." He stepped in front of her to prevent her from running off. "I stayed away from you for this long because I knew I was the last thing you needed, but I never changed my mind. No matter how long it takes, I'll win your trust again."

"Is this about you being vindicated?" Lily asked. "Because I'm not interested in suffering anymore so you don't feel bad about what you've done."

"This is about you trusting me, loving me and marrying me."

Lily gasped. "Marry you?"

"If you've been feeling even a fraction of the loss I have this past month, then you'll understand how there could be nothing to deter me. I don't care if it takes another ten years. I may not deserve to be, but I am somewhere down there in your heart and I'm going to move the earth if that's what it takes to make you realize it."

Lily had to hold on to him to steady herself. She looked up at him and saw in his eyes everything she'd ever wanted despite wanting to believe the opposite. "Marry you?"

"That's what I'm here for, Lily. Marriage, family, all of it stems from the preciousness of your forgiveness."

Her father's words filtered through her mind, but her heart had already made its decision. Being honest with herself, it made its decision the second she saw him standing in the doorway.

As his lips came down on hers, all the pain Lily was feeling was wiped away. Having known for a long time that she truly loved him, it was in that second she truly forgave him.

"I love you," she whispered into his ear before her lips found his again. "I love you so much."

FORGED OF STEELE

The sizzling miniseries from
USA TODAY bestselling author

BRENDA JACKSON

*Sexy millionaire Morgan Steele has
his sights set on sultry Lena Spears.
But when Lena is less than
impressed he must go to plan B!*

BEYOND TEMPTATION

AVAILABLE JANUARY 2007
FROM KIMANI™ ROMANCE

Love's Ultimate Destination

Available at your favorite retail outlet.

Chase Dillard broke Laura Masterson's heart when he left her to pursue his Olympic dreams.

Winning her love won't be so easy the second time around!

HERE

and

NOW

Michelle Monkou

AVAILABLE JANUARY 2007

FROM KIMANI™ ROMANCE

Love's Ultimate Destination

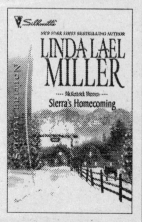